D0725416

By Private
Invitation

By *Private* Invitation

STEPHANIE JULIAN

HEAT | NEW YORK

THE BERKLEY PUBLISHING GROUP
Published by the Penguin Group
Penguin Group (USA) Inc.
375 Hudson Street, New York, New York 10014, USA

Penguin Group (Canada), 90 Eglinton Avenue East, Suite 700, Toronto, Ontario M4P 2Y3, Canada (a division of Pearson Penguin Canada Inc.) • Penguin Books Ltd, 80 Strand, London WC2R 0RL, England • Penguin Ireland, 25 St Stephen's Green, Dublin 2, Ireland (a division of Penguin Books Ltd) • Penguin Group (Australia), 707 Collins Street, Melbourne, Victoria 3008, Australia (a division of Pearson Australia Group Pty Ltd) • Penguin Books India Pvt Ltd, 11 Community Centre, Panchsheel Park, New Delhi–110 017, India • Penguin Group (NZ), 67 Apollo Drive, Rosedale, Auckland 0632, New Zealand (a division of Pearson New Zealand Ltd) • Penguin Books, Rosebank Office Park, 181 Jan Smuts Avenue, Parktown North 2193, South Africa • Penguin China, B7 Jaiming Center, 27 East Third Ring Road North, Chaoyang District, Beijing 100020, China

Penguin Books Ltd., Registered Offices: 80 Strand, London WC2R 0RL, England

This book is an original publication of The Berkley Publishing Group.

PUBLISHING HISTORY
Heat trade paperback edition / January 2013

Library of Congress Cataloging-in-Publication Data

Julian, Stephanie.
By private invitation / Stephanie Julian.—1st Heat trade pbk ed.
      p.   cm.—(A salon games novel)
ISBN 978-0-425-26287-0 (pbk.)
1. Antique dealers—Fiction.   2. Hotelkeepers—Fiction.   I. Title.
PS3610.U5346B9 2012
813'.6—dc23
2012029691

PRINTED IN THE UNITED STATES OF AMERICA

10 9 8 7 6 5 4 3 2 1

For David, again and always.
And for Kate, who didn't live to see this published,
but whose notes on early pages led me to the book it's become.
Miss you.

Acknowledgments

Writing is such a solitary endeavor but publishing is not.

Thank you, Leis, for seeing what I see in this story. And for what I didn't.

Thank you, Elaine, for your rock-steady guidance.

Thank you, Judi, just because.

Thank you, Deb, for the shoulder to whine on.

Thank you to the women of VFRW, who are always there with hugs and cheers and stickers and chocolate.

And thank you to my sons, who know I still love them even when I don't always feed them.

One

"Jesus, I really hope I don't get arrested for indecent exposure. Could you have made my neckline *any* lower, Kate?"

Staring into the mirrored doors as they waited for the elevator in Haven Hotel, Annabelle Elder barely recognized herself. If not for the pale green eyes and the auburn hair, she wouldn't have.

The woman in the reflection looked freaking amazing with her overflowing breasts and miles of leg. But she didn't look like any version of the Annabelle she thought she knew.

"Of course I could have," Kate Song huffed. "But then you *would* have been arrested. Stop fussing. You look fine, Annabelle."

Kate reached out to fluff Annabelle's skirt for the hundredth time, exposing more thigh than Beyoncé on Grammy night.

"Enough already." Annabelle swatted at Kate's hands. "I barely recognize myself as it is."

"Well, that was the point, wasn't it? A new you."

Annabelle pulled a face at her best friend. Yes, yes. She'd said that, but—

"Hey!" She yelped and grabbed her skirt as Kate pulled it higher on her thighs. "Do you *want* me to get arrested for soliciting? Gary the Asshole would love to see me locked away."

"Oh, please." Kate sighed loudly but stepped back, moving her straight black hair off her shoulders. "That jerk deserved whatever you threw at him." She paused and Annabelle glanced up to see Kate's grin. "Including his file cabinet."

Annabelle's nose wrinkled. "Too bad it only grazed his shoulder, the ass."

She wished she'd taken the two-timing jerk's head off with the thing. Or aimed a little lower and caught his dangling bits. Little itty-bitty bits that'd been on full display three weeks ago when she'd caught the bastard with his head between his secretary's legs.

Kate snapped the elasticized hem of Annabelle's off-the-shoulder sleeve, pain zinging up her arm.

"Ow!" She turned to Kate with a frown. "What was that for?"

"That jerk's not worth one more second of your time." Kate flicked her on the shoulder for good measure. "Except to thank him for busting you out of a rut. Think of tonight as your coming-out party."

Annabelle tried to take a deep, calming breath but could barely manage against the tight lacing. "I'll be coming out of this dress if I *breathe* too deeply."

The matching silk-and-satin fairy costumes created by Kate were masterpieces. But where Kate's blue bodice had a demure little dip in the front, Annabelle's green one angled down nearly to her belly button. Kate's short, filmy skirt hit just above her knee. Annabelle's barely made it to mid-thigh. She was afraid to look at her rear view again. The skirt was a little longer in back so she wasn't showing off her ass, left naked by a green satin thong, but still . . .

"Thank God for big-busted pop singers and all those rappers who love big-ass girls," Annabelle said with a sigh.

"Oh, please." Kate snorted. "You've got a great figure."

Yeah, if she was one of the women in her Victorian erotic art collection. She loved those paintings, not only for their unabashed sexuality but because those women weren't skinny little girls with no tits or ass. Both of which she had in abundance.

Not that she'd ever flashed so much of it. Her friends and neighbors in Adamstown would be scandalized if they saw her now. They only knew quiet, sedate Annabelle who'd been so damn busy keeping her business afloat for the past year. Poor, stupid Annabelle who should've dumped Gary the Asshole long ago.

At least she no longer resembled that girl. Rita Shumacher had quivered with joy from her platinum beehive to her open-toed Manolo knockoffs when Annabelle had told her to cut off her waist-length braid. Then the sixty-something hairdresser had worked her magic and tamed the remaining unruly mass into sleek curls that just brushed her shoulders.

Now Annabelle looked sexy. Confident. Ready to find a man to share her bed and her fantasies for the night before reality returned Monday morning.

Kate yanked on the laces on the back of her dress, making Annabelle squeak.

"I know what you're thinking and you can stop right now," Kate said. "No business tonight."

Annabelle sighed. "I know, but don't you dare."

Kate gave an eye-roll worthy of a teenager as her hand froze midway to Annabelle's hem.

"You know," Kate said, a distinct challenge in her tone, "if you want to chicken out, we don't have to go to the party. I'm only here to keep you company. I don't need a man. I already have a fiancé."

The two tickets for the New Year's Eve Masquerade at Haven Hotel in Philadelphia had cost a small fortune. More than Annabelle ever would've considered spending for any party.

She'd seen the ad boasting gourmet food, fine champagne, live music, and a night to remember in a piece of newspaper wrapping an antique vase months ago. She'd thought that it sounded like fun, but dismissed it because Gary would never agree to go, the cheapskate. After she'd dumped him, she'd called for tickets.

The bell dinged and the elevator doors opened, whisking away her reflection as they stepped into the empty cage for the ride to the lobby.

Annabelle squared her shoulders. "We're going. And I *will* have fun tonight. It's been too long since I had a good time. No one knows me here. I can flirt with a gorgeous guy, dance all night. Maybe even get laid." She looked down at Kate. "Do you know how long it's been since I had good sex?"

Her best friend since college, Kate had her Korean father's dark eyes and his sleek, straight hair. The rest of her was pure Italian from her late mother. The combination gave her an exotic beauty that always made Annabelle feel like a limp dishrag next to her.

If they hadn't been best friends since their freshman year at Gettysburg College, Annabelle would try to hate her. But Kate was too nice to hate. Even with her sharp tongue, occasional foul mood, and inexplicable taste in fiancés.

"Unfortunately, yes," Kate said. "I know how long you went out with Gary."

"Well, I'm sick of being plain, pathetic Annabelle. Tonight, I'm going to be fun, flirty Annabelle."

At least, I'm going to try.

The door opened again, depositing them in the sinfully elegant lobby of Haven Hotel, and Annabelle touched the antique pin on her bodice for luck. The six-carat, teardrop-shaped orange citrine glowed as if lit from within.

Her grandfather had given it to her a decade ago. After her world had collapsed.

"No second thoughts." Annabelle nodded. "It's a new year."

"Good for you." Kate smacked her on the rear, making Annabelle laugh as they stepped out of the elevator. "Now get out there and get laid."

* *

Jared Golden loved beautiful women, cold champagne, and the hum of a well-run party.

Not always in that order.

Tonight, it was the reverse.

From his vantage point at the Italian marble bar in the second-floor ballroom, he surveyed Haven Hotel's annual New Year's Eve Masquerade.

Excited laughter filled the air, along with good music, the mouth-watering aroma of gourmet food, and dry-mouthed sensuality. Beneath it all, he heard a satisfied hum.

Jared loved that hum. It gave him a measure of satisfaction comparable only to the buzz from good champagne. Or great sex.

After five years in the hotel business, he and his brother, Tyler, had done exactly what they'd set out to do. They'd created a hedonist's playground.

From the swanky Frank's Bar and Asian fusion restaurant Dome on the first floor to the fourth-floor, invitation-only Salon. From the fantasy suites that were booked solid all year to the Indulgence Spa on the third floor.

Haven was a place to have fun, let loose, give in to your fantasies. The ultimate adult playground.

Nothing at all like the stuffy grandeur of his father's hotels.

"Jared, love, dance with me."

He turned, smile already in place for the luscious blonde dressed in a slinky red gown reminiscent of a Golden Age starlet. "Sorry, Jane. I'm on duty tonight."

Jane Collins pouted her collagen-enhanced lips. "I can't believe how much of a bore you can be when you're having so much fun."

Jared took a sip of champagne to stifle a laugh. *Weird but true.* "I'm sure there're more than enough single men here to amuse you."

Trailing blood-red fingernails down the front of his shirt, the twice-divorced boutique owner sighed theatrically. "Of course. But I wanted to play with you tonight."

Jared swallowed a sharp-edged retort. His grandmother had instilled too many manners for him to deliberately brush off a lady. But tonight he refused to be tied down. Tonight was for mingling and dancing and, later, even more pleasurable activities.

It was not for dancing to Jane's tired tune all night. *Been there, done that, smacked that ass*, he thought. Thank God he'd been smart enough not to invite her to the Salon later.

"As much fun as that sounds"—Jared injected just the right amount of regret into his tone—"I do have a job."

Luckily, after another unsuccessful minute trying to garner his undivided attention, Jane spotted another eligible bachelor, this one a lawyer, and glided off in his direction.

Allowing Jared to return his full attention to the only mistress he'd never tire of—the hotel.

New people in and out every day. Challenges to overcome. Problems to solve.

Parties to plan. Jared lived for a good party.

This one was off to a good start. But it was the invitation-only event scheduled for later tonight that put a true smile on his lips.

Last year's first Salon Games had been a carefully guarded secret. He'd chosen each of the ten participants personally, laid out the rules explicitly, then let it happen.

Everyone had left the next afternoon with a smile. And not one word of it had leaked. Amazing, considering the nature of the games.

But then, those who'd been there had wanted to be invited back.

Looking out over the ballroom, he picked out several of the guests invited to the Salon tonight. A few caught his eye, nodded, then went back to what they were doing. Men and women Jared had known for years, some for most of his life. People who shared the same interests.

People he trusted and who trusted him. There weren't many he counted in that category.

As his gaze continued around the large room, he saw two new arrivals approach the arched entrance of the ballroom. Two women.

He watched as the maître d' greeted them and showed them to a table close to the dance floor.

As host for the evening, Jared felt compelled to greet everyone at the party. He started toward the women's table, speaking briefly to a few people along the way but never losing sight of his original target.

When he reached their table, he waited until they looked up at him before bowing his head.

"Ladies, welcome to Haven. My name is Jared. I hope your table's satisfactory?"

Pale green and midnight black gazes locked onto him from behind feathered masks. Dressed in fairy costumes, complete with wings, the women had natural beauty that couldn't be bought at a plastic surgeon's office.

The brunette in blue was sleek and slim, delicate. Her exotically shaped eyes hinted at an Asian heritage, her mouth a wide bow.

But the redhead . . . Damn. Her green eyes flashed and held on his, wide and inquisitive, her hair a rich autumn red that fell in curls around her shoulders.

She stared at him for a moment, assessing. Then her smile broke free, a beautiful sight on full lips he'd bet had never been artificially enhanced.

"Thank you," she said. "It seems the party's in full swing. We were a little late arriving."

Jared's smile widened. "Well, I'm certainly glad you made it. Is this your first time at Haven? I believe I'd remember such beautiful women."

"Yes, it's our first time," the blue fairy answered. "We're just here for the night."

"Then I hope you enjoy your evening," Jared said. "And I'd appreciate if you would each save me a dance tonight."

When he turned to the redhead, her smile had turned down-right sultry. And his body tightened as if she'd stroked a hand over his cock.

"I'd like that dance." Her voice held no trace of guile, no simpering fakery.

Jared's heart started a slow, familiar rhythm as he held her gaze. Her smile widened as he straightened.

He liked that smile. It was sexy but uncomplicated. Completely natural.

So unlike the women he typically dated.

As he nodded again, ready to leave, a glint of color caught his eye and his gaze dropped past spectacular breasts to the pin at the bottom of the vee on her dress. The pin looked familiar somehow, pinged something in his brain, some memory. He'd ask about it. Later.

"I'll be back to collect." Jared signaled a waitress to their table and headed back to the door, trying to shake off the feeling he'd missed something.

"Jared, honey, this is a lovely party."

Beatrice Golden sat on a barstool, a Manhattan in one hand, a delicate silk fan in the other. The fan matched the authentic Japanese kimono she wore.

"Hello, Nana. I'm glad you're enjoying yourself."

His seventy-five-year-old grandmother put her deceptively frail hand on his sleeve, bringing him closer. "The young woman you were just talking to, is she your date?"

He smiled ruefully. "No date, Nana. Not tonight. I'm working. Besides, there are too many beautiful women in the world to tie myself to just one."

Beatrice tsked and rapped his arm with her fan, her short

gray hair swaying around her still-youthful features. "You are going to live to eat those words. I've had to give up on Tyler. For the moment. But I plan to see you fall. And soon. Then we'll see who has the last laugh." She sighed. "I just wish I had the pin or the ring to give you. The legend—"

"Nana," he cut her off gently. "You're going to live forever." At six-two, Jared had to bend to kiss his tiny grandmother's wrinkled cheek. "And the legend is just that, a story—"

"No, it's not." Beatrice's voice held firm. "Since those jewels were stolen, our family has had horrible luck in love. Your parents have had such a rough time." She sighed, shaking her head. "And Tyler's fiancée. Her death was such a tragedy."

"You're right, Nana," Jared soothed. "Mia's death was a tragedy." *As is my parents' marriage.* "But believe me, when the right woman shows up, I'll know it."

He felt a twinge of guilt at the outright lie. He didn't believe in soul mates, much less everlasting love, but the smile on his grandmother's face was worth the white lie. "But I won't find her because some piece of rock tells me. Besides, I like my life as it is, uncomplicated by fairy tales of true love."

His grandmother sighed. "I just want you and your brother to be happy."

Jared hated to see his normally vibrant grandmother so defeated, especially at a party. "We are happy. Look at everything we've accomplished." He waved a hand around the room. "Tyler and I put Philadelphia on every pleasure-seeker's map with Haven. The spa is world-famous, the restaurant is five-star, and you know we give the best parties."

And what she didn't know wouldn't hurt her.

Her lips curved in a small smile.

"Come on, Nana," he cajoled. "I'm only twenty-nine. I've got

plenty of time to find the right woman and get chained for life."
He suppressed a slight shudder. "When I meet her, I'll know."

That made her expression brighten. "Yes, Jared. You will. Your
fall from love god to love slave will make my day. Go on, now."
She waved a hand laced with blue veins at him then reached for
her drink. "I know you're busy. I'm going to sit here and soak in
the sights. Just be open to possibilities, sweetheart."

If she only knew . . . "I live for possibilities, Nana."

Over his grandmother's head, he nodded to the bartender, who
nodded back. Fred Carvell, a retired, twenty-year police veteran,
wouldn't let anyone hassle Beatrice. She'd refused his earlier offer
of a table, saying she liked the constant ebb and flow of atmosphere at the bar.

He had a lot in common with his grandmother.

"Yes, you certainly do." Beatrice patted him on the arm, and
he was sure she'd read his mind rather than replied to his last
statement. "I'll see you later, dear."

"I'll be back. Don't go dancing with any strange men."

He swept into a low bow that never failed to make her laugh,
then meandered through the crowd, stopping to greet a few friends
before he made his way to the guest register, stopping next to his
brother.

"Hey, Jed." Tyler didn't look up. "How's Nana?"

"She's fine. *She's* enjoying the party." Jared threw a mocking
glance at his brother. "Are you going to glue yourself to this spot
for the rest of the night or are you going to try to have a good
time?"

Tyler actually deigned to look at him for a brief second, and
Jared saw a glimmer of humor in his eyes. "I plan to make the
rounds in a few minutes. We're still waiting for a few stragglers."

"You know we actually pay people to man this station, right?"

Tyler gave him his big-brother look, designed to intimidate. At one time, that look would've pissed off Jared. Now, Jared was merely unimpressed. He waited, one eyebrow raised.

Tyler returned his gaze to the touchscreen set into the stand. "I'm waiting for Mom and Dad. I figured one of us should actually show some decent manners and invite them."

Every muscle in Jared's body tightened. "God damn it. Why the hell did you invite him? Mom, sure, but that bas—"

"Be a big boy and try to behave."

Jared gritted his teeth even as he smiled at an arriving couple. "I thought we agreed. The old man tried to run our lives for too long. We don't need him. We didn't need his money to build this hotel and we certainly don't need his phony attempts to bond, now that we're grown."

Tyler shook his head, another wry smile on his lips. "You know, you're a lot like him. Now, don't get all ticked off." Tyler raised his hands as if to ward off a blow, which made him look idiotic because he stood six-three and was still built like the linebacker he'd been in high school. "But you are. You're both stubborn to the core and too intelligent for your own good. Be an adult for two hours tonight and let the old man believe you're happy to see him for a change. At least pretend and make our mother happy."

Jared grimaced at the thought of playing nice with his father but, even though he hated to admit it, Tyler had a point. It would make his mother happy. And she needed all the happiness she could get.

Still, he didn't have to make it easy for his father.

"Fine. I'll be nice to Mom and Dad tonight if you ask one woman to dance with you."

Tyler laughed, but it had a hollow sound to it. "Sure, why not. But I get to pick her, and you have to dance with Mom."

Jared smiled. "Agreed." He knew he'd gotten the easier end of the bargain. Tyler hadn't come close to a woman since his fiancée's death from cancer eighteen months ago.

"Enjoy yourself tonight, Ty. It's the start of a new year. Maybe this will be the year Nana's dream comes true and she can marry off one of us. Not me, of course. But maybe I'll get lucky tonight."

"What? With the brunette you seated a few minutes ago?"

Jared's gaze locked onto his brother, whose attention appeared to be glued to the screen. He wasn't buying the act.

"Actually, I don't have my eye on the brunette. Why don't you ask her to dance? You could fulfill your part of the bargain."

Tyler grinned and looked out at the lobby. "Yeah. And so can you." He nodded toward the entrance.

"Hello, Tyler. Jared." Glen Golden strode toward them, a hearty smile on his still-handsome face, his white hair gleaming. "How are you both tonight?"

Their mother, Helena, walked beside him, her slim hand tucked into her husband's elbow.

To the world, they looked like the perfect couple. His mother's ash-blonde hair was perfectly styled, her evening gown a designer original. His father's tuxedo was Italian and handmade and the lines around his blue eyes only added to his air of stately appeal.

But Jared knew it was all a farce.

Suppressing a groan, Jared forced a smile to welcome his parents, sliding one more glance at his green fairy.

It was still early.

Two

"Did you see that man's smile?"

Annabelle couldn't help but stare at Jared as he spoke to an older couple by the entrance. "He has a body to rival a Michelangelo. And that face. I've never seen anything so perfect."

Handsome didn't come close. He looked like a young Paul Newman, with lean, chiseled features, wavy blond hair cut short to control the curl, and blue eyes that looked like reflections of a fall sky.

She sighed. "Too bad he was just being polite. Probably has women falling all over him. What would he want—*Ouch!* Hey, you kicked me." She bent down to rub at her ankle, then glared at Kate.

"I'll do a lot more than that if you don't stop putting yourself down." Kate huffed. "Didn't you get a good look at your reflection before we left? I specifically made that dress to enhance your attributes. And the man definitely noticed. Of course he wants you. You're beautiful. The goons in college never looked beyond the glasses and the braid." Kate's nose wrinkled. "Of course, that braid was kind of goofy."

Annabelle tried to look indignant, but thinking about college still made her cringe. "Okay, so I looked like Princess Leia on a bad-hair day. All I wanted was to get my degree and get out. Guys were a distraction I couldn't afford."

Her granddad had first suggested college overseas, where she might not be so easily recognized. But she'd insisted on Gettysburg because the program had what she wanted. And she'd be close to him.

Besides, she'd grown and her appearance had changed so much in the three years since the pictures the tabloid scum had taken of her, no one at college would make the connection between Graceanna Belle O'Malley and Annabelle Elder. No one could make her life a living hell by exposing her secrets.

A waitress interrupted Annabelle's thoughts by placing two glasses and an ice bucket with a bottle of champagne on their table. After making sure they didn't need anything else, she left.

Annabelle took a sip of the champagne, rubbing her nose at the unaccustomed bubbles. She'd traveled all over England and Europe, bits of Africa and the Far East, but until tonight, she'd never imbibed to excess, never flirted with a gorgeous man, and never . . . jumped off a cliff.

She sighed. Well, she was going to fix at least two of those. "Tonight, I'm going to live a little."

Near the end of his life, her granddad had harped on her lack of extracurricular activities.

"Get a life, Annie, my belle," he'd bellow at her. "You can't spend your days wasting away in this musty shop. Go out, find a man, live a little."

Bill Elder had died suddenly a year ago, in his sleep, exactly the way he'd wanted to go. He'd lived life to the fullest and one day he was just gone—leaving her orphaned for the second time in her life.

Which probably explained the ill-advised affair with Gary. Damn, if only she'd figured that out five months ago. Would've saved her that scene in his office when she'd tossed the filing cabinet at him.

She hadn't meant to hit him. Not really. She'd only meant to express her displeasure. Except her aim had been a little better than she'd expected. Years of manhandling antique furniture in the shop had given her strong arms.

The metal box had sailed through the air and the edge had glanced off Gary's narrow shoulder, knocking him to the ground. His eyes wide, he'd scrambled away on the floor, like a crab. The wuss.

His secretary had calmly pulled down her dress, patted him on the head like the dog he was, and walked right past Annabelle.

"Nice throw, Annie," Carla had drawled as she slinked out the door.

Annabelle had wished she could make as elegant an exit but she'd worked up a good mad by then. That bastard had never gone down on her like that. He'd claimed not to like it.

But there he'd been, with his head between Carla's thighs. Acting like he loved it. Hell, he hadn't even looked like that when they'd had *sex*. It'd been more like porn sex—lots of noise and motion but no substance.

She should've known the bastard was cheating on her but she'd been so busy with the shop and . . . Okay, if she were truthful, she'd admit she just hadn't cared enough to wonder why he'd break off dates on short notice with lame excuses.

"Would you like to dance?"

Annabelle blinked out of her thoughts to see a blond man dressed as a pregnant nun standing by their table, smiling at her. He had a drink in one hand and a whip in the other, handsome in a bland, vanilla-milkshake sort of way. Not that vanilla milkshakes were bad. Until now, they'd been her favorite. But that was before. Tonight, she'd decided it would be banana splits all the way.

Jared appeared behind the nun, towering over him. "Sorry, Bill, but the green fairy promised this one to me."

Her gaze met Jared's, and lust drenched her from head to toe at the sensuality smoldering in his eyes.

No one had ever looked at her like that.

When he extended his hand, she took it without a second thought.

Vaguely, she heard Kate turn down the nun as Jared drew her onto the dance floor. Then a slow, dreamy jazz standard shut out the rest of the noise of the large crowd.

"I didn't mean to be rude." Jared's warm whisper caressed her ear as he eased her against his lean body. "But I couldn't stand the thought of you in another man's arms. I hope you can forgive me."

A laugh escaped her before she could catch it. "That's a wonderful line. Did you make it up on the spot or have you used that one before?"

Jared blinked, just once, as Annabelle bit back a groan. She couldn't believe she'd said that. She'd been raised to speak her mind but that . . . She definitely was no good at flirting, and she was too long out of the loop.

Jared's face split in a huge grin. "Actually, I just made it up. But you're right. It's a line. It also happens to be true."

She took a deep breath, thankful he hadn't abandoned her on the dance floor. "I can't believe I actually said that. Please let me add that I'm glad you asked. I'd hoped to see you again."

Jared's fingers tightened around hers. "And why wouldn't I ask? You're the most beautiful woman here."

She laughed again, unable to help herself. She knew it was another line, but really, what did it hurt? She was determined to have a good time tonight and Jared seemed determined to give her one. "And you are the most proficient dancer I've ever had the pleasure of partnering. Did you take lessons?"

"No, my grandmother taught me." He held her a little closer, the warm material of his pants leg brushing against the inside of her bare thigh, making her want to clasp both thighs around it. "She believed any young man who could dance had a leg up on the riffraff who never took the time to learn."

"Your grandmother sounds like a great lady."

Jared winked at her. "She's one of a kind. So, I didn't get your name earlier."

"It's . . . Belle." She didn't want to lie, nor did she want to reveal more just yet. This was a night for fantasy, after all. "What do you do at the hotel, Jared?"

"I facilitate various activities, like tonight's party. And you?"

"I'm an antiques dealer."

"Really." His brows raised in interest. "What kind?"

"My shop specializes in early American and European furniture but my true passion is art."

"Is the pin one of your finds?"

Mesmerized by his voice and those blue eyes, his question puzzled her for a moment, until she followed his gaze down to the pin on her dress.

"Oh, no. Not mine. My grandfather acquired it several years

ago. It's beautiful, isn't it? Granddad couldn't believe it was mixed in with a load of costume jewelry. The large stone is an orange citrine. The smaller ones are diamonds and sapphires. The intricacy of the metalwork shows a fine hand, we think European. I've occasionally tried to discover its maker but I haven't been able to so far."

Jared tried not to stare but couldn't help himself. It seemed like such a far-fetched idea but he couldn't ignore the voice in his head telling him this was one of Aphrodite's Tears, part of the set his grandmother had mentioned earlier. The pin and matching ring had been stolen so many years ago, he'd never seen anything but pictures. Still, this pin fit the description exactly.

If it was . . . Holy shit. How much of a coincidence would that be?

"I'm sorry." Annabelle's voice broke into his thoughts. "I must be boring you talking shop."

His gaze lifted to catch embarrassment staining what he could see of her cheeks beneath her mask. Her gaze slid away across the crowded dance floor.

"You're not boring me. In fact"—he surprised her by spinning her in a tight circle before drawing her close again—"I find it fascinating. Tell me more."

Belle's eyes lit up as she smiled. Not a sexy smile, designed to seduce, but a grin of pleasure. She started talking about antiques, provenance and historical significance, words that held no meaning at the moment.

Her bright eyes held his attention. He would gladly drown in that green gaze. Typically, women attracted him first with their looks. He was a man, after all. But he bored easily if there was nothing but air behind the beauty.

This woman's intelligence intensified her beauty.

And she could be wearing his grandmother's pin.

No, it couldn't be. His grandmother mentioning it earlier had just made him think it was. That's all.

"So where is this shop of yours?" he asked when she paused.

Her gaze faltered for a second. He would have attributed it to the dance, but they weren't doing more than a slow circle at the moment.

"Outside the city." She shrugged. "It's not huge but we—I do a decent business. I travel a lot. Granddad and I were never in the same place more than a few months when I was growing up. I traveled the world with an antiques dealer and a tutor with a doctorate in history. It was an unorthodox upbringing."

He wondered what she meant by that. Unorthodox. "Sounds interesting."

She smiled, but it was perfunctory, as if she'd shut down her emotions. "It was. Unfortunately, my grandfather died a year ago." She shook her head and her smile began to warm. "I'm sorry, I've monopolized the conversation. Tell me about you. And"—her eyes widened as she realized they'd just danced through three songs nonstop—"I don't want to get you in trouble with your boss. Do you need to get back to work?"

Jared quashed a smile, shooting a glance at the door to see if Tyler was sending lightning bolts his way. But his brother wasn't at the entrance.

"Actually, my boss must've stepped out." He spotted his parents, sitting at a table in the corner, but Tyler wasn't with them either. "There really isn't much to tell. I've been with the hotel since it opened. I enjoy my job and the people I work with. And it has its perks."

He flashed her one of his most charming grins, and she laughed.

"I bet." Her teeth sank into her lower lip, making him want to do the same. "You must meet a lot of people in a job like this."

"Yes, I do. Though I've never met anyone like you."

He didn't realize how true that was until he said the words. He frowned at the thought, and Belle dropped her gaze. She took a deep breath, drawing his attention again to the pin.

Damn, what was he going to do about that? However, he knew exactly what he wanted to do with the woman.

"Sorry to interrupt." Tyler clapped him on the shoulder, startling him and causing Belle to step out of his arms. They had danced to the opposite side of the room. "I need you at the door for a few minutes, Jed." Tyler lowered his voice. "And you have to honor our agreement."

With a raised eyebrow for Jared and a slight smile for Belle, Tyler moved away.

"I should get back to my friend, anyway." Belle made a slight wave in the direction of her table. "Thank you for the dance."

The fact that her flirtatious smile nearly made him go caveman and toss her over his shoulder threw him for a second, and he didn't say anything until she started to move away.

"Wait." He caught her upper arm gently, smoothing a thumb over her silky flesh. "I'd like to see you later."

"I . . . I really shouldn't have deserted my friend like that." Consternation clouded her expression, but she paused. "When are you finished for the night?"

"Meet me at twelve thirty in the lobby, by the courtyard entrance. The garden is beautiful."

Her smile brightened again. "I'd love to see it."

She turned and walked away and he couldn't tear his gaze from her.

Twelve thirty couldn't come fast enough.

* *

"I don't believe I recognized the woman you were dancing with. Should I?"

Jared waltzed his mother sedately around the dance floor, sliding glances when he could at Belle, irrational outrage swamping him when she smiled at another man standing by her table.

While *he* danced with his mother.

Amazingly, Mom had behaved herself so far. Smiling into her pale green eyes, he noted their clarity.

And breathed a silent sigh of relief.

"No, no one you know. So, how's the Arts and Artists benefit ball coming along?" That should distract her for a while. Helena loved to talk about her projects, especially the yearly ball she helped chair for one of the local colleges.

Unfortunately, her sons held the top spots on her list of projects.

"Very well, actually." She smiled, and guilt hit him in the gut at the thought that he could make his mom so happy with a simple question. "We've got the guest list worked out and we only need confirmation on the date from the college."

Jared relaxed even more as his mother talked about her favorite charity. He didn't want to discuss Belle. He was still trying to figure out what had happened between them.

They'd made an instant connection and she'd returned to her table looking somewhat dazed. That was good. However, the minute she'd sat down, some guy in a penguin suit—not a tuxedo, but an actual penguin outfit with flippers—started hitting on her.

His reaction had been immediate and completely unlike him. He'd been jealous.

Jared had a very long fuse. Only his father ever managed to infuriate him with his lies and overbearing arrogance. But right now, he would have gladly tossed the penguin out on his ridiculous flipper.

"So, I told the chaplain . . ."

As his mother continued, he nodded at all the appropriate places, trying to decide his next move with the lovely Belle. He didn't want to wait until twelve thirty. He wanted to monopolize her entire evening.

But that wasn't his style. He didn't do exclusive. He refused to give any woman the false impression that he'd pledge his undying love for her. Or even commit to more than another date.

Tyler was right, though Jared would never admit it. Jared was a lot like his father. Neither of them had the gene that allowed them to love. Jared, at least, was honest. He'd never lied to a woman the way his father lied to his mother. Jared would never put a woman through what his father had put his mother through.

He tuned back in to Helena, still talking about her charity ball. She lived to volunteer, found the appreciation she craved there, which she never got enough of from her husband. Helena and Glen Golden were the only offspring of two very wealthy families. Their marriage had cemented their place in Philadelphia society. But Jared knew his mother would trade it all for her husband's love, which he was incapable of.

Jared couldn't understand why she allowed herself to be hurt like that.

When the song ended, he escorted her back to her table and exchanged civilities with his father, whose subdued responses were so unlike him Jared wondered if he'd gotten caught in one of his affairs again.

Old anger flared, but he submerged it under thoughts of one beautiful redhead and made his way back to Tyler at the entrance, flipping again through the guest book on the computer.

"I've held up my end, big brother." Jared sent a brotherly elbow into Tyler's side. Tyler didn't flinch. "It's your turn."

"I already did my part." Tyler tapped the screen. "I asked and got rejected."

Rolling his eyes, Jared sighed. He should have known his brother would find a way out of his end of the bargain. The man had graduated top of his class at the Wharton School of Business. He hadn't wanted to dance, so he'd found the one woman in the room who'd say no.

"You're a coward." Jared leveled the only truthfully disparaging remark he could at his brother.

One corner of Tyler's mouth curled up. "Nah, I'm just smarter than you."

In some ways, Jared agreed. Though he'd never admit it. "Who'd you ask?"

Tyler stiffened for a moment. "The blue fairy."

Jared snorted. Yeah, that was what he'd figured. She hadn't danced with a man all night, though several had asked. She'd only gotten on the floor with Belle for a few faster numbers.

Tyler shot him a hard look, his fingers stilling on the screen. "What was that for?"

"You *are* a coward," he repeated. "I'm going to orphan that little blue fairy again. If you don't want her to be hit on by another ten guys, why don't you go keep her company? On second thought, don't bother. She promised me a dance. I think I'll go collect."

His brother's gaze narrowed on him. "It's not gonna work, Jared."

"No idea what you're talking about." Jared countered with a

grin as he headed back to Belle's table. It only took two strides for Tyler to catch up. Jared didn't comment. He'd made his point.

The women's conversation halted when they arrived. They both looked up at the same time and Jared caught his breath. Belle had finally removed her mask. He had an almost uncontrollable urge to take if from her so she couldn't put it on again.

While she wasn't conventionally beautiful—her features were a little too broad for that—she was pretty. The phrase "girl next door" fit her perfectly. Not at all his usual type.

Pale freckles splashed across her short, upturned nose, while high cheekbones defined her oval face. The costume fit perfectly. She looked like an Irish fairy just back from dancing under a full moon. Her cat-green eyes sparkled and her wide smile rocked him back on his heels.

He returned her smile and winked, introducing Tyler only by first name. Then he held out his hand to Belle.

"Will you dance with me again?"

She flashed a quick glance at her friend, who nodded before turning back to Jared.

"I'd love to."

Jared didn't know whether to thank Kate or his brother. He was pretty sure if Belle would've had to leave Kate alone again, she would have said no. The women were true friends, a foreign concept to most of the females in his circle who saw other women as rivals, first and foremost.

"I hope Kate's enjoying herself." Jared brought her tight against his body, heat rising at the feel of her breasts, soft and curved, pressing into his chest. His cock twitched, already half hard. She'd be able to feel his erection soon. "She seems . . . shy."

Belle smiled, but there was a hint of sadness in it. "Not really. I think she's just overwhelmed. There've been a lot of guys hitting on us tonight, and it's a little disconcerting. If I thought she really loved her fiancé, I'd think she missed him. He left on a business trip yesterday. It looks like she and Tyler hit it off, though."

He glanced at the table, surprised to see Kate and Tyler engaged in conversation. And, amazing but true, Tyler was smiling. Too bad she was engaged.

"What makes you think she doesn't love her fiancé?"

Belle shrugged. "When Kate decided it was time to get married, she settled for the first man who asked her. Big mistake, if you ask me. The woman's a fabulous seamstress. She made our costumes. She could have her own business but she settled for working at a dry cleaner while she waits for her wedding day. It's a shame."

"That she's getting married?" Jared nodded. "I'd have to agree with that. There's not enough time to tie yourself to one person. Life's too short."

It was his standard response whenever anyone talked about marriage, but he realized the words sounded trite and kind of cold when he spoke them to Belle. He watched her expression, but his comments hadn't seemed to make any impression on her at all.

Good. That was good, right?

"No, not that she's getting married." Belle shook her head. "But she's settling for less than she should. I refuse to compromise. If I ever get married, it'll be after I've secured my career."

Ah, a woman with a life beyond landing an eligible bachelor. This one was *special.*

"And how do you plan to do that?" His hand inched down her back, closer to the rounded curve of her hip. Because of her wings, he had to be careful to keep his hand low on her waist. She didn't even feel like the women he typically dated. She felt soft and curved, instead of hard and angular.

"By having the best goods on the market and letting everyone know it." Her lips curled at an enchanting angle, and she batted her eyes at him, flashing green fire from beneath full brown lashes. "You have to be sharp in the antiques business. Fakes and reproductions can ruin your reputation."

"Sounds like you know your stuff."

"I do. I had the best teacher."

She shook her hair over her shoulders, drawing his attention to her pale skin. Jared wanted to lay his mouth on the few freckles he could see dotting her shoulders. He wanted to play connect the dots with his tongue.

"My turn to ask a question," she said. "I'm getting a lot of, shall we say, negative vibes from many of the women in this room. Have you dated all of them?"

Firming his jaw before it dropped open in amazement, Jared managed to breathe before laughter consumed him. This woman amazed him.

He bent low to whisper in her ear, "If I let you in on a secret, will you promise not to ruin my reputation?"

Annabelle shivered as Jared's heated breath caressed the sensitive skin beneath her ear. She hadn't meant to be so outspoken or rude, but once again her mouth had gotten away from her. This gorgeous man hadn't taken offense, though. In fact, he seemed amused.

"I've had relationships with less than five percent of the women here. And none of them intrigue me the way you do."

As he spoke, the hand on her back swept a caress down the curve of her hip and pressed her even closer. She drew in a breath. *Oh boy.*

"So, there's no one in your life right now?"

He gazed into her eyes and her heart stuttered. "No one."

Jared's smile faded, his expression more serious than she'd seen him all night. Swallowing, she dropped her gaze and rested her cheek against his shoulder as they continued to dance.

Nerves made her lungs draw in a sharp breath unexpectedly.

Yes, she wanted him. Her nipples tightened and her stomach clenched as she brushed against the erection he didn't try to hide when she was in his arms. Her thong was already damp and if he asked to go to her room, she'd say yes.

This was why she'd come here tonight. To meet a man and have fun. Reduce her stress through a little sexual indulgence. Why not?

Jared seemed like the perfect candidate. He knew women, seemed to know what they liked, what they wanted.

Could she go through with this? Did she have the guts?

To hell with doubt.

She concentrated on the feel of Jared's hands on her waist, on the way his broad shoulder shifted beneath her cheek. On the rigid erection pressing into her hip.

He wanted her and she wanted him. Wanted him to ask her to leave with him. Better yet, she should ask him to her room.

Sex with this man would be the best end to this evening.

One ballad segued into another as they continued to dance. How many songs passed? She didn't know or care but Kate must be bored out of her head. She chanced a look at the table to see Kate and Tyler, their dark heads closer than they had been before.

She hadn't told Jared yet, but one of the men she'd danced with earlier had spilled the beans about his identity and his relationship to Tyler and the hotel. The brothers looked nothing alike, she realized. Jared's wavy hair and classic features made him look like one of her grandfather's prized Italian sculptures. But his smile was warm, and those eyes . . .

She wondered what he saw when he looked at her. Did he see a confident, sexy woman? Had she inherited any of her mother's genes other than her hair color?

Jared stopped abruptly and, with a start, she realized Kate stood beside them, Tyler at her side.

"I hope you don't mind," Kate said with an apologetic smile, "but I'm going to go up to my room."

"Is something wrong?" Annabelle asked, immediately worried.

Kate's lips curled ruefully. "No. It's just that it's late and I'm tired."

Excusing herself, Annabelle pulled her friend away from the men to talk quietly.

"Is everything okay?" Annabelle asked. "It's not even midnight."

Kate shook her head. "There's nothing wrong and this is just another night of the year for me. I'm not really into all this New Year's stuff. I did have a good time, though." Kate leaned forward for a hug and Annabelle obliged, but they ended up giggling like schoolgirls when they entangled their hands in their wings. Funny, Jared had managed to avoid them all night.

Annabelle gave her friend a rueful smile. "I'm sorry I was such awful company—"

"Actually, I enjoyed talking to Tyler." Kate sliced a quick glance at the other man. "It was . . . enlightening."

Annabelle took a close look at her friend, only now noticing the flush on her cheeks and the sparkle in her eyes. She raised her eyebrows in question.

"Oh, don't get the wrong idea," Kate rushed on. "I'm an engaged woman. I just think it's time for me to head up. Annabelle . . . have fun."

Annabelle's smile was slow to form but it *was* there. "I plan to. I'm so glad you came with me. Tomorrow we'll hit the King of Prussia mall and do a little damage to our credit cards."

Kate nodded then turned and said good night to the men. Tyler walked her to the door but stopped there. Annabelle watched Kate shake hands with Tyler then disappear down the hall as he stared after her.

Annabelle raised her gaze to Jared's. Holding his hand out to her, he waited until she reached for him, her warm hand clasping his.

"Would you like to see the garden, Belle?"

Three

"It's like a little piece of England transplanted here."

Belle stood in the center of the hotel's deserted courtyard, looking around. Jared lingered near the edge of the lawn.

She looked perfect in the formal garden.

Surrounded on three sides by the hotel, the courtyard retained a touch of summer in the winter. With its huge glass-dome ceiling and paneled wall of glass at the rear, the enclosed garden was Tyler's pride and joy. With the temperature hovering around seventy degrees, flowers bloomed and shrubs and trees thrived, even in winter.

Jared called it the petri dish just to needle Tyler, but he had to admit, the damn thing was amazing.

A boxwood hedge surrounded the garden and divided it into four distinct areas with a circular area in the center where a marble fountain bubbled.

Belle stood there now, staring at the fountain's intricate carving in the dim glow of the gas lanterns high overhead.

She trailed her fingers along the lip of the pool at the bottom of the fountain, then wandered down the brick path, toward the herb garden. She bent to rub mint leaves between her fingertips, drawing Jared's gaze to the length of her legs.

He wanted to wrap those legs around his waist as he lifted her up against a wall and found out what exactly she was wearing under that little skirt.

Still moving, she entered what was the rose garden in the summer, now filled with potted poinsettias of every color. From there, she wandered through the perennial garden, until she came to Jared's favorite section, the topiary garden. Tyler took care of the topiaries himself. He hated when the gardeners messed with his trees.

Belle leaned in to sniff a fragrant rosemary bush forced into the shape of a heart, and he wanted to bend her over the nearest bench and sink his aching cock into her.

"Did you have anything to do with the garden?" she asked, not looking at him.

He chuckled at the thought. "No. My . . . ah . . . One of the owners designed it, actually."

"It's gorgeous. You should be very proud of your brother's work."

Well, shit. Someone had ratted him out. Probably one of the other men she'd danced with tonight. Too bad. He'd enjoyed having someone treat him like a normal person for a change. He wondered if she was going to go bubbleheaded on him now.

"I take it someone gave you an earful." He moved closer to see her expression.

"Oh, yes." She faced him, nodding solemnly. "Several of the men I danced with were quick to point out why I didn't want to get involved with someone like you." She smiled and something uncoiled in his chest. She wasn't going to take their advice. "I understand why you did it. It's nice to be someone else for the night, isn't it?"

He nodded, wondering who she wanted to be. He couldn't think of anyone he'd rather spend time with at this moment. "Yeah, it is."

"It's a new year." She winked at him. "You can be anyone you want tonight."

Breaking out in laughter, Belle released the velvet shawl she'd wrapped around her shoulders, which caught on her wings before slithering to the ground. "It's not even cold out here. That glass ceiling is magnificent. Was the courtyard enclosed when the hotel was built?"

Forcing himself to go slow, he walked to the wrought-iron bench nearest Belle and sank onto the plush cushions. The bench sat in a shadowed corner behind one of the larger topiaries. Anyone passing through the garden would never see him.

"No, we installed that in the renovation." Then, because he couldn't stand to have her so far away, he asked, "Are you sure you're not cold? It can get chilly out here in the winter."

She wiggled a finger at him. "I have to be careful around you. You're a charmer. And no, I'm not cold. I want to look around a little more."

She turned her back on him and wandered down the path, stopping to admire a statue of two lovers entwined in a kiss.

"Mmm." Belle's voice sounded even more seductive in the near-dark. "I could stay out here all night, but then I wouldn't get to sleep in that decadently huge bed in my room." She flashed him a look that burned, then sent her gaze over the garden again. "You look comfortable."

He quirked a brow at her. "Why don't you come over here and I'll show you just how comfortable I am."

Her lovely face tilted to the side as if she were contemplating his request. Then she smiled and walked back to him. Easing onto the cushion beside him, she tried to recline, but her wings got in the way.

Presenting him with her back, she asked, "Would you mind?"

"Not at all."

After a quick assessment of how they were attached, Jared freed her from the wings, dropping them to the ground at his side.

"You're entirely too good at that." She tried to turn, but he placed his hands on her shoulders, mesmerized by that expanse of creamy white skin.

"And your skin is so soft," he whispered against her neck.

A chime sounded from inside the building and the faint roar of a crowd reached them.

He leaned closer, let his lips caress her ear as he said, "Happy New Year, Belle."

She shivered against him, though he was pretty sure she wasn't cold. Her skin felt warm beneath his hands and he leaned in until his nose almost touched the curve of her neck. Her hair fell away as she tilted her head to give him access.

Drawing in a deep breath, her fragrance made his heart pound. He loved the way women smelled. Some spicy and heady, others light and delicate. Each one different. Yet underneath it, similarities.

Belle sighed and that tiny sound broke the control he'd been exerting since he'd asked her out here.

Lowering his mouth to the tender spot where her shoulders and neck joined, he surprised her by nipping the skin there. She gasped, the sound stroking along his libido.

Wrapping his arms around her waist, he pulled her against him. The next kiss he placed on her neck wasn't as soft as the first, and he wasn't surprised when she pulled away.

But then she turned in his arms and slid her arms around his neck. With a growl, his control snapped and he lifted her over his lap.

She straddled him, her knees on either side of his thighs, and dropped her mouth back on his, her hands on his shoulders.

This kiss held none of his usual finesse, but it served the purpose. Her mouth opened at his urging, letting his tongue slide into her warmth, teasing along her tongue.

She wasn't at all hesitant about kissing him back, and her eagerness made his cock throb. As if she'd felt it, she lowered herself that last vital inch and settled her mound against his erection.

Heat flowed from that point, and she broke away, gasping. Her eyes opened and stared into his, bemused but hungry.

With a grin curling the corners of her mouth, she slid her hands from his shoulders to the short hair at his nape. Scraping her nails along his neck until his skin tingled and broke out in gooseflesh, she settled another millimeter closer on his lap.

He leaned in to kiss her again and ran his hands down her arms—noticing now that her skin felt cool. He leaned back, trying to break the kiss. But she wouldn't let him. She followed, nipping at his lips, until he kissed her again.

"You're cold," he whispered in her ear as his hands rubbed up and down her arms. He bit the lobe then blew lightly over it, feeling her shiver.

"Really?" She shivered again, but he didn't know if it was

from the chill or a belated reaction. Her eyes remained closed, her breath coming in short gusts. "I feel like I'm on fire."

So did he. Every nerve ending flared with pleasure, making him want to rush instead of savor. There was something about this woman, something that made him lose his edge.

Yes, he wanted her. Possibly more than he'd wanted a woman in a very long time.

And he was going to have her.

Releasing her, he sat forward to shrug off his tuxedo jacket and wrap it around her shoulders.

She smiled as he leaned back then settled her hands on the soft white cotton of his shirt. Without a word, she stroked downward along the fabric, making him want to shed his shirt so she could put her hands on his skin.

And speaking of skin . . .

He set his hands on her hips, giving them a squeeze before letting them glide up over the tight, silky material of the dress to the point at which her breasts began to overflow. Trailing his fingers over the pale mounds, he watched as she arched into his hands.

Whatever restraint he'd had left blew apart at that second, and he molded his hands to her breasts with one purpose. Since the dress was fashioned like a corset that lifted her breasts but didn't cover them, a filmy green material had kept her decent all night. Now, he pulled that material away to reveal ruddy nipples, already hard.

He bent to take one in his mouth, sucking on the firm tip and rubbing his tongue on the pebbled flesh. She moaned and his cock hardened into a thick shaft, aching for her touch. But he knew if she did, this would be over too soon, and that was unacceptable.

She had to come first. At least once, if not twice. Those were his rules.

With one hand holding her breast to his lips, he let the other graze back down her side to her thighs, where he burrowed under her skirt.

He felt the heat of her pussy against his fingertips as they brushed against the slick material. She was already wet. He groaned against her breast, strung a series of hard kisses across her chest, and set on the other nipple.

The hand at her mound turned to cup her through her panties, and he felt the bare skin of her ass as she attempted to get closer.

A thong. So easy to get rid of.

The heat in his body turned into a raging fire that wiped out everything but the need to get inside this woman. To make her come, to have her enclose his cock in her wet heat until he exploded.

Since she seemed to be on the same page, he set aside the rational part of his brain that wanted him to slow down and gave in to the impulsive urge he usually kept on a short leash.

The hand on her ass stroked across her soft skin, making her moan again. Except this sounded more like a purr. With each stroke, he got closer to his goal until finally his fingers brushed against the wet fabric.

"Touch me, Jared," Belle whispered in his ear as she bent to nip at his earlobe. "Don't be a tease."

"Oh, but I like to tease." He spoke against the warm swell of her breast, the scent of her arousal overpowering the faint floral scent on her skin.

Easing one finger under the edge of her thong, he felt only slick skin. No hair.

She was bare. His heart pounded harder.

When he paused, she rolled her hips, only a fraction of an inch, but enough to let him know she wanted him to continue. He slid his hand completely under the material, one finger parting the slick folds of her sex, his thumb pressing lightly on her clit.

Lifting his head, he wanted to see her expression. The sheer pleasure on her face tightened every muscle in his body, and the need to make her come had him working his finger into her body in a slow, steady push. Her eyes drifted closed and her back bowed as he fucked her with first one, then two fingers. After a second, her head dropped onto his shoulder and her tongue licked the warm skin of his neck.

He shuddered at the sensation and increased the pace of his thrusts.

Her cream on his fingers made him want to lick them. Better yet, he wanted to lick her. But that was out of the question here. Later . . .

Her clit was a hard little nub that he flicked mercilessly, only easing up when he felt her near the edge of orgasm. Then he pulled back. He wanted to control her every response, to wring every last drop of pleasure from her before he took her over the edge. Then he wanted to work his cock inside her still-pulsing sex and fuck her until neither of them could see straight.

He had a momentary flicker of caution, a brief second where he realized this wasn't like him, but Belle chased it out of his head by biting his neck. The sharp, brief pain made that inner caveman roar and he lost all reason.

He lived only to make her come.

The hand on her breast kneaded in time with the fingers he tunneled into her, squeezing the nipple as he rubbed her clit.

Her panting breaths hardened his cock until he swore the zipper on his pants protested.

"Come on, baby. Come for me."

His whispered words did the trick. She cried out, nails digging into his shoulders, and he felt her juices release over his fingers.

As she collapsed against him, he tried to catch his breath, wanting to rip open his pants, pull his aching cock out, and settle her down over it. He'd palmed the condom he always had tucked in a pocket then forced himself to slow down.

He had to ask. He couldn't just take. Another rule.

"Belle, may I?"

He felt her lips curve in a grin just before she lifted herself away from his chest.

Her gaze found his first then shifted to the foil packet in his hand. Her grin grew into a full-blown smile as she reached for the condom with no hesitation.

Then she lifted it to her bodice and set it between her breasts, just beneath that damn pin, letting it rest there while her hands drifted down to his zipper.

She took her own good time getting his pants open, caressing him through the material for what seemed like forever, until she finally released the button and slid the zipper down.

Released from some of its confines, his cock tented up through his tight black boxer shorts.

She looked down, then back up into his eyes. "Very nice."

He grinned. "Thank you. I'll make it feel even better, Belle. Pull my underwear down."

He heard the demand in his voice and wondered how she'd take it. Would she balk now?

The women he typically had sex with knew what he wanted. What he liked. What they were getting into.

Belle was an unknown. What would she say if he told her everything he wanted? Would she give him what he wanted?

He never made false promises. He would make it good for her. He knew enough about sex and women to make this very good for her.

When she smiled and slipped her hands under the waistband of his underwear, he almost sighed in relief. Until she wrapped a hand around his cock and started a wicked pump. Then he could barely breathe.

Her smooth hand created just enough friction to set his nerve endings on fire. Letting his eyes close, he leaned his head back against the bench and absorbed the sensations.

The feel of her naked thighs under his hands, the slight flex of her muscles as she worked him. When she shifted, he felt her breath along his cheek as she bent to lick at his jaw, nipping at the skin, then moving to his mouth. She kissed him this time, and it was a reversal he enjoyed.

Typically he kissed a woman and she let him. This . . . almost blew his mind.

She wasn't as demanding as he would have been. Her lips were softer, gentler, but still managed to make his heart pound. He didn't realize his hips had started to thrust in time with her caress until the tip of his cock brushed against her still-covered mound.

He leaned back just enough to be able to speak. "How attached are you to these panties?"

"Not very."

"Good."

In a split second, he'd snapped both sides of her thong and drew the now-worthless scrap from between her legs, leaving her naked to his fingers.

While she continued to stroke him, he petted the small triangle of hair just above her clit.

She rewarded him by tightening her hand around his cock and shivering. "You're not as civilized as you pretend to be, are you?"

If she only knew. "There's a time and place for everything. It's time for you to fuck me."

She shuddered in his arms, the sound of her labored breathing telling him she was just as close as he was. His cock felt like iron and throbbed like a son of a bitch.

"Then I guess you'd better make use of that condom."

He reached for the packet, making sure he tweaked her nipples before he drew it from between her breasts. She moaned again as the sound of foil tearing ripped through the silent garden.

He had a momentary hesitation for their location but, tucked in the topiary garden, they were pretty well concealed by the trees. And his coat hung down her back, covering his knees as well. No one would see anything that would embarrass Belle.

He barely had the condom rolled on before she positioned herself over the tip and started a slow, sensuous slide down his shaft.

The heat of her pussy seared him through the thin casing of the condom, her tight sheath pulsing around him, easing only enough to let him in. He wanted to thrust and he felt her take a deep breath, as if waiting for him to move. But he knew anticipation was a powerful aphrodisiac.

"Jared." He heard the plea in her tone, felt the contained desire in her body, and his thighs tightened. But he forced his muscles to relax, his fingers to release their tight grip on her hips.

"Ride me, Belle. Slow and easy. Make me beg for it."

Usually, it was his pleasure to make the woman beg. But Belle wasn't anywhere near usual. She was unique, unknown but completely open, and so damn sensual.

She took him at his word and began to lift her body off his cock without fully seating him. She pulled up until only the tip was still lodged in her sex. Then she shifted again and he pulled free. Rubbing her lips over the head, she teased herself with him, moving to stroke her clit against him.

She started to pant after the first minute or so, matching him breath for breath, but she didn't take him in again. Sweat began to seep down his back and bead on his forehead, his balls pulled up as tight as rocks.

He bent his head to pull a nipple into his mouth and suckled hard. Her cry echoed around the garden, and she shuddered just before she reached down to pull his cock away from his body. Then she sat on him and took him deep and fast.

She froze and he released the tight tip to look into her eyes. Hers were glazed with passion and he figured he probably had the same look in his. He thought she was going to say something so he waited, watching her, his body screaming for release until finally he broke.

"I'm begging. Please, Belle. Fuck me."

Her smile combined with the almost brutal pace she set made his eyes roll back in his head and for the first time in his life, he gave his pleasure over completely to another person.

And she didn't let him down. She rode him hard, kept up the pressure, her thighs working her body up and down. He tried to hold out, to hold on, but his body wouldn't listen.

He came with a deep groan, lifting his hips into her downward thrust to seat himself high and tight inside her.

He pulsed his release into the condom, listening to her breathless moan as she jerked against him, her sex milking him as she came.

The vague regret that he wasn't naked inside her passed through his head.

Next time.

He really hoped there was a next time.

He'd make damn sure there was.

"Belle, would you like to accompany me to an after-party?"

Four

Annabelle read through the waiver a second time, though she knew she was going to sign it.

Her pussy still rippled with aftershocks from that amazing orgasm. And she wanted more.

She looked up into Jared's bright blue eyes. "What type of party requires a legal waiver?"

Sprawled in a matching art deco leather club chair in a small but decadently furnished room on the fourth floor, Jared watched her with an intensity that should have worried her.

Her bodily response was far from it, as it made her wet and hot to have him again. In any and all ways possible.

He smiled. "The waiver's not only for your protection but for the other members'. This party isn't like any other you've ever been to, Belle. Its only reason for being is pleasure. There are no rules except those against physical violence. If you want to leave at any time, you only have to say the word. But the waiver requires you not to reveal who else is in the room.

"You have my word no one will hurt you or do anything you don't ask for. Or beg for." He paused and she could barely swallow as her heart began to pound in anticipation and her sex clenched. "This is only about pleasure. As much as you can stand. In any way you want."

Oh, hell. Where had all the air in the room gone? She certainly needed more.

From the moment Jared had whisked her into the private elevator at the rear of the garden and up to this fourth-floor room, she'd known exactly what type of party he'd asked her to attend.

"How many people will be there?"

His steady gaze never faltered. "Ten were invited but I'm not sure all of them will show. Eleven if you decide to join us."

"And no one will know my identity?"

"Everyone wears a mask the entire time."

Kinky, she thought. *And arousing.* Maybe she had inherited some of her mom's sensuality. "This isn't the first time you've done this, is it?"

His lips curved in a wicked grin. "No."

Oh, my, when he looked at her like that she wanted to jump him where he sat. Unzip his pants and ride him until she passed out. He made her feel sexy, beautiful. Wanted.

And so freaking horny. She could very easily get addicted to his touch.

She picked up the pen from the side table and signed her name on the bottom line, illegible but still legal. Beneath the paragraph that stated she was free of any sexually transmitted diseases.

Jared didn't even look at the paper as he took it.

Leaning back into the chair, she stared at him. "I'm surprised you don't require a clean bill of health from a doctor."

"We do. All members of the Salon have legal waivers from their doctors, which are updated every six months. I'm trusting you were honest about your medical history when you signed that form."

She nearly blushed, embarrassed to reveal how long it'd been since she'd had sex. Or the reason for knowing she was disease-free. "I'm clean. When my last . . . relationship ended, I had an exam and all the requisite tests."

"Sounds like the relationship didn't end well."

Her mouth twisted in a grimace. "You could say that. Fortunately, I was more pissed off than hurt." Which she couldn't say about Gary. He'd had to see a doctor for his shoulder.

Jared shifted in his chair and her gaze was drawn to the bulge in his slacks. He made no effort to hide his erection. Her blood heated like lava.

She couldn't relax, his blatant lust made it impossible. She wished he would move, pace, take her to wherever they were going. But he made no effort to get up. Spontaneous combustion became a distinct possibility.

She took a deep breath as something occurred to her. "Will Tyler be there?"

How weird would it be to do anything sexual with his brother? Even unknowingly, though she was pretty sure she'd recognize his voice.

Jared shook his head. "He doesn't attend the Salon games."

Something clicked in her sex-addled brain, some piece of information that focused her away from sex. "Salon as in Victorian salon?"

He nodded. "That's right."

Her smile made his gaze burn a little brighter.

"What's that smile for, Belle?"

"I never told you about my specialty in antiques, did I?"

If he was surprised by her change of subject, he didn't show it. "I don't think it came up."

"The shop's main focus is early American and European furniture. That was my grandfather's passion and where most of my income comes from. My focus is erotic artwork."

He blinked once, but his smile never faltered, and he raised his eyebrows just enough to let her know he wanted her to continue.

"Most of my collection is eighteenth-century European, Japanese, and Chinese." And some very special modern American works. "I'm well versed in European because of my degree in art history, but I also have a few other pieces, like Greek redware and Roman marble."

Now he moved, shifting in his chair, leaning forward. "How did you get into the field?"

He looked so relaxed, so at ease, with his shirt sleeves rolled up and his collar open. She had no idea where his tie was. Was it so wrong to be so turned on by the hint of T-shirt she could see under his shirt? To be panting after the naked skin of his forearms?

The man was made to be touched. And she planned to.

But first, she'd make him beg again. She'd never made anyone beg and it felt so damn good.

She burned for him. Not just between her legs, but her breasts ached for his lips to suck at her nipples and her skin tingled with the remembered touch of his hands. She wanted him to burn for her, to crave the taste and feel of her.

"My granddad accepted a set of Paul Avril engravings for *Fanny Hill* as payment for a nineteenth-century Lancaster County chest. I happened to open the box when they came. I was . . . fascinated."

Jared's smile widened. "I know the ones you're talking about. I have an entire set. How old were you?"

Her smile turned into a full-out grin. "Seventeen. My grand-dad lined the paintings up against the wall, completely ignored the content, and discussed the techniques used by the artist. I've been fascinated with erotic art for years. How the turn of a head or the curve of a lip can convey so much passion in the hands of a master."

"And you're a collector?

She nodded. "As well as a dealer. I have several clients who love art as much as I do. They enable me to expand my own collection. And I work with a few museums around the world. It doesn't pay all the bills but it's my passion."

She'd chosen the word deliberately and was rewarded by heat flaring in Jared's eyes.

"I've always believed passion is the only thing that makes life worth living." Jared stood and her gaze flicked, for one brief moment, to his crotch and the impressive bulge there. When she looked up his smile was gone, but lust showed in the tight line of his jaw. "Let me show you my passion before the others arrive."

She really didn't want him to think she was a nympho, but she really hoped he meant they were going to have sex again. It'd been months since she'd broken up with Gary and frankly, she'd never had sex as good as she'd had with Jared.

A little voice in the back of her head wanted to intrude, wanted her to question what she was doing. But she shut it down before it could become a nag. Tonight was all about pleasure.

If there was one thing she'd learned from her parents, it's that pleasure was sacred.

And damn it, she deserved some.

She took his outstretched hand and let him draw her to her feet.

Tilting her head back to look into his eyes, she smiled and he bent to give her a quick kiss. Not long enough to satisfy. And no tongue.

A tease. She wanted to tease and torment him.

He nodded toward the back wall of the room. "Through here."

While this room was the size of the one she'd checked into for the night—and which she probably wasn't going to be sleeping in—there was no bed. Two couches and six chairs were arranged around the room in seating areas, the art deco style repeated in the side tables and decorations. Not gaudy, as some deco could be, but elegant and tasteful.

Annabelle saw no door in the wall but Jared touched a piece of the ornate molding and, like magic, the seam she'd thought was from the wallpaper cracked open to reveal another space beyond.

Jared stepped in ahead of her, flicking switches on the wall.

A warm glow suffused the room and Annabelle's breath caught at the scene spread out before her.

Like a scene out of *Pride and Prejudice* or, more appropriately, *Fanny Hill*, the large room looked like someone had transplanted a drawing room straight from Victorian England.

From the ornately decorated ceiling to the plush carpets, the octagonal room dripped with elegance.

Lush fabrics covered the chaise lounges, chairs, and ottomans. Silk wallpaper gleamed in the light of the crystal chandelier in the center of the room. Directly below the chandelier sat an octagonal game table with eight chairs.

A baby grand piano held court in one corner, lit by a leaded glass piano light, and a large glass-front walnut display cabinet across the room held a collection of items she couldn't see from where she was standing.

Several other seating areas lay scattered around the room, most shadowed in darkness, including one in front of the majestic marble fireplace burning with a gas fire.

"All the furniture is reproduction," Jared said. "We can get . . . a little enthusiastic and I didn't want anyone to feel like they had to hold back for fear of breaking an expensive antique."

She glanced over her shoulder and watched as Jared headed for the writing desk on the opposite wall from the piano. He withdrew two pieces of black cloth from one of the drawers and turned to face her.

Walking over to him, she let her hips sway just a tiny bit more, the action helped along by the fact that she wasn't wearing any underwear. She wasn't sure what had happened to the ones he'd ripped off her. She suspected they were in his pocket.

And that really shouldn't make her pussy tingle.

Reaching out, she took the mask from his hand and examined it. It reminded her of a blindfold but with holes cut out for the eyes. Sitting on the edge of the desk, he circled one finger in the air, signaling for her to turn. She did and he slipped the mask over her eyes, waited until she adjusted it, then tied the strings behind her head.

The material felt like silk, sinful and sexy.

When he was done, she turned to fasten his.

What would it feel like to have my hands bound behind my back with these?

She'd never told Gary about that little fantasy, had worried he'd think she was perverted. Or worse, that he'd tell one of his idiot friends and it'd be spread all over town the next day.

She knew what it was like to be the object of vicious gossip and she didn't want to live through that hell ever again.

Here she could indulge with no fear of repercussions.

She drew in a deep breath, and Jared turned, his eyes narrowing.

Grabbing her around the waist, he lifted and turned her until she sat on the edge of the desk. Her skirt fluttered up and her bare ass settled onto the desk. The cool surface made her shiver, but her entire body shuddered when Jared put his hands on her thighs. Under her skirt.

"Are you cold, Belle?"

Not at all. "If I say I am, will you offer to warm me?"

The corners of his mouth quirked but the rapid pulse at the side of his neck belied his seemingly outward cool. She wanted to lean forward and bite him right there. Mark him in some way.

His hands slid forward by the tiniest increments, each slight motion making her legs fall apart just a little more. "You don't feel cold. In fact, your skin is so warm, I want to soak in your heat."

The throb between her legs made her ache to move his hands higher, faster. Leaning back on her hands, she spread her legs until she could accommodate his body between them. When his fingertips nearly touched the lips of her sex, he pressed her open even more, rubbing his hard cock against her mound.

She tilted her hips up so he brushed against her sensitive clit.

Swallowing a moan, she fought to keep her eyes open, to watch him. She wanted him to push her back and flip her skirt to her waist. "Maybe you need to take my temperature."

He grinned this time. Not a sophisticated smile, but an honest-to-God grin that made his eyes narrow to slits. "And how would you like me to do that?"

"Oh, I'm sure you could think of something."

His fingers moved closer, every centimeter they covered fueling her lust. "Should I use my fingers?"

"Yes, please. Touch me, Jared."

"I am touching you."

Damn the man, he wanted her to spell it out. As if he knew how excited she could get just from talking. How he knew that, she had no clue. Gary had never picked up on it in all the months they'd been seeing each other. "I want you to put your fingers in my pussy and fuck me with them."

Jared's smile turned hard and a dark flush tinged his cheeks. "Oh, I will, sweetheart. Lay back, Belle. And don't move."

Jared watched as Belle did exactly what he wanted without question or hesitation.

And his cock throbbed with a fierce need to get inside her now.

Damn, he wanted to fuck her. No preliminaries, no foreplay.

Just ram into her and thrust until he exploded.

Jared prided himself on his restraint, on being a considerate lover, one who gave his partner several orgasms before he came. Yeah, he was a little—okay, he was a huge control freak. Most women enjoyed it. They let him have his way and he fucked them until he got bored and moved on. Or they did. He didn't hold grudges on that account and hoped they didn't either.

He'd bet his life this woman wouldn't just let him fuck her and take it. She'd want to return the favor and make him lose his control.

That made her dangerous.

And Jared dealt with danger in one way. He subdued it.

For the briefest second, he let his fingertips brush against the lips of her sex, barely enough to feel the moisture coating them.

Belle arched toward him and he withdrew until his hands rested on her knees.

"Touch your breasts. Pull your dress down so I can see you play with your nipples."

She flushed a bright, pretty red and, for a second, he thought she'd refuse. His breath caught and held, waiting, until finally she did as he asked.

Legs spread, her back flat against the desktop, she kept her gaze locked to his as she lifted her hands to her neckline. Slow and steady, she pulled the gauzy material down until her bare nipples showed. The tight corset around her middle helped push her breasts into mounds.

Barely able to breathe, he watched as her long, slim fingers played over the taut nipples. She had beautiful breasts, full and round. Her nipples pebbled as she touched them and he wanted to lick them and bite them. Make her scream while he did it.

Right now, though, he was content to watch her as she caressed, hesitantly at first, then with more confidence. Her eyes drifted closed and her teeth lodged into her bottom lip.

His hands tightened on her legs and he started a slow caress of her thighs, up and down, falling into the rhythm she used to fondle herself.

His dick throbbed and his jaw ached from being clenched. The breathy moans escaping her lips inflamed his lust even more.

Tearing his gaze from her breasts, he looked down her body, at the bare lips of her pussy, shiny with moisture. Moving his hands, he stroked her, flicking her clit as he barely penetrated her with his fingers.

She moaned, louder this time, and her hips thrust up, trying to get his fingers to sink deeper.

Not yet. He wanted her wild. He wanted her complete surrender to sensuality before he made her come.

He sensed she was holding back. And he wanted her complete surrender.

"Belle, open your eyes. Watch me."

Slowly, her lashes flickered and those pale green eyes peered at him, lazy and full of heat. She struggled to breathe, her chest rising and falling in a heavy pattern that made her breasts quiver. He wanted to suck those tight nipples into his mouth and he would. But first, he needed this.

Leaning down, he put his mouth on her stomach just below her belly button. The soft skin contracted as she drew in a sharp breath, but she froze, as if worried he would move if she did.

He kissed her, running his tongue up to her belly button then down to the soft triangle of hair on her mound. A light brown, almost the same shade as her hair, she kept it trimmed.

He rubbed his nose against it, drawing in her scent, then flicked out with his tongue, catching the tip of her clit. With a cry, she writhed, arching up toward his mouth. Catching her hips in his hands, he pinned her to the desk and covered her clit with his mouth, sucking on the little nub until he could nip at it with his teeth.

His own lust caught him off guard as he ate at her. Her earthy taste and scent hit him like a punch in the gut. He nipped her clit harder, then used the flat of his tongue to lick it. His heart pounded in his chest as her fingers slid into his hair. The slight pain as she pulled at the short strands caused his cock to throb with his heartbeat.

Rational thought deserted him and sex consumed him.

He alternated biting her clit with soothing licks of his tongue, keeping her body on the edge of orgasm. Tension filled the air around them. Hers, his.

And someone else's.

He didn't stop to see who was standing behind him but he knew someone was there. And Belle knew it too because her breath caught and she froze for several seconds.

Would she ask him to stop now that the reality of what she'd agreed to hit her? Christ, he hoped not. He wouldn't let it.

He didn't let up and continued to work her body with his mouth. And when he used his tongue to fuck her, she cried out, her hands reaching above her head to hold on. Her body arched off the desk and her taste flooded his mouth.

His cock so hard it hurt, he rose and unbuttoned his slacks, releasing his cock from the confines of his underwear.

Behind him, someone moved.

Jared recognized Dane Connelly by his hair, long enough to brush his shoulders and dark as night. Dane had shed his coat but wore his mask.

Best friends since high school, Dane didn't wait for an invitation to join. He just cupped Belle's breast in one hand and bent to take the nipple in his mouth.

Belle's short gasp made Jared pause to watch her closely. If she freaked, he'd get her the hell out here.

She didn't. After several long seconds, she closed her eyes and let another man suckle her breast.

Damn, she was beautiful, with her lips parted and a blush tingeing her cheeks. He'd never wanted a woman more.

Pulling a condom from his pocket, Jared covered his cock, watching as Dane worked her breasts with his mouth and his hands.

With her eyes closed and her hair spilling all over the desk, she looked like one of the paintings on the walls of the Salon. Abandoned. Wild. Lost in pleasure.

He wanted to feel her come all over his cock again. Once hadn't been enough.

Sliding his hands up her legs, he waited until she opened her eyes. Glazed with passion, she stared at him, her mouth slightly parted, lips red from biting them. He saw no fear, no doubt, no unwillingness.

He stepped closer to the desk and rubbed the tip of his sheathed cock against the heat of her pussy. She tilted her hips, offering herself up while at the same time pushing her breast further into Dane's mouth.

His cock pierced her lower lips until the head disappeared into her flesh. Molten heat surrounded him and he wanted to bury himself in her. At the same time, he wanted to draw this out, wanted her to lose all control and know he was the one who made her do it.

Pulling out, he watched her watch him, watched her eyes dilate just a little more as he pushed back in, a little further this time. Her eyes flickered shut briefly, catching on Dane for several seconds before lifting to reconnect with Jared's gaze.

She reached for him, catching the tail of his shirt and tugging. "Take me."

"I'm planning to, honey. Just tell me how you want it."

Her gaze flipped to Dane again as her lips curved into an enticing smile. "Make me beg."

Out of the corner of his eye, he saw Dane glance up at him. His friend had no idea who he was fucking but it wouldn't matter. Dane was a pure sensualist. As long as it felt good, Dane didn't care where the pleasure came from. And Dane knew Jared well enough to know how much he loved a challenge.

Jared let his own lips tilt just the slightest bit. "Be careful what you wish for . . ."

He pressed forward again, sinking into her tight sheath a tiny bit more, watching as her eyes closed.

"Oh, no." He pulled out and her eyes flashed open. "You have to watch, baby. Don't look away or you won't get what you want. No matter what happens, you don't look away from my eyes."

Dane bit her at that moment, not hard but just enough, knowing it was exactly what Jared wanted him to do. Her mouth parted on a gasp but she kept her gaze locked to his.

He rewarded her by seating himself deep in one thrust.

Her blissful cry sent a sizzle of heat from his balls through his spine. Sweat popped onto his forehead as he started thrusting at a slow, deliberate pace.

His body wanted him to hurry, to pound into her and find his release. But Jared never let his body dictate his actions.

Out of the corner of his eye, he saw Dane glance at him, questioning.

Did he want Dane to put his cock in her mouth?

No, he didn't.

He shook his head once, just enough of a motion that Dane got the hint. He could play but she was Jared's. For now.

Dane's eyebrows quirked up in surprise, then he released Belle's breast for just a second to grin at him. Dane would want to know why later and Jared didn't know if he'd be able to explain.

He only knew he wanted her to feel only his cock, to know only his taste. Dane was only there to add to the pleasure. Not benefit from it. Dane could find his own woman later.

Just not his Belle.

He thrust harder and faster, sweat gathering at the base of his spine and coating his skin with a fine sheen.

Still staring at him, Belle sighed on each exhale, the sound both tortured and filled with bliss. He had the caveman urge to make her scream his name as she flooded his cock with her juices.

She shuddered, her body clenching around him tight as a fist. Heat radiated from her, soaking into his skin until he felt like he stood under a heat lamp.

He barely noticed Dane. He only had eyes for Belle.

And she looked transported. Her eyes glittered brilliantly through her slitted lids, just barely enough for him to see. One hand left her hip to smooth over her belly and down to her mound. His thumb brushed against her clit, once, twice, then pressed the hard little nub until she squirmed, causing his cock to twitch.

His release imminent, he rubbed her clit harder and thrust faster, watching her face.

She was trying to hold on; he saw it in the lines of her face. He wanted to rip her control away. He pumped faster and a little harder, watched her gasp as the base of his cock hit her clit on each inward thrust.

Almost there.

"Come on, baby. Let go."

She bit her bottom lip, drawing it into her mouth for several seconds before letting it ease out, glistening with moisture.

The sight sealed his fate.

His cock twitched and he felt his release explode through him. Hot cum spewed into the condom and, at that moment, he hated being confined. Then she cried out, wiping his mind of everything but the sight of her face as she came.

Her eyes closed then and her back arched, pushing her mound hard against his groin. Her sex squeezed him, milking him, and he stood there, knees locked against the quiver in his legs, watching her and letting pure ecstasy pour through his veins.

His eyes must have closed because when he opened them, he noticed Dane had gone and Belle was staring at him.

Her tight pussy still held his dick, her breasts quivered with each breath, and her smile nearly blew his mind. Again.

"Belle. Are you okay?"

He realized he was holding his breath and forced himself to relax as he withdrew.

Moist towels were stashed throughout the room, including the desk drawer. He should clean up. He didn't want to move but he forced himself to do exactly what he would have done if this had been any other woman.

He reached for the drawer and cleaned himself off discreetly. He did the same for her as she lay there, watching him with those bright green eyes.

Then she smiled and he swore his heart actually tripped over in his chest. "I'm fine."

Giving her his hand, he helped her back up to a seated position, smoothing her skirt down over her thighs and adjusting the top, the pin glinted in the light. He had the almost overwhelming urge to hustle her out of here, take her to his room and keep her there, locked away all night. All to himself.

But he didn't know that she'd appreciate that. She looked excited, ready to have fun. And that had been the whole point in inviting her.

Fun.

Her gaze darted over his shoulder and he heard the hum of a soft conversation behind him. Others had arrived and he hadn't noticed.

"Do you want a drink?" he asked. "Champagne?"

Her gaze flicked back to his and her smile curved again. "I'd love some."

He held out his hand. "Then come with me and I'll show you around. We got distracted. I didn't get to show you my collections."

She slid off the desk, fluffed her skirt and took his arm. "And what do you collect?"

Steering her away from the growing crowd on the other side of the room, where Dane was holding court, he led her to the first collection.

He watched as her eyes widened and a delighted smile lit up her face. "You have the Borel Les Mémoires de Saturnin series. Were did you find it?"

"From a dealer in France." He pointed at the next set of framed etchings. "And the Carracci Loves of the Gods series."

Like Belle, he had a collection of erotic artwork. Unlike Belle, his parents hadn't been as tolerant of his less-than-acceptable—at least to his parents—interests as a teenager.

He'd learned not to upset his mother with his fascination with sex and all the ways in which you could do it. But he'd lived for the times he could royally piss off his father by throwing it in his disapproving face.

Who had no room to talk, the cheating bastard.

"How long have you been collecting?" Belle had moved ahead of him, her sharp gaze examining each piece thoroughly. She looked engrossed.

Jared wanted her again, wanted to bend her over the rolled arm of the nearest sofa and take her.

He was becoming obsessed. And that could be dangerous. And then there was that pin . . .

He shook off the thought. "When I was twenty-one and came into my inheritance from my grandparents. Every penny I made working for my father at his hotel went into an account for the day

Tyler and I bought this place. Most of the money from my grand-parents went into the hotel as well but I saw a Beardsley piece at a shop when I was looking for the furnishing for this room and I was hooked."

"I'm not much of a Beardsley fan, but I do love Fendi. His work's so bright and playful."

She stopped finally before his most prized possession. She'd lost her smile but her expression had turned soft, almost yearning.

"You have an original O'Malley." Her voice had lowered to an almost reverent whisper.

"He's one of my favorites, though I only have this one original. I do have a few sketches but he's hard to come by."

"Some people only buy him because of the scandal attached to his name."

He heard the question she didn't ask. "Not me. His death was a tragedy. And his wife's and lover's."

"You don't think they deserved what they got? For the lifestyle they lived?"

He frowned, trying to figure out what exactly she was ask-ing. And why? "Everyone's entitled to live their life the way they want, as long as they don't hurt anyone else. From what I know, O'Malley and his lovers never hurt anyone. All the nontabloid accounts of their lives say they were passionate, wild, and totally in love. All three of them. The woman who killed them should've just taken herself out. She robbed the world of a great talent."

Nodding, Annabelle's gaze practically caressed the painting of Catrina O'Malley and Danton Romero by Peter O'Malley. It was one of a seven-part series featuring Catrina and Romero in various sexual positions. Jared hoped one day to own all seven.

"She was beautiful, wasn't she?"

He nodded, though he doubted Annabelle was expecting an

answer to her question. "I think so, yes. And O'Malley painted her beautifully."

"The right artist, the right muse."

"Do you have any of his work?"

Now Annabelle turned her attention back to him. "A few pieces, yes."

"Are they for sale?"

"No," she said, and turned to continue her examination of the rest of his collection.

They talked art for a while longer and he held up his end of the conversation. But mainly, he watched Belle.

Others were arriving, a few couples already pairing off and heading for dark corners.

Belle didn't seem to notice. Her entire attention was focused on the artwork. And on him. The thought occurred to him that she was avoiding the other couples.

Until she turned away from his collection and focused those bright green eyes on him.

"So, are we going to join the rest of the party?"

Five

Annabelle felt as if she'd had restraints removed.

As if she'd been given a free pass into a world of sensual pleasure, a world she'd never experienced.

Tomorrow, she'd return to her dusty antiques shop and her sheltered life. Tonight, she didn't want to waste a second.

From the moment the other man had joined them, from the moment he'd put his mouth on her breast, she'd let go of her inhibitions.

Or, more correctly, Jared had released her from them.

She'd never had sex in front of other people before, had never had the opportunity or the inclination.

Tonight . . . Tonight, she wanted to experience everything.

Her body still tingled from the most explosive orgasm of her life. She wanted Jared to touch her again.

And she wondered if she was a latent exhibitionist. And possibly a voyeur.

Because she knew the others who had entered the room were pairing off. Some of them in more than pairs.

And she wanted to watch.

"Would you like to join the rest of the party?" he asked in response to her question.

She let her smile be her answer.

Jared obviously came to the right conclusion and he pulled her against him. Even in her heels, she still had to tilt her head back to look into his eyes. And when she did, he kissed her. A deep, lingering kiss that made her pussy clench and her blood sizzle. Again.

She wanted to melt into him, into the hard contours of his chest and the thick muscles of his thighs. The man had a body worth worshipping and she still hadn't seen him naked.

She wanted to. Needed to.

But anticipation was a good thing.

After he eased back from the kiss, Jared turned her in his arms and leaned down to speak directly into her ear. "Watching is sometimes almost as much fun as participating."

His warm breath brushed against her skin, making her blood pressure rise again. With one finger under her chin, he directed her gaze to the left, toward the piano.

A man had taken the seat and started to play while a woman knelt at his feet, sucking his cock. His eyes were closed in ecstasy but his fingers flew over the keys, never hitting what sounded like a wrong note.

The woman's blonde head bobbed up and down to the rhythm of the music, one hand beneath her skirt.

Jared's finger nudged her chin again and she focused on the threesome on one of the chaise lounges. The woman lay on her back, her head hanging off the end as she sucked the man standing above her while another buried himself inside her.

She caught sight of the man who'd joined her and Jared seated on a plush, armless chair seemingly designed for exactly what he was doing—letting a woman ride him, her fingers clutched in his hair, her blue silk dress pulled up around her waist, his pants puddled around his shoes on the floor.

Her lips parted, her lungs unable to get enough air. Heat drenched her body, threatening to make her overheat. She knew she couldn't hide her reaction from Jared and didn't bother to try.

She'd never been so turned on in all her life and the more she watched the others around her, the more she wanted Jared.

Her sex began to throb, clenching in need and wet with desire. Without her panties, her juices would be running down her legs soon.

As if he'd read her mind or sensed her need, the hand he'd had resting on her hip moved down her thigh, stroking along her filmy skirt before sliding his hand under it. He teased along the outer flesh of her leg for several seconds, making her breath catch, before he curled his fingers around her thigh. He let his hand rest there for several seconds as she continued to stare at the other couples. Her focus started to blur as her entire attention focused on his hand.

The anticipation as she waited for him to move built like a slow-acting drug in her blood, her heart pounding and her lungs struggling for air.

And when he finally did, she drew in a deep breath and held it as his fingertips brushed along the inside of her thighs. Light as a feather but as tantalizing as his scent.

She felt the stiff rod of his erection nestle between the cheeks of her ass, and she ground back against him, wanting to torment him just a little in return.

But he got back at her, his fingers finally moving, if only to brush against her clit so lightly she couldn't honestly say he'd touched her at all. It was more like the whisper of a touch.

When she moaned, so softly she barely heard herself, the finger he had at her jaw took a leisurely path down her neck, coaxing shivers from her overheating body. He traced the hollow of her throat and the line of her collarbone. From there, it was only inches to her breast. He stroked the upper slope of her breast, tantalizing her already over-stimulated nerves with more pleasure.

"Jared." She barely whispered his name, but she knew he heard her when his hand obeyed her unspoken command and slipped into her bodice to cup her breast.

She moaned again when his fingers lifted her out of the material, baring her to the air, and tweaked her pebble-hard nipple. Her sex clenched, needed something to fill it as she nearly came from his touch.

And just as she had the thought, he slipped two fingers between her slick lips and thrust.

Caught against his hard body, held in place by his hands in her pussy and around her breasts, Annabelle came again, her body shuddering, her cry of completion lost in the music of the piano and the sounds of the other couples and threesomes enjoying themselves.

Jared drew out the sensation, his fingers thrusting inside, rubbing that spot that made her mindless, and rolling her nipple almost to the point of pain.

And when finally he removed his fingers from her body, she thought she might just fall in a puddle of satiation at his feet.

But Jared had other ideas.

"I think you need to get off your feet, Belle." In the next second, she was in his arms. She barely had time to realize they were moving before he set her on her feet and turned her away from him again. The next thing she knew, he'd bent her over the rolled arm of the nearest couch.

"Stay right here, sweetheart," Jared crooned as he shifted behind her. "Don't move."

Moaning, she heard the metallic slide of his zipper, the slight crinkle of a condom wrapper, then his hands flipped her skirt up to her hips.

"You have the most beautiful ass, Belle. I've been dying to smack it all night."

She couldn't produce a sound at how hot that made her. She wanted to feel his hand spank her, make her skin heat and tingle. It was something she'd never experienced, had never felt comfortable enough with another lover to even express this particular fantasy.

And then Jared's hand came down.

She bit her lip to stop from crying out as the sting traveled straight to her pussy, making it clench and moisten. Her breath hitched as the air behind her stirred and she tensed in pleasure, waiting for the next blow.

When it came, she moaned, her eyes closing to fully enjoy the sensation.

A few more gentle slaps followed, each one tightening her sex until she thought she might come.

But he must have sensed her nearing orgasm and instead brushed his hand over her hot skin.

"Oh, no, you're not getting off that easy. I want to feel you come around my cock again, baby. Right now."

He grabbed her hips and sank home in one fluid motion. Her

sheath clenched around him, grabbing hold of his cock and milking him.

"Shit, you're tight." Jared was practically panting. "And I'm not gonna last."

"Don't. Do me. Now. Hard."

His groan sounded tortured as he began to thrust with slow, deliberate movements.

She felt the head of his cock rub against that spot high in her channel, which was exactly what she needed.

Crying out, she began to come.

"Oh, God. Faster." She could barely force the whisper from her mouth as Jared pumped in and out, no more finesse. Just a wicked, wild ride that had her clutching the back of the sofa.

"Come on, baby," Jared chanted. "Come on. Come on."

Pleasure burst and streaked through her body, tightening her muscles and speeding like acid through her veins. The sensation stole her breath, nearly stole her consciousness.

Until Jared gave one final thrust and released inside her. Then she went boneless, slumping over the arm of the couch like a very limp rag doll, thinking, *Now, I know.*

* *

"What's up, Tyler?"

"We have a situation with one of the guests. I need you to come downstairs."

Rubbing sleep out of her eyes, Annabelle took a few seconds to orient herself as she listened to the brothers in the living room of Jared's apartment on the top floor of the hotel.

After Jared had carried her out of the Salon last night, he'd brought her back to his apartment and proceeded to strip her naked. She'd returned the favor, and the last time she'd noticed the clock on the bedside table, it had read something like 5:18.

It was now . . . 8:09. *Ugh.*

"Fine. Give me a minute."

She heard a pause, then Tyler said, "She's in your room, the redhead from last night. Jesus, Jed, did you take her to the Salon?"

"She signed the waiver. What the hell are you pissed off about?"

"Christ, Jed, she's not one of your reprobate friends. Why the hell did you drag her into your sick games?"

"She's not a child. She's a grown woman who had a hell of a good time last night. What the fuck is your problem?"

"My problem is Kate and Belle aren't the kind of women who get into your sort of fun."

Tyler was absolutely right about Kate but he didn't know Belle at all. Heat flooded her cheeks as images from last night crowded her brain. What she'd seen. What she'd done. What had been done to her.

She'd enjoyed every damn minute it of. Maybe a little too much if the ache between her legs was any indication. She refused to regret any of it.

But Tyler made her sound like a child. Or, worse, a rube.

She was no innocent. And last night . . .

Last night had been amazing.

"Okay, that's it," she heard Jared whisper. "What the hell is going on with you? Christ—"

"Damn it. God *damn* it. I don't know what the hell's wrong with me." Tyler sighed so loud, she actually heard the sound through the slim crack of the open door. "You're right. I shouldn't have jumped you. This situation downstairs has me pissed off. You need to deal with the guy before I say something I shouldn't."

"Hey, no problem, Tyler. I'll handle it. Did something happen last night, bro? You okay?"

"I'm fine."

"You know, it used to be your sort of fun, too. What's going on?"

"Nothing. Nothing's going on. Get dressed and meet me downstairs. We gotta take care of this other thing."

"Wait. I . . . need some advice."

"About what?"

Jared paused and Annabelle stilled, not wanting to miss what he had to say. "What if I told you my interest in Belle wasn't entirely sexual?"

Her breath caught in her throat. Was he saying he had feelings for her?

"Jed, what—"

"Did you notice the pin on her costume last night?"

Annabelle felt her face screw up in a frown. Her pin? Her gaze automatically fell to her fairy costume, lying on the floor by the bed. She'd been too busy to care what had happened to it after Jared had taken if off her last night.

"No, I didn't notice any pin. What does that have to do—"

"I think it's Nana's pin, Ty. I think it's one of Aphrodite's Tears."

"What? The set was stolen decades ago."

Annabelle swallowed a gasp at the last second. Her pin had been stolen? From Jared's grandmother?

"I know it sounds crazy," Jared said, "but I'm pretty damn sure that's what it is."

"Did you ask her where she got it?"

"She said her grandfather found it years ago at a flea market in a box of costume jewelry."

"So . . . what? You wanted her so you figured you'd have her and tell her in the morning, 'Oh, by the way, your jewelry's hot?' You don't even know if her pin's real. Christ, Jed, you're an idiot."

"Of course I'm not gonna say that. I'm not stupid. But the pin fits Nana's description perfectly and you know how much she wants it back. I'll pay Belle for it, of course. Anyway, last night was a one-off. It was fun but you said it yourself. She's not part of our crowd. I doubt I'll ever see her again. She doesn't exactly run in the same circles."

Indignation, hot as lava, flooded through her. Did Jared think she was some hick who just fell off the hay wagon? A laughable diversion?

Bastard.

She heard the brothers continue to talk but she shut out their voices. As quickly and quietly as she could, she jumped out of bed and pulled on her dress. With a pen and pad from the bedside table, she jotted down the address of the post office box she used for her lawyer.

Then she removed the pin from her dress.

Did he want the pin so badly, he felt he had to sleep with her to get it?

Just another asshole. She took a deep breath and pulled open the door.

Jared didn't notice her right away, standing with his back to the door. "That's not—"

"Jed." Tyler nodded toward her, his expression solemn, and Jared turned to face her.

Even with too little sleep, his hair mussed, and his eight o'clock shadow, the man was beautiful. Even if he had been exposed as a prick.

Jesus, did guys like this have some kind of radar that pointed her out to them?

"Belle—"

"All you had to do was tell me about the pin, Jared." She held the piece out in front of her, ignoring Tyler. "If I'd known it was stolen, I would've returned it to its rightful owner years ago. I do have scruples. If the pin actually *isn't* your grandmother's, I've included the address to my lawyer. You can return it to him."

Jared didn't take the pin, his eyes staring straight into hers. "I don't know what you think you heard, but—"

"Basically I heard everything." She forced ice into her tone, feeling it run through her veins as well. "The night's over, Jared. It was fun. Thanks so much for inviting me to your party." She made sure he understood exactly what she now thought of that party. "And please don't worry. I have no desire to be sued. Your secrets are safe with me. As I hope mine will be with you."

Then, instead of throwing it at him like she wanted to do, she flipped the pin to him like she was flipping a quarter. As if it didn't matter. As if she wasn't losing a piece of her grandfather. But she couldn't keep it. Every time she looked at it, she'd be reminded of tonight. And her gullibility.

Jared caught the pin, his mouth opening as if to speak, but she walked by the brothers, stepped through the door into the hallway, and headed for the elevator. Luckily, she saw no one in the halls. At this point, she didn't think she'd even care. Forcing herself not to think, she went straight to Kate's room and knocked. After a half minute or so, Kate cracked open the door. Her sleepy eyes widened, probably at the sight of the tears forming in Annabelle's eyes. Kate waved her through and Annabelle let the tears flow.

Six

"Jared, oh my goodness. The pin! What . . . How did you find it?"

A few hours later, Jared smiled at his grandmother's stunned delight when he placed Belle's pin in her hands.

"So it is yours?"

Her eyes wide, she flipped the pin in her hand, staring at the back before flipping it over again. "It's been so many years since I've seen it but yes, it is. Where did you get it?"

Fuck. He'd almost been hoping the damn thing wasn't the right pin after all.

"One of the women at the party last night was wearing it. When I recognized it and told her its history, she insisted I return it to you."

Beatrice's pale blue gaze lifted and pinned his. "She just gave it to? Did you offer to pay her for it?"

"I don't think she would have taken any money." Belle

would've rather had his head. He could still see the betrayal in her eyes before she'd closed the door in his face. She thought he was a snake.

God damn it, he wasn't. He'd planned to tell her about the pin that morning. He hadn't invited her to the party with the intention of seducing the pin away from her, though it was pretty obvious that's what she thought.

"Well, who is this woman?" Beatrice demanded. "I want to meet her."

Jared couldn't sit still any longer so he moved to the kitchenette in his grandmother's suite for a Coke. His grandmother didn't drink coffee and Jared would kill for a whole pot right now.

"I'm not quite sure how to contact her." He hated lying to his grandmother. He popped the top on the can and chugged half of it. "But she gave me the pin, and I'm returning it to you. I thought you'd be thrilled."

Beatrice's eyes narrowed. "Do you know where she found it?"

"She told me her grandfather found it at a flea market."

"Really? A flea market? Did you ask her if there were any other pieces?"

He shook his head and turned to set his soda can on the table to avoid meeting her gaze. "I honestly didn't think about that, Nana."

"So," Beatrice said slowly, "you're telling me you told her that this pin had been stolen almost forty years ago, was rightfully mine, and she simply gave it to you?"

With nothing to do but grin and bear it, Jared looked her straight in the eyes. "Yeah. Amazing, huh?"

His grandmother paused, staring back at him. "Yes, a little too amazing." Beatrice shook her head as she held the pin out to him, her mouth a straight, flat line. "This pin is no longer mine, Jared.

You have to give it back to the woman you took it from. Then you have to beg her to forgive you for being a complete jackass. I know you. You're hiding something, something that wouldn't reflect kindly on you. How *exactly* did you tell her the pin was stolen?"

Yes, his grandmother knew him too well.

He sighed but didn't reach for the pin. "I didn't actually tell her. She overheard a conversation I had with Tyler that she . . . misinterpreted. And"—he pushed forward before his grandmother could say whatever she'd opened her mouth to say—"I am planning to apologize. But I'm sure she'd want you to have the pin. Of course I'll compensate her—"

Beatrice cut him off with a sharp hand motion. "You will do no such thing. You will take this pin back to her. You will apologize for whatever you did and you will find a way to make it up to her." Shaking her head, Beatrice sighed and her shoulders sagged. "Didn't you listen to anything I've said about the legend in all these years? Jared, you may have thrown away your one chance at true love."

Silence filled the room as that four-letter word floated in the air.

Love.

She didn't really believe that. Did she? Jared stared at his grandmother, trying to figure out when she was going to laugh, to tell him she was joking.

But hadn't there been something there, some spark with Annabelle that you've never felt with another woman?

Chemistry, yes. Amazing chemistry. But love?

No.

They'd had a good time last night. Yes, he'd fucked up by not closing the door tightly enough to talk to Tyler. He certainly hadn't meant for her to overhear his conversation.

You hurt her feelings and didn't even bother to try to make it right.

Yes, he'd been an asshole not to apologize right away. He'd walked away with her pin, thinking . . . What? What the hell had he been thinking?

He hadn't been thinking. He'd simply decided to avoid the whole mess. He didn't do drama. Life was too short and he had enough in his life already.

He started shaking his head and couldn't stop. "Nana, if you want me to, I'll gladly return the pin. She's a very nice woman, but please don't read any more into this than there is."

"Oh, there's already more here than meets the eye." She nodded primly. "Tell me something. Was the pin the first thing you noticed about her?"

Jared could see where this was going. "No, Nana, it wasn't. But . . ."

"But what?"

With a sigh, he walked to the window and placed one hand on the cold glass. It was freezing outside at almost two in the afternoon. So different from last night's mild temperatures in the garden. And the warmth of the Salon. With Belle.

Which wasn't her real name. In fact, he wasn't sure who Belle really was. Her credit card was listed in the name of a business. He'd checked before coming here, knowing Nana would want to know who had found the pin.

Bullshit. You wanted to know who she was.

He wanted to tell his little inner voice, his conscience, to take a flying leap.

But he had to admit, there'd been something about Belle, something that drew him . . .

Silence surrounded him like a wet blanket, his grandmother's displeasure nearly tangible as he felt the heat of her glare on his back.

"Alright, alright." He spun from the window. "I admit I found her attractive before I noticed the pin. But, Nana, that doesn't mean I'm going to marry the woman."

Beatrice smiled as she lifted her hand, holding out the pin again. "Tell Belle I'd like to meet her. Have a nice day, dear."

* *

"Are you sure you're going to be okay? I could stay, if you want. We could do some damage to a bottle of wine and a box of Double Stuf Oreos."

Idling in her car outside Kate's home in Adamstown on Sunday evening, Annabelle forced a smile and shook her head. "I'm fine, Kate. Really. I'm just tired. I'm going to take a hot bath, watch a little TV in bed, and probably fall asleep in ten minutes. Shopping all day wore me out."

Yeah, right. Shopping. Sure.

Kate's eyes narrowed and Annabelle began to silently beg her best friend not to push. They hadn't spoken about what had happened, not since this morning when Annabelle had woken Kate and spilled the whole story.

How the only reason Jared had seduced her had been to get the pin.

Kate had been shocked, then furious. She'd wanted to tear Jared a new one. She wanted Annabelle to demand he give back the pin.

But Annabelle had only wanted to get the hell out. Humiliation burned like acid. She'd dealt with it before, and she knew the only cure was to shore up her defenses and she could only do that alone. Where no one could see her pain.

Pain was not for public consumption. The public twisted pain, consumed it like candy and left only ashes behind.

Finally, Kate sighed as she grabbed her overnight bag and shopping bags from their trip to the King of Prussia Mall. "Alright. I'm going. But I'll be by to check on you tomorrow. And you *will* let me in."

Kate's fierce expression actually made Annabelle's lips curve in a tiny, true smile. "I'll be fine tomorrow. Just make sure you bring doughnuts."

After a kiss and a hug, Kate reluctantly left the car, her expression worried. Annabelle drove home in silence and parked her car in front of the sturdy brick building that housed Elder Antiques.

Through the large front window of the first floor, she traced the controlled chaos of the store. The faint glow of the security lights outlined the larger furniture and display cases. She knew exactly what each case held and where to find every piece of inventory.

Her gaze then lifted to the second floor where she lived.

Home, sweet home.

For years after her parents' deaths, she'd felt adrift, anchorless. She'd lived all over Europe during those first three years with her grandfather, never staying in one place more than four or five months. Then she'd moved to Gettysburg and a series of dorms and apartments at college. She'd felt safe there. Insulated.

Now, finally, she had a place to call home.

But no family to make it one.

Pushing out of the car and gathering her stuff, she made her way up the stairs at the side of the building to the private entrance to the second floor.

Once inside, she did a quick check to make sure nothing had been disturbed and that the security system had registered nothing out of the ordinary. Dumping her bags by the door, she headed straight for the kitchen and the bottle of red wine on the counter.

Glass in hand, she made her way to her bathroom and turned the taps to fill the old-fashioned claw-foot tub her grandfather had had restored for her. As it filled, she wandered back into her bedroom to gather underwear but found herself stopping to pick up the photo on her nightstand.

It was candid, not a studio shot. Three adults gathered around a child who could've played the lead in *Annie* without the curly red wig. The girl was blowing out eleven birthday candles on a homemade cake that leaned to one side.

Everyone was smiling. Happy.

She remembered later that night, she'd crept out of her bed in the loft to go to the bathroom and caught a glimpse of the adults continuing the party.

Which had reminded her very much of last night's party.

Liquor flowing, couples, threesomes. Mom and Poppa on a bench by the wall, bodies entwined.

Daddy with his ever-present pad seated beside them, sketching, watching.

She remembered being transfixed by the sight, like a deer in the headlights. Not by her parents having sex. No, she'd been a fairly normal preteen and that was just too icky for her.

But her dad, the intensity in his eyes, the way his hands moved over the paper, the picture that slowly emerged from a series of lines and curves . . . That was amazing to her.

Her gaze lifted to the painting hanging on the wall. The one her dad had done from that sketch.

Only, instead of two people in the painting, there were three. He'd added himself.

It wasn't nearly as explicit as most of his other work. And it was one of his only watercolors, so it was hazy, almost indistinct. Lovely.

Annabelle thought it was one of his best pieces. It was certainly her favorite.

Peter O'Malley had had an incredible talent. And an incredible capacity for love, which had included her mom and their lover, Poppa Danton.

Until a crazy woman had murdered the three of them in a jealous rage.

Leaving one Graceanna Belle O'Malley an orphan.

* *

"So far, I got nothing. She's either a ghost, Jed, or she's got a lot to fucking hide."

Dane tossed a manila folder on Jared's desk the Tuesday after the party, then stood there looking pissed.

"I'll be damned." Jared picked up the folder and flipped it open to see exactly why Dane looked so furious. "Something you can't do."

Dane shot him the finger and started to pace. "It's no skin off my ass if I can't find her. And I've spent too much time on this already. I have paying customers."

"No, actually, you don't." Jared's gaze narrowed on the slim amount of information in the folder. "You don't charge anyone therefore you have no paying customers. What the hell does this mean? How can there be no actual people listed as owning this corporation?"

"Because the corporation doesn't actually exist." Dane finally threw himself into the chair opposite Jared's desk, shoving his hand through his dark hair to push it out of his face. "Whoever set this up was a fucking genius. I think I need to hire him."

"So you can't find her?"

Dane shot him a dirty look. "I didn't say that. It's just going to take a little time."

"How much time?"

"Maybe a week. Maybe more to sift through everything. I'm telling you, whoever did this did not want to be found."

Well, shit. Why the hell would an antiques dealer from some small town in Pennsylvania not want to be found? It sounded like the plot to a mystery novel.

And seriously pissed him off.

"Are you working the antiques store angle?"

Dane flipped him off with both middle fingers this time. "Stick to hotels and let the professionals handle the heavy lifting. Of course I am, but like I said, it'll take some time to wade through."

Jared sighed and tossed the file back on the desk. He was tempted to tell Dane to forget it. He'd tell Nana he couldn't find her and that would be the end of it.

But the look on her face as she'd tossed him the pin. The hurt . . .

And last night, he'd dreamed about her, naked and writhing under him while he thrust into her. She'd begged for more, bit his skin, licked him, sucked him. And he hadn't been able to get enough of her.

The dream had been so real he'd woken on the verge of orgasm, like a goddamn teenager.

He'd had to finish the job in the shower, thinking of Belle.

Christ, when the hell had he last dreamed about a woman? It was pathetic and he didn't do pathetic.

But . . .

"Keep digging. Let me know when you find her."

Dane's gaze narrowed. "Why?"

"Why what?"

"Why are you so determined to find her?"

"Nana wants to talk to her about the pin."

"That's not all." Dane sat forward in the chair, a smile starting to curl his lips. "There's something else. You actually liked this woman, didn't you?"

Jared rolled his eyes. "What are you? Twelve? This isn't high school."

"No, but you never acted this way in high school, either. You're always moving on to the next woman, the next party, the next project. You don't ever get stuck on one thing."

"I'm not stuck on her. Christ, Dane, Nana wants to talk to her. That's all."

Well, maybe not all. He wanted her back in his bed.

"Just find her."

Seven

"Damn the man, anyway. I hope he pricks himself with the pin and gets blood poisoning."

Annabelle ran a brush through her hair, twisting the unruly mass into a tight bun on the back of her head. Monday mornings she typically slept in because the shop was closed. Today, she had business.

She stuck in a few pins to hold the mass in place, then stepped back to check her appearance.

Minimal makeup. Brown suit, cream camisole that revealed no hint of cleavage. All buttons done up tight. Stockings, no runs. Brown and cream spectator pumps.

Should've kept my damn buttons closed New Year's Eve.

She looked . . . boring as all hell.

"No, not boring. Respectable," she told her reflection. Who stuck out her tongue.

Had it really been only two weeks since that night? A night

filled with more pleasure than she'd experienced in her whole life.

A night that had ended in humiliation.

Damn, Jared Golden. She had to stop thinking about him.

Today she needed to have her head in the game. One slip up and her carefully crafted life crumbled.

She pulled a face at herself. "Overdramatic much? Jeez."

Still, she had to be careful. Especially with collectors.

"Talking to yourself again, Annabelle?" Kate's voice floated into the room from downstairs. "I thought I told you to stop that. It's making me nervous."

Sighing, she turned from her reflection and headed down the steps to the shop. Kate waited at the bottom of the stairwell, grinning at her.

"I thought you were working today." Annabelle gave Kate a hug, holding on a little longer than usual. "Are you here for moral support?"

Kate's rueful smile was her answer. "Sorry, but I can't stay long. I just wanted to see how you're doing."

Annabelle tugged at the hem of her tailored suit coat. "I'm fine. Okay, maybe I'm a little nervous. I don't want to screw this up and have her realize who I am. Jesus, why the hell did I ever think becoming a freelance appraiser for Carmen Moran was a good idea? She *knew* my parents. She commissioned pieces from Daddy. I don't remember ever meeting her and I can't imagine that she'll connect me with them but—"

"Annabelle." Kate reached out to squeeze her hand. "Everything will be fine. Just calm down. Your grandfather made damn sure your background would stick when he had the lawyer draw up the papers for your new identity. Carmen Moran will have no reason to look beyond that."

Annabelle took a deep, calming breath. "You're right. I know you're right." She looked down at herself and tugged on her skirt. "Do you think I should have worn the blue suit? But the blue one makes me look fat. Of course this one makes me look like a spinster. But I—"

"Annabelle, please." Kate laughed, holding her hands over her ears. "My brain's going to bleed. Carmen Moran isn't coming to critique your wardrobe. She's coming because she knows you're good at what you do."

"I know, I know." Groaning, Annabelle hurried through the shop and into the front room. "I just want this to go well. If she adds me to her list of appraisers, my reputation will be set."

She cursed as she banged her left shin on an 1876 Philadelphia highboy and nearly knocked over a 1787 primitive rocker on her way to the counter in the front of the store.

"You'll be fine." Following behind, Kate smoothed a hand over her shoulder, brushing a spec of lint from the fabric. "Don't lose your cool. You know your stuff. You have a double major in art history and design. You've been collecting art all your life and you've got a file folder full of recommendations from satisfied customers who you've done appraisals for. You've got the credentials."

Taking a deep breath, Annabelle held it for a moment before letting it out. "I know you're right. I know it. It's just . . . My head's been all messed up lately. I wish I'd never met that damn man."

"Ah." Kate nodded sagely. "Now I know what's going on."

"I can't believe I fell for his line." Annabelle sighed, wishing she could just forget New Year's Eve. "I should have realized he was after something. He was just too good to be true."

And, oh, it had been good. Every night since that party, she'd dreamed about Jared. Dreams that owed more to her imagination than memory. He hadn't been that good.

Which is a complete crock.

She almost told herself to shut up, but then Kate would really think she was nuts.

"Just put him out of your mind for now," Kate said. "Focus on what you need to do. After you've been added to Carmen Moran's stable, I'll fix you up with some nice, quiet friend of Arnie's." She paused, wrinkling her nose. "Then again, maybe that's not such a good idea."

Annabelle saw something flicker through Kate's expression, something she'd never seen there before. Doubt about her relationship with Arnie.

Annabelle wanted to do a victory dance even though she shouldn't be so happy that her friend was having doubts about the man she'd agreed to marry.

Maybe their night in Philadelphia had been good for something if Kate was questioning her relationship. Which was a huge mistake just waiting to happen, Annabelle believed. But one she couldn't convince Kate of.

Seems all Kate had needed was one night at a swanky hotel party. If Annabelle had known that was all it would take, she'd have booked them a weekend away a year ago. Before she'd said yes to Arnie.

"You're right. It's not a good idea," Annabelle agreed. "I'm swearing off guys for a while."

At least she was swearing off playboys who made her hotter and hornier than she'd ever been in her life.

The bell over the door dinged, making Annabelle's breath catch in her throat.

Just her luck the woman would be early . . .

Turning, she swallowed a groan as Teddy Walters waddled into the room like a two-hundred-pound duckling.

"Hello, Annabelle," he chirped in his high-pitched squeak. "So, today's the big day, huh?"

She managed not to roll her eyes, but just barely, and forced a smile for her fellow antiques dealer. Teddy and his mom, Dolores, owned a shop just up the road where Dolores had a collection of Staffordshire china to die for.

"Good morning, Teddy. I thought you were visiting your sister this week in Pittsburgh?"

"Oh, I am, I am." He nodded to Kate, but never took his eyes off Annabelle. Well, Annabelle's chest. "But I wanted to be sure I said good-bye before I left."

Annabelle and Kate exchanged a look, which Teddy never noticed.

"Well, I hope you have a great time," she said. "Say hi to your sister for me."

"I will. Mom asked if you'd come visit her while I'm gone." He nodded sagely, the perfect copy of his elderly mother, who he still lived with. "You know how lonely she gets when I'm not there."

Annabelle now had to work to keep from rolling her eyes. Dolores actually loved to have her little house to herself. Said she enjoyed the peace and quiet.

When Teddy turned to look around the shop, she made a frantic face at Kate, who bit her lips to stop laughter from bubbling over.

Annabelle hated to be rude to anyone but she couldn't take Teddy today. He made no bones about the fact that he wanted to date her. But as much as Annabelle adored his mother, Teddy didn't do a thing for her. Which never stopped him from trying.

And after Jared—

No. The man had no place sneaking into her thoughts today.

"I'll be sure to stop by," she said with a gracious smile. "Now, I'm sure you need to get on the road so don't let me keep you. I know how your sister looks forward to your visits."

Teddy's bright smile made him almost handsome. Almost. "Alright, Annabelle. I'll be sure to stop by when I get back." He smiled again, and with one last quick glance at her chest, he walked out the door.

Kate and Annabelle sighed simultaneously, then broke out in bemused laughter.

"I swear, that man would attach himself to your leg if he ever cut his mother's apron strings," Kate said. "You should put him out of his misery and go out on a date with him. Just once."

Annabelle shook her head. "Wouldn't help. He'd never leave me alone then. But I did need the laugh. I should thank Teddy for that. I'm a little calmer now."

Kate gave her another hug before moving to the door. "Think about good old Teddy's face if you get nervous. That'll help you smile. I gotta get back to work. Just remember, Annabelle, no one knows your stuff better than you. Make sure you come and tell me how it goes."

Kate closed the door behind her, leaving Annabelle alone again to run a critical eye around the shop.

Situated on a side road off the main antiques drag, the building's former life as a small hotel built in the 1890s had been eradicated except for the main desk her granddad had turned into the checkout counter. He'd gutted the first floor for the shop and renovated the second and third floors into a living space.

The first floor, with the exception of the rear gallery, was an open space filled with furniture. Annabelle closed her eyes for a few seconds then opened them, trying to see the room as a casual observer would.

It was crowded, but what antiques shop wasn't. Granddad had alternately cursed and blessed their many treasures, but Annabelle had never seen the jumble as anything less than heaven.

Lancaster County chests mingled with Philadelphia sideboards and an authentic Gruber Wagon built in Berks County took up a large area near the front of the store. Grandfather clocks made in Reading near the turn of the nineteenth century towered over the folk art made by an itinerant farm worker in the 1940s.

She had a couple of Benjamin Austrian paintings on the wall and several local landscapes that, remarkably, still looked the same as they had a hundred years ago.

Since it was Monday, and the shop was closed, she didn't have to worry about visitors interrupting. But that left her with an hour to fill before Carmen Moran was set to arrive.

Carmen had agreed to come to the shop instead of interviewing Annabelle at her New York gallery because Carmen was traveling back from Ohio to visit family by car and it'd worked for her schedule.

That had suited Annabelle just fine. She loved the city but it'd been years since she'd been back.

Heading back to the front room and the CD player beneath the counter, Annabelle dug beneath the tasteful classical music she typically played when the store was open until she found what she wanted.

She smiled at the posturing cast of *The Matrix*. The obliviously cool Keanu Reeves. Sexy Carrie-Anne Moss. All that black leather.

Slipping the CD out of the case and into the player, she queued up her favorite song and cranked it.

Marilyn Manson blared from the speakers hidden throughout the shop. Closing her eyes, she let the hard-driving drums and guitar pound at her brain. She couldn't help herself, her feet wouldn't stay still, and she started to sway to the music.

Hairstyle be darned. They didn't call it head-banging for nothing. Music had been one of the few normal teenage things she'd been into. And she couldn't seem to cure the addiction to industrial metal she'd picked up when they'd lived in Germany for several months in her teens.

The music throbbed in her blood, lending itself to a total release of inhibitions. Thank God no one could see her—a grown woman dancing like she was a fourteen-year-old in the concert pit. Pins flew from her hair and she raked her hands through the mass to take out the rest. She'd fix it later. After she got this restlessness out of her system.

It felt good to let go. She'd been living in a fishbowl since breaking up with Gary. A young woman with no family, no boyfriend, and very few friends living in a tight community was cause for speculation.

If she hadn't—

Someone started clapping.

Eight

With a gasp, Annabelle stumbled over her now schizophrenic feet, grabbing onto the nearest piece of furniture to help her regain her balance. She froze, lungs gasping for air, and scoured the room until she found the intruder.

Silhouetted against the front window, Jared Golden glimmered like a mirage in the morning sun.

He wore a denim shirt under a black leather jacket and a pair of jeans that clung lovingly to his thighs. He looked so different out of his tuxedo she had to wonder if she wasn't seeing things at first.

Until he smiled.

Then a rush of heat swept over her, so devastating it threatened to make her knees buckle.

Elation rose before she could squelch it, followed by intense disappointment, embarrassment . . . and a little fear. He'd caught her with her guard down.

And he shouldn't have been able to find her in the first place.
Old fears tried to swamp her.

After the murders, her grandfather and his lawyer had hidden
her identity so well, not one of the tabloids or the news programs
had been able to find her. But that didn't mean she didn't have
panic attacks about being found. About having her identity, the
one she'd built around herself, ripped away.

Damn, damn, damn that man.

How the hell had he found her? She'd used her personal credit
card to charge the hotel bill, the card her lawyer had set up so that
neither her legal name nor any other was attached to it.

He'd assured her it was perfectly legal and no one would be
able to track her down through it.

Yet, here stood Joshua Golden.

Had he discovered who she was? Was that why he was here?

Don't assume anything. He can't know for sure.

Drawing herself up to her full height, she pushed her unruly
hair behind her ears and stuck out her chin. No way would she
let him see how flustered she was. After a deep breath, she walked
to the CD player and turned down the volume. She wouldn't turn
it off because that would leave a silence to fill. And this was going
to be bad enough.

"What the hell are you doing here?"

She'd meant her tone to be hard, unconcerned. And mentally
smacked herself when it came out breathless.

That smile of his pumped her blood pressure even higher.

"I have something of yours." His strong voice conquered the
music and his smile had disappeared. Staring straight into her
eyes, his intensity shuddered through her like an electric shock to
her system.

She swallowed and wet her lips before attempting to speak again. His gaze burned as it followed her tongue's path.

"You have nothing I want," she answered, proud of her now-steady voice.

That made his lips quirk at the corners in a staggeringly handsome way. God, the man was too good-looking for her peace of mind. He had to go. Before she—

No, he just had to go.

"I thought I'd made it perfectly clear that I had no wish to see you again. In fact, I never gave you my name."

Jared just smiled. "I know that. But I'm happy to report that I have a friend who's a pretty decent investigator. You'd told me you were an antiques dealer so it became a process of elimination. Next time, maybe you want to pick Mary or Kathy. Belle was just too close to Annabelle."

Okay. She could deal with this. She could deal with him knowing her name as Annabelle Elder.

What she couldn't deal with was his presence here. In her shop. Her world.

With what she hoped was just enough haughty disdain, she lifted her chin and prepared to brazen it out. "If I ever decide to go incognito to another party, I'll remember that. Now, I have a busy agenda today, so if you—"

"Actually"—he grinned, and that really was a crime against women—"I do have something that belongs to you. Two things, really."

She frowned. Heat drenched her and her cheeks began to burn as he tugged on a small swatch of green silk showing just above his front jeans pocket. The bastard *did* have her thong.

"But I'm only giving one back." He left the silk where it was as he reached into his shirt pocket with his other hand. The pin reflected the sunlight pouring through the front windows.

Holding her gaze, he walked toward the counter. Even though she stood behind it, she felt the need to step back, away from him. It was too easy for her to get lost in his warm—or perhaps lying—gaze. She resolutely held her position.

He set the pin on the counter and nudged it toward her with one long finger.

"The pin belongs to your grandmother," she stated, hoping her voice sounded as hard as it did in her head.

"Not according to my grandmother."

She frowned. "What do you mean? Are you telling me that's not your grandmother's pin?" She laughed, but it sounded like gravel grinding under tires. "So your little scheme was all for nothing."

He never even blinked. "I never had a 'scheme,' Belle. I only wanted you. Naked and under me. Naked and over me. Naked and next to me."

Oh, God, how could he make her thighs clench and sex contract by just talking? "I can't believe a word you say."

He shrugged. "I don't really expect you to. But the pin is yours, regardless of the fact that it was stolen from my grandmother."

Her fingers itched to reach for it, so she clasped her hands together in front of her behind the desk. "Please take it and leave."

He shook his head. "We have unfinished business."

"There is nothing unfinished between us."

He smiled that smile again. "Honey, I don't think you give yourself enough credit. I might have come, but I wasn't finished. Not by a long shot."

Pure lust swamped Annabelle's entire body in a wave of remembered pleasure, even though she didn't want to remember.

"I want you to leave."

He cocked his head to the side. "Are you so sure about that?"

She gasped. "Can you really be so arrogant? You played me for a fool that night. You expect me to welcome you back with open arms?"

"Annabelle, I wanted you from the first moment I saw you, before I noticed the pin. And you wanted me."

No way would she respond to that one. "Just leave, Jared. I don't want you here."

But she did. At least, her body did. Her body ached for him. And she couldn't allow that.

He couldn't be here. He made her want—Well, he just made her *want* so badly.

And she couldn't. She couldn't let herself be taken under by uncontrolled desire.

She turned from him and walked. Anywhere. She just had to get away from him. Her head was spinning and it was all his fault. She couldn't have this. Not now, not with Carmen Moran on the way—

She froze as she realized where her feet had taken her. Her gallery.

And she knew he'd followed her.

"Yes, you—" Jared stopped in mid-sentence.

She stood there staring straight ahead, feeling him behind her, knowing he took in everything—the paintings, the statuary, the tapestries.

This room held her life's work. Her passion.

And the only way out was through the doorway Jared now stood in. She would have to go by him to get out.

If she so much as touched him . . .

She managed to stop herself before that thought went any further.

But her treacherous mind began to replay their night together. In full, sweaty color.

Her. Him. The man who'd joined them. The other couples in the room.

Her lungs began to struggle for air.

"I guess you weren't kidding when you said you had quite a collection of your own." His tone was awestruck. "My God, Annabelle, this is amazing."

"Please leave." She'd plead if she had to. He needed to be gone. Or her resolve was going to fail spectacularly. "You're going to ruin my entire day."

"I would never want to do that, sweetheart."

She jolted as she felt his finger trace the line of her left cheekbone, trailing warmth. Her eyes closed, shutting out the room, but that only enhanced her sense of him. The heat of his body seeped into her, making her want . . .

A shiver coursed through her, which she knew he felt.

Distance. She needed to put some distance between them, but the only way to do that was to go further into the room. And she didn't want to do that either.

She turned her head, breaking the contact with his finger. His hand dropped to his side.

Remorse tried to rise but she fought it back with anger.

"Jared, if you came to apologize, fine." She tried to sound hard, cold. She was pretty sure she didn't succeed. "If I accept it, will you leave?"

"I apologize for not returning the pin immediately," he said without a moment's hesitation. "I would have come sooner, but there was that little matter of tracking you down. However," he said, holding up his hand, "I refuse to apologize for making love to you."

She shook her head, furious that tears had crept into her eyes again. "I don't want to talk about that. It was all a lie, anyway."

Jared clamped his mouth shut on his immediate denial. He knew she wouldn't believe him. Not yet.

And he'd rather show her how wrong she was. He wanted to kiss her and be done with it. He'd wanted to since the moment he'd walked into the shop. Hell, he'd craved it since the morning she'd disappeared.

That worried the hell out of him. But he was damn good at ignoring things he didn't want to deal with.

And when he did have to deal with something unpleasant, he could usually charm his way through it.

But for the first time in his life, he worried his charm might not be enough to get him out of this situation and back into Belle's good graces.

"How could you doubt exactly what I was feeling?" he said. "I never lied about that."

That brought her gaze around to him. How could he have ever thought she was merely pretty? With her cheeks pink-tinged with anger, her green eyes flashing and her chest heaving, she was gorgeous.

"Oh, please. Men are ruled by their sex drives." She flung out a hand. "Doesn't all of this prove that?"

He swung his gaze around the room again, taking a closer look this time. The artwork in the display cases appeared to be Asian. Couples in various sexual positions, some he'd never imagined. That was slightly humbling.

And holy shit, she had two O'Malleys. Both from the same series.

He'd check those out later, along with the rest of her collection, but now one particular small object caught his eye. He moved away from her, hoping like hell that she didn't leave, and walked to a shelf on the other side of the room.

"What I see is a collection of artwork celebrating love-making," he said.

He turned to catch her expression and was again struck by how much he wanted her. Even in the straight-laced suit with all the buttons precisely done up and the blocky square-heeled shoes, she exuded sexuality. She seemed to draw it from her surroundings. Especially in here. She lit up in this room.

Right now, though, she looked a little flustered. It puzzled him.

"Most men see it as a sign that I'm easy."

His brows flew up. "Oh, yeah? Then they're not really worth the time, are they?"

She crossed her arms over her breasts, her expression firming. "What do you want, Mr. Golden?"

He smiled. He had an easy answer to that one.

"I want you . . . to accept the pin and my apology. I never meant to hurt you."

Her expression didn't change, though she blinked twice. "Accepted. Now please leave."

He grinned, baring his teeth. No way.

He knew she wouldn't give in easily, but he had no intention of losing her so quickly this time around. This time, he would decide when they were through.

"Why don't you show me around a little first? I'd really like to see your collection."

Her pretty chin hitched up another notch. "There's nothing here I want to show you."

"Really?" He turned to pick up a large wooden object from the display case beside him then held it out to her. "How about this?"

She flushed but he didn't think it was in embarrassment. No, she was pissed. And that was much better than hurt.

She swallowed hard and met his gaze.

"Do you know what you're holding?" That husky voice of hers took on a schoolteacher tone.

He took another look at the object. "Yeah, I'm pretty sure what it's supposed to represent. But why don't you tell me about it?"

She fought the urge to answer, fought it so hard, he could almost imagine her biting her tongue to keep from answering. Finally, she walked near enough to gently pluck the precisely detailed phallus from his palm.

"Not that you care, but that's five hundred years old and African." She turned to replace it to the shelf and quickly stepped away from him, as if he might bite.

And he just might.

He turned to the display shelves again and examined the beautifully detailed netsuke. She must have more than a hundred of the tiny Japanese carvings, representing almost as many variations of the sex act. They were some of the finest work he'd ever seen though he didn't collect them.

He collected paintings and etchings and he'd thought he had a damn good collection of erotic art. Annabelle's put his to shame.

He recognized pieces by Romano, Paul Emile Becat, Antoine Borel, and Agostino Carracci. No Beardsleys, which made sense. He remembered she didn't like him. There were a few by artists he didn't recognize, one or two he'd like to buy.

Especially the O'Malleys.

Not that he considered even broaching that subject now. He had designs on much more than her artwork.

He wanted her. She'd become a craving, one he needed to work out of his system. Maybe because she'd been the one to walk away first. That didn't happen to him often. Usually women wanted to keep him and used any and all weapons at their disposal.

But he wasn't looking for a relationship. He only wanted her again. At least one more time.

He turned to find her watching him, her mouth pursed but her eyes . . .

She could pretend all she wanted but she wanted him too. She couldn't hide the heat in her gaze. Not when she looked at him like that.

But first he had to make amends.

"Annabelle, I am sorry I hurt you that night. My only excuse . . . Well, my only two excuses are that I love my grandmother and I wanted you. I still want you."

When she didn't say anything, he took a step closer. "I dream about you. I can't go into the Salon without replaying that night in my mind." He bent close enough to nip her earlobe if he wanted. "I go into that room a lot and it's damned inconvenient to walk around with a hard-on all day."

Now he did catch her lobe between his teeth as he heard her breath catch. He let the silky skin slide through his teeth then blew on it. She shivered and her lips parted to allow a heavy sigh to escape.

Then she moved away again. "I don't want anything you have to offer, Jared."

"Yeah, I'm not buying that, sweetheart." He traced a line from her shoulder to her hand then back up, until he came to the first button on her jacket. "I think you dream about me. I think you dream about that night and want more."

When she didn't knock his hand away, he flicked open the button.

"I think you burn for me like I do for you." Another button gave up the fight. "I think you want me to show you. Right here. Right now."

She didn't answer. She didn't do anything, just stood there, still as a statue, those green eyes glazed and staring straight ahead.

"I am so sorry I hurt you, Annabelle," he breathed into her ear, meaning every word. "I never meant to hurt you. Let me make it up to you."

He touched his mouth to hers, brushing their lips together, trying to get a response from her. When she only stood there, he turned his head to slant his lips over hers and delve deeper.

He wanted her to respond, wanted her to feel as out of control as he did.

And when she moaned and threw her arms around his neck to draw him closer, harsh desire broadsided him. He thrust his tongue between her lips and stroked her tongue, her teeth, the roof of her mouth. She welcomed him, opening her mouth wider to accept him, and it was his turn to groan.

Grabbing her hips to bring her against his raging erection, he felt a strange mixture of relief and heightened desire twist his insides into knots.

He would gladly leave them that way, content for the moment to kiss her, to have her cling to him and to feel her body against his. But he wanted so much more than a kiss, especially if it only took her kiss to affect him like this.

He raised his hands to finish unbuttoning her suit coat and

bumped into hers, scrabbling at his shirt placket. His heart started to pound against the wall of his chest.

It became a race. By the time she had his shirt unbuttoned to the waistband of his jeans, he had her suit jacket on the floor and her shirt around her elbows. Breaking off the kiss, he looked down. The plain white bra confining her breasts made him that much more determined to get rid of it fast.

He lifted his hands to remove it, but stopped before he ripped it away. He heard his breathing, hard and heavy, and lust pumped through his body.

Slow down. Take it easy. She's not going anywhere. And you're not a teenager.

Hell, even as a teenager, he'd never been this out of control.

And it was all her fault.

He stared down at Annabelle, his cock throbbing as she stared up at him. She wasn't smiling but the heat in her eyes seared him, made him burn.

She held on to his gaze as she bared his chest, pushing aside his shirt. He swore she should be able to see his heart pounding through his ribs.

As she watched, she leaned forward, pressing her lips to the center of his chest and nuzzling her nose in the hair, then kissing a path to his left nipple.

Slow down. Slow down.

The words chanted through his head, even as his body urged him to lay her on the floor and take her.

As slowly as he could, he reached for the front clasp on her bra. Feeling as unsteady as a teenager, he snapped it open and watched the cups part to reveal a tantalizingly small portion of creamy skin.

When he reached up to nudge them open even more, Annabelle's gaze lifted to snag his. She didn't say a word, but he caught a hint of something vulnerable, something cautious in her eyes. Something he'd put there by his actions on New Year's Eve.

He brushed his hand across her eyes, urging her to close them, then fastened his mouth over hers again. Wrapping his arms around her, he lifted her into him, her breasts crushing against his chest.

He heard the thump as her shoes hit the floor, felt her warm hand move to the zipper of his jeans. She slipped her fingers into the opening and caressed him through his boxers, shivers of pleasure making his flesh leap toward her.

If she kept that up, he'd come in her hand.

Holding her against him with one arm, he reached for her skirt zipper with his free hand and pushed her skirt to the floor. The pantyhose would be tougher, he knew from experience, but nothing he couldn't handle. He reached for the waistband . . . and found a garter belt instead.

Jesus. His cock gave a hard pulse as he realized there was still a little bit of the woman he'd met on New Year's Eve under all these prissy clothes. Releasing her mouth, he trailed kisses over her jawline and up to her ear. "Annabelle, I want you to leave those on."

She nodded. Or she shuddered. He wasn't sure which. Either way, she didn't argue. He never looked to see what underwear she wore. He just hooked his thumb into one side and pulled, letting them drop to the floor.

Setting her on her feet, his mouth took hers again as one hand wrapped around her neck and the other landed on her mound, petting the pretty little patch of curls there before sinking lower to her bare lips. Her bare, wet lips.

She moaned around his tongue as he breached her mouth. The

taste of her made his blood run thick, and the hand on her pussy stroked between her folds, his fingertips slick from her moisture.

The scent of her arousal acted like a drug, making him oblivious to everything but the smell of her, the feel of her.

He had to have her. He lifted his head, his eyes searching . . .

Christ, there's so much stuff. Not as much as in the front room but still . . . Wait, there. That would do just fine.

"Jared, wa—"

He kissed her again, cutting off what he was sure would've been "wait."

He didn't want to wait. Hell, he didn't think he could. She'd infected him like a virus. And he knew she wanted him. She arched against him, pushing her mound into his hand, her body telling him she didn't really want to wait.

Lifting her again, he strode toward the ornate velvet chaise in the corner by the far wall. Luckily it had a cushion, but he wouldn't have cared at this point if it were covered in nails.

But instead of placing Annabelle on it, he set her on her feet as he sat. Drawing her between his legs, he feasted on her breasts, now at the perfect height for his mouth.

He felt her fingers dig into his shoulders, her deep moan incentive to suck harder. His fingers kneaded flesh wherever they landed, sliding down the sensuous silk of her stockings. He stroked her bare bottom, her hips, and up to her breasts, where he suckled until her nipples stood out in tight peaks.

From his shoulders, her hands swept down his arms and up into his hair, her fingers tugging him closer.

"Jared."

Her husky voice stroked along his skin, pouring more gasoline on the fire.

He felt the rapid rise and fall of her chest, the restless movements of her body. She wanted to press even closer but he held her steady, enjoying the slight burn as she pulled harder on his hair.

Finally, with a not-so-gentle nip, which made her shudder, he released her breasts and began to string kisses across her abdomen.

Her hands skated across his shoulders, then her fingernails dug into his skin as he slid a hand between her legs again.

He brushed against her hard little clit, eliciting a cry from her that made his heart thunder. Her hips thrust forward, the little patch of curls on her mound brushing against his lower chest and making him crazy.

Faster. He had to go faster.

With his jeans still clinging to his hips, he grabbed for his wallet in his back pocket. Setting it next to him, he used his free hand to shuck out of his jeans then released her altogether to lay back on the chaise.

Standing beside him, Annabelle watched him with the sharp eyes of a cat. Her gaze traveled the length of his body. Like hot candle wax, heat dripped all over his body, sharp and stinging, but erotic as all hell.

She stared at the condom in his hand for several agonizing seconds before reaching for it, her expression almost fatalistic. But the heat in her eyes scalded him.

"You know," she said as she ripped open the packet, so slowly Jared wanted to grab it and do it himself, "I would have been perfectly happy if I'd never seen you again."

He spoke through gritted teeth as she reached for his cock, held it away from his body and rolled the condom into place. "I had to see you again. You've haunted me."

Okay, maybe that was a little too honest. He froze for a brief second, but the sweet smile that barely curved her lips made him forget he'd said anything.

"Good answer, Jared. Very good answer." In one sleek movement, she straddled the chaise, her knees on either side of his hips, and positioned herself over him. Gripping him in one hand, she guided him to her and sank onto him in a moment of perfect bliss.

His hips thrust up to meet hers and he sank as far into her as he could get. Her tight sheath gripped him like a fist, pulsing around him, egging on his climax.

He felt it building in his balls but forced it back as he reached for her hips to hold her steady, to keep her from going too fast.

"Slow down, baby. I don't want this to be over before we really get going."

Her expression glazed with passion, she stared down into his eyes as she continued to lift and lower her body over his. "And I don't have the time to let you play. I shouldn't have let you start this but I couldn't . . . I couldn't *not* . . ."

She never finished. Instead, she covered his hands with her own and drew them up her body to her breasts. She molded them to those plump curves, her eyes closing as he squeezed them, his thumbs caressing the hard tips.

Her deep moan made his balls tighten even more.

Then, as if she couldn't stand it anymore, she moaned and her eyes drifted closed. Her back arched, thrusting her breasts into his hands. He let his gaze drop to watch his fingers pinch those pointed rosy nipples.

Goddamn, she had beautiful breasts, the kind a man should worship. He thought about sitting up so he could get his mouth on them again but didn't want to disturb her.

She rode him so deliberately, so achingly slowly, as if she were testing him. Testing his control. And this was a test he would pass.

Even though, as he watched her curls bounce on her bare shoulders and the slight curve on her lips, his caveman instinct began to rear its head.

He wanted to make her beg.

Releasing her breasts, he let his hands drift down her sides to her hips. Her skin slid against his like silk on steel. Without warning, he braced her with his hands on her hips and thrust upward. She gasped, her eyes widening and locking with his.

"Jared."

"Did I hurt you, Belle?"

"Oh, God, no." She sighed. "Do it again."

He did, several times, until her lips curved into an outright smile.

Flat on his back, Jared watched her, his hands caressing her breasts, making her arch into his hands.

She maintained eye contact as she worked him in and out of her body, her green gaze slumberous and hypnotizing. Every movement pushed him closer to the edge of his control.

But he wanted her to break first; he needed her to.

Releasing one breast, he stroked down her body until he had his hand poised just above her mound.

Her breath caught in her throat and she froze in mid-thrust, waiting.

Holding on by a thread, his heart beating like a racehorse, he finally pressed his thumb over her clit and started to work it.

Her sheath clenched around him as her eyes closed, her head fell back, and she sank down onto him. The wet lips of her pussy met the root of his cock, her moisture seeping onto to his balls.

"Now, baby," he said. "I want to feel you come on my cock. Right now."

It seemed she'd only needed his permission. Her body shuddered around him, her orgasm a flurry of contractions that built in intensity.

Without warning, he sat up. The motion brought her clitoris hard against the base of his penis, and she cried out, her fingernails stinging his shoulders.

Jared rode out the need to come, counting backward from one hundred by sevens until he felt her internal spasms fading.

As their harsh breathing resounded through the room, she let her head drop onto his shoulder. He let her rest, enjoying the feel of her surrounding him, the warmth of her.

When she sighed, her body growing heavier on him, he moved just enough to let her know it wasn't over.

She moaned, and he thrust harder, but the position started to take its toll on his back.

In one fluid movement, he swung his legs to the side, still imbedded within her, then rolled until she was on her back on the chaise.

Raising her legs to clasp him around the waist, she opened herself wider, letting him ease deeper. Sweat broke out on his forehead as he fought back his own orgasm. He felt it gathering in his balls, boiling in his blood, and he forced it back, shoved it down.

Too soon. Not yet.

He froze, fingers digging into her hips. When he finally had himself under enough control to open his eyes, he found Annabelle smiling at him.

Then she moved. More like wriggled.

Jared groaned, his head dropping into the curve of her shoulder and neck. He put his mouth over the delicate spot where they met and bit down just enough to make her gasp. She tightened her sheath around his cock.

She turned her head, her lips brushing against his earlobe, raising gooseflesh over his entire body.

"Come on, Jared," she whispered. "Move. I want you to. I dare you to. You know you want to. I want to feel you moving inside me."

His body took up the challenge his mind tried to ignore. He moved. And then he couldn't stop. The need for her, the feel of her, swamped him in a rush of pleasure so sharp, it took his breath away.

His hips pistoned against hers, his cock shuttling in and out, the friction with each thrust heightening the sensation.

Until he felt his balls tighten to the point of pain and he came, his body and mind exploding in a pure adrenaline rush of sensation.

Nine

Still trying to catch her breath, Annabelle clung to Jared's naked shoulders.

In the back of her mind, she heard a little voice screaming, "You idiot! What the hell were you thinking?"

Well, that was pretty obvious, wasn't it? She hadn't been thinking. Or she never would have let him fuck her senseless.

No, that wasn't right. She hadn't "let" him. She'd wholeheartedly participated in their mind-blowing sex.

In her *shop*. Right before the interview that could push her career to the next level.

She felt a groan building in her chest, cushioned against Jared's.

Jesus, I'm crazy. Crazy about him. No. Absolutely not.

She refused to believe that. Sure, he was great in bed . . . or on a chaise, as the case may be.

But that didn't explain why she'd practically devoured the guy.

Holy hell, the sex had been explosive. Amazing.

She still felt him lodged inside her, and she tightened around him just thinking about it.

Above her, Jared groaned and nuzzled his nose against her shoulder.

She had to get up. She had to get him out of here before Carmen Moran showed up.

"Jared."

Sprawled on top of her, the man gave no indication he heard her. His warm breath blew against her neck, raising goose bumps. The heat of his body along hers made her want to close her eyes and drift in a post-coital haze.

But she couldn't. She gave his shoulders a shake, trying not to admire the sleek, hard muscles under all that silky skin.

"Jared, we need to get up."

His arms tightened around her, as if he knew she was going to try to get away.

"No, we don't." His voice rumbled out of his chest, fresh arousal zinging through her veins.

God, she had to get the man out of here before she lost what few brain cells she had left and boffed him again.

God, was she deliberately trying to sabotage her meeting?

That made her pause before she mentally shook her head. No, that wasn't true.

"Yes, we do." She pushed against his shoulders and this time he moved, barely enough so he could see her.

His eyes were slits of sky blue as he stared down at her.

"Hey, babe. You okay?"

No, she wasn't okay. She was so screwed. "What time is it?"

He frowned but grabbed his pants to look at his phone.

"Quarter of ten. You have somewhere you have to be?"

She sighed in relief. She still had fifteen minutes—

The bell over the front door rang.

Her mind blanked and a terrifying darkness yawned at the edges of her consciousness.

"Hello, Annabelle," Teddy Walters called, his voice strangely deeper than normal. "There's someone here to see you."

Oh, my God.

"Oh, my God."

With a shove, she pushed Jared off her and scrambled to her feet. Jared hit the floor with a loud thump, and she scowled down at him as she looked for her clothes.

"Be quiet," she said. "They'll hear you."

Jared lifted an eyebrow at her as he stood, brushing off that perfectly formed, naked ass. "Just let me pull on my pants and I'll get rid of—"

"Oh, my God, *no*." Her heart skipped a beat as she pulled on her underwear. She wanted to yell at him but she had to keep her voice to a whisper. She heard Teddy and a voice that could only be female talking in the main shop area. "Don't even think about it, Jared. Just stay here."

Where the hell was her skirt and shirt? She spied her bra under the chaise and dragged it on as hysterical laughter wanted to erupt along with an impending sense of doom.

"Belle, what—"

"Damn it, Jared."

"Just be quiet."

She shot him a glare meant to shut him up, but her addled brain got caught on the sheer animal magnetism of his body. Could the man be any sexier than he looked right now, standing naked among her erotic collection? He resembled a piece of art himself, even with his cock spent and his watch the only thing on his body.

"Annabelle?" Teddy called again. "Are you here?"

She gasped and grabbed the first thing within reach—Jared's jeans. She tossed them at him, uncaring when they caught him in the face.

Her blouse. Her coat. She needed to find them. Right now.

Her skirt was within reach and she pulled that on. Her coat was by the door. *Screw it.*

Doom sounded with every approaching footstep.

Behind her, she heard clothing rustle, the metallic snick of a zipper, then Jared slipped her blouse up her arms.

His warm hands caught her shoulders and turned her so he could button the placket of her shirt.

"You were expecting someone?"

With her brain still numb, she merely nodded as she shoved her top into her skirt and fumbled for her shoes. She couldn't do anything about her hair but finger-comb it and hope to hell it didn't look too bad.

Now, if she could just get Jared to stay hidden.

She nearly squealed in shock as he moved toward the door to the front room but caught herself before any sound emerged.

Oh, my God, she was going to kill—

"Jared?" A female voice she didn't recognize called out as Jared disappeared from her sight and into full view of Teddy and whoever he'd brought into the shop. "What are you doing here?"

"Carmen! Hey, nice to see you. How have you been?"

"Fine, I've been fine. How are your parents?"

Her mouth dropped open as realization shot through her when they carried on a short conversation.

Jared knew Carmen Moran.

Well, of course he did. He collected art. It wasn't much of a stretch to believe he'd dealt with Carmen Moran at some point.

"I take it you're here to see Annabelle?"

Jared's question jolted her into action.

Shit, she needed to get out there now.

Stopping in front of the display case, she checked her reflection as best she could before scooping her jacket off the floor and quickly buttoning it.

With one last finger-comb through her hair, Annabelle pasted on a smile, stuck out her chin, and headed out into the fray.

* *

Two hours later, Annabelle's temples throbbed and she swore her face was going to permanently freeze into this smile.

"Thank you again for taking the time to come out here, Ms. Moran. I appreciate it."

The other woman smiled as she pulled on her overcoat and grabbed her Coach tote, holding Annabelle's carefully crafted resume. "I very much enjoyed meeting you and I'll be in touch soon."

Probably with a "Thank you, but no thanks."

As Annabelle closed the door behind the woman, she smiled pleasantly and waved until Carmen started her car and drove away.

Then she released a long, pent-up sigh and wilted back against the door.

Cold air seeped into her back, making her shiver in reaction.

"Well, that sucked."

Carmen Moran probably thought she was an idiot. She'd sounded like an idiot.

All that preparation blown to hell.

And nothing she could do about it now.

Pushing away from the door, she headed for the counter and realized the pin was no longer there.

Drawing in a quick breath, she hurried behind the counter, thinking maybe it had dropped behind.

"Looking for this?"

Annabelle shot straight up, gasping when she saw Jared standing in front of the door. He must have let himself in just a second ago.

In his outstretched hand, he held the pin. "I didn't think you'd want it lying unprotected on the counter so I picked it up. How'd your interview go?"

Her mouth firmed and her cheeks heated with anger. "I need you to go, Jared. Tell your grandmother I want her to have the pin and just go."

"No. We have unfinished business." Crossing his arms over his chest, he leaned back against a display case, his face a cool mask.

"No, we don't." She spoke carefully, as if she was afraid she'd let her anger get the better of her. "You need to go."

Jared wasn't going anywhere. God, she was gorgeous when she was angry, even with her beautiful mouth pursed in a straight line. But he saw tears in her eyes and that made his stomach churn.

Damn it, one of these days he'd put a smile on this woman's face that would stick.

He shook his head, knowing it would anger her even more, but there was no way he was leaving.

Walking over to her, he set the pin on the counter between them. "Why don't we go somewhere and talk? Do you live upstairs or is there somewhere else we can go? We need to talk, Annabelle."

She shook her head again and pointed at the front door. "You need to leave."

"Sorry, not happening." Letting his gaze roam the shop, he looked for the stairs to the second floor. He knew she lived above the shop and she wasn't going to get rid of him so easily.

"Jared, what— Oh, no. Don't you *dare* go up those steps."

As he blatantly ignored her, he heard Annabelle huff and the sound of her angry stomps on the stairs behind him.

"Where do you think you're going?"

"You need a drink. Got any alcohol in this place?"

He reached the top and found himself in her living room. The décor had the look and feel of a romantic country inn with lots of floral fabrics, chunky wood tables, and overstuffed furniture. It felt comfortable. Like home.

Well, not his home, but it certainly fit Annabelle.

A little eclectic, a little traditional, the red velvet accent pillows on the couch added a hint of sensuality.

Beyond the living room, he spied the kitchen through an open door and headed for it.

Behind him, he heard Annabelle reach the top of the stairs.

"I do not want a drink." The strength was returning to her voice. "It's barely noon, for heaven's sake. I want you to leave. If you don't, I'm calling the cops."

He reached the kitchen, which didn't have any windows big enough for her to push him through, so he stopped in the doorway and smiled at her. "Honey, you don't really want to do that. Besides, I've got a proposition for you."

Her mouth dropped open. "A proposition? What the hell are you talking about?"

He turned to reach for her refrigerator. "You look a little uncomfortable in that suit, hon. Why don't you go get changed, then we'll talk."

He hadn't been lying to her. He did have a proposition. Just not of a sexual nature.

With the great-sex buzz still zinging through his body, even after he'd spent two hours waiting in his car for Carmen to leave, he had to be careful not to overtip his hand and have Belle physically toss him out. She was upset and angry and he didn't want to make it worse by grinning like a fool. He had no doubt she'd try to eject him if she decided she wanted him gone.

Of course, there was no way he was leaving. Not now.

He pulled open the fridge. A gallon of milk, a carton of orange juice, and a bottle of white Zinfandel were the only beverages. He pulled out the wine just as something hit him in the back. Turning, he caught a breath-stealing glance of a furious Annabelle as she stomped away. A pillow lay on the floor by his feet.

For a brief second, he considered following her but decided against it. She needed a little time to calm down.

He set the wine bottle on the table, scrounged up glasses from a cabinet, and waited. A minute later, she stomped back, dressed in green army fatigues and a tight Penn State T-shirt that'd seen better days. The faded pink cotton lovingly outlined every single one of her abundant curves.

And given how his cock stirred, you'd think he was a teenager the way his body responded around her.

Thankfully, he'd sat at the dining room table and his erection was hidden.

Watching her approach, he saw her emotions plainly on her face, defeat clear in her eyes.

Annabelle dropped into the seat across from him, her mouth set, but her eyes suspiciously wet. He poured her a glass of wine, topped his own, and then said, "Tell me."

Without speaking, she reached for the glass and took a healthy swallow. She looked ready to tell him to go to hell.

He braced for a fight, then released his tightly held breath when she started to talk.

"Carmen Moran was here to interview me for a position as a

freelance appraiser. I am *damn* good at what I do and Carmen's firm is the most respected in the field. I wanted that job, Jared."

Surprisingly, he heard no condemnation directed toward him in her voice. Only self-recrimination.

No way would he let her feel bad about the attraction that registered off the charts between them. He might not believe in true love or soul mates or anything so prosaic. Pleasure as intense as what they'd experienced wasn't something you just tossed away.

"Are you in financial trouble?" he asked.

She shook her head. "I'm in no danger of losing the shop. Yes, business has taken a hit in the past few years but I'm not struggling."

"So you don't really need the job?"

Sucking in her bottom lip, she just stared at him, as if she didn't want to say anymore.

Okay, fine. With a smile, he picked up his glass and walked into the living room.

"I'd love to see your home. Why don't you show me around?"

"No."

"Gee, Annabelle, is that any way to treat a guest?"

"You're not a guest."

"You wound me." His eye caught on a grouping of paintings in the hallway that probably led to the bedrooms and he headed over to look at them. "But don't worry, I heal fast."

"Jared, stop."

He did, but only when he reached the hall.

"Holy shit."

He stopped dead in his tracks, staring at the painting.

She had another O'Malley.

He moved down the hall, his heart starting to pound for no good reason.

She had two. The smaller painting wasn't signed but he'd bet his reputation that was an O'Malley, too. One he'd never seen. One he'd never heard mentioned or catalogued.

"Jared!" Annabelle grabbed his arm and pulled him back in the direction of the kitchen. Away from the paintings. "I want you to leave. Now."

Annabelle's heart threatened to pound out of her chest as Jared stared at her father's paintings in the hall.

She could explain being in possession of another O'Malley. She'd told him she had a few. But Jared was smart and he knew O'Malley's work.

She'd have a damn hard time explaining the unsigned portrait of her mother if he realized what it was. And he would. She knew he'd be able to tell it was one of her dad's just by looking it. Everything about it screamed O'Malley, from the color of the paint he used for her mom's hair to the blue settee she lay on.

She needed him to leave now. Before he looked at her and began to ask questions. Questions she couldn't answer without risking everything she'd built here.

He didn't put up a fight as she practically dragged him to the door that led to the stairs on the outside of the building.

Maybe she should have realized he was making it too easy on her. But all she wanted to do after that interview with Carmen was sit in her room and devour a pint of Turkey Hill rocky road ice cream.

Flinging open the door, she shoved him through. "Keep the pin. Just don't come back."

She went to slam the door in his face but he put one hand on the door before she could. With the other, he snagged the waistband of her sweats and pulled her closer.

Those blue, blue eyes stared into hers with an intensity she couldn't break.

"I'll be back to take you to dinner at seven," he said. "Make reservations wherever you want but be sure you're here when I get back. You don't want me to come looking for you."

Opening her mouth to tell him in no uncertain terms there was no way in hell she would ever go out with him, Annabelle gasped when his mouth covered hers for a kiss that took her breath away.

Hard, forceful, and utterly wicked, his mouth moved over hers with a possession she should have fought.

But didn't.

Shocked, she let him kiss her until her body began to respond. Her nipples peaked and hardened, her sex moistened, and she had to force her arms to stay straight at her sides, otherwise she would have wrapped them around his shoulders.

Then he released her.

She stared up at him, her lips parted as she drew in much-needed air. She felt the weight of the pin in her pocket where he'd slipped it.

He looked cocky as ever, his grin lopsided. "And wear the pin. It looks good on you."

* *

Stepping out of Annabelle's building, Jared walked across Main Street so he could take a look at the entire building.

Built from square-cut stone blocks, the two-story structure looked like a box, but its clean lines, large windows, and oak-plank door spoke of another time. A cornerstone on the front proclaimed the year 1829. Good, strong bones. Like many of the other buildings in the town.

Mayberry couldn't hold a candle to Adamstown. He looked first left then right up Main Street. He didn't see a car coming either way. Way too quiet for a born-and-bred Philadelphia boy.

The town probably rolled up its sidewalks by nine o'clock. Shaking his head, he started walking east on Main. He'd driven in from the west and hadn't seen much more than houses. The rest of Main Street, all ten blocks of it, contained two small factories—Goods Potato Chips and the Bollman Hat Factory. Each looked like they'd been entrenched for years.

Annabelle's was the only antiques store on Main and not visible from Route 272, which bypassed the town. Most of the antique stores that were this area's claim to fame sat along that road. She did have a sign on the main highway, but it wasn't large. He wondered what kind of advertising she did to keep the business going.

Or maybe she didn't need to. Maybe . . .

Maybe he was crazy for thinking what he was thinking.

He knew Peter and Catrina O'Malley and their lover, Danton Romero, had been killed by an unstable woman with a fixation on Danton. He knew Peter and Catrina had left behind a daughter who'd been in her teens at the time.

And he knew that Annabelle Elder owned three O'Malley paintings, one not even known to exist.

Bypassing his car parked along the street, Jared decided to take a walk. Clear his head.

He'd love to add those paintings to his collection. He wanted them almost as much as he wanted her.

Other than Annabelle's shop, the town boasted two churches—beautiful brick buildings with stained-glass windows—a VFW, a beauty salon, a tailor, a café, and less than a hundred private residences. Not two blocks from Annabelle's was a small inn.

The Horse-and-Carriage Inn had Victorian gingerbread trim and about four different paint colors. In the summer, the grounds and building would be shaded by mature trees. The gardener had an eye for landscaping and there was enough winter interest in the surrounding gardens to avoid appearing barren.

Not what he was used to but it certainly ranked above the motel he'd seen on the drive in.

He headed back to his car for his cell phone to make a reservation.

And give Dane another call.

* *

"Annabelle! Annabelle, are you here? Do you know who I just saw walking down the sidewalk?"

Kate's voice rang out from the shop, forcing Annabelle out of the stupor she'd fallen into. "Up here," she called.

In seconds, Kate bounded up the stairs, her eyes wide and shock plainly written on her face. "You are never going to believe—"

"Jared's in town. I know. Wine?"

Kate froze, then sank into the chair Jared had occupied not that long ago. "Did you know he was coming? What's he doing here?"

Annabelle poured herself another glass. "No, I didn't know he was coming but he had impeccable timing. Showed up just in time to screw up my interview with Carmen Moran."

Kate's eyes widened even further. "Oh, jeez, I completely forget about that. How'd it go?"

Annabelle just shook her head.

"Oh, wow." Kate grimaced. "What happened?"

After another healthy swallow of wine, she spilled the whole sordid story, cringing as she thought about what she must have looked like, just fucked and probably smelling like sex.

"I'm screwed," she muttered. "You know that, right? Carmen Moran will never talk to me again."

"Please." Kate rolled her eyes. "Who cares what that old biddy thinks, anyway? You're doing just fine on your own. What are you going to do about *Jared*?"

Annabelle frowned at her best friend. "Are you kidding? I'm not doing anything about him. There's no way I'm going to dinner with him." She shook her head. "Jesus, Kate. He saw the paintings in the hall. What if he figures out who I am?"

Kate waved that comment off. "Why would he even think that some random antiques dealer might be the daughter of a famous painter because she has a few paintings by the guy? You're a collector."

"Because he's smart as hell. He's going to realize the portrait of my mom is something he's never seen mentioned. Not ever. He's going to want to know where I got it." Annabelle wanted to tear out her hair. "Hell, he's going to want to buy it and I'm going to have to tell him no. Jesus, everything's messed up. The man is a complete menace. I can't believe I fell for his act. Again."

"Alright, Annabelle." Kate's voice had the same tone she took with naughty children and dirty old men. "Take a deep breath. You've got to snap out of this. This is not the end of the world. He's not going to figure it out."

"God, I wish I could believe that."

"Okay, so what if he found out? Would *that* be the end of the world?"

Icy fear coated her veins as she remembered back to just after her parents' murders. "I couldn't go through that again. The gossip, everyone talking about them like they were deviants. It was hell the first time."

"Oh, sweetie." Kate reached across the table to grab her hand. "I can't imagine how awful that was. But Jared is not a tabloid reporter."

"No, he might be worse. He's a collector."

Kate's eyes rolled again. "How is that worse?"

Because what if he figures it out and only wants me because of who I am?

Annabelle didn't say that aloud. She barely wanted to think it. Because like it or not, she had feelings for the man.

"Annabelle? When is Jared coming back?"

"Seven. But there's no way I'm going out with him. How can you even suggest that? After everything that's happened?"

Kate's expression softened. "Are you really saying you don't want to see him again? And tell the truth."

Of course I want to see him again.

She bit back her immediate response, shaking her head. God damn it, it just wasn't fair.

The truth was her heart beat a little faster and her panties got wet each time she thought about him. And she'd been thinking about him a lot.

So not fair.

Sighing, she threw her hands in the air. "Of course I want to see him again. The man makes me hot. But everything's already so messed up. When I'm with him, I don't think straight. And that's not good. He's a playboy. I don't want a man like that."

"So what do you want?"

She opened her mouth to answer and closed it just as fast because she didn't have a quick answer. "I don't want a guy at all."

"Right." Kate smirked. "If you weren't looking for a man, why did we go to a party so you could meet one?"

"That was just sex."

Kate was getting pretty good at that eye roll, Annabelle noticed.

"So what's stopping you from having 'just sex' with Jared while he's here? It's not like the man offered to marry you. And it's not like you want him to. But why not take what pleasure you can while you can?"

Logically, she knew that. Emotionally . . . Hell, emotionally, she was a mess. She wanted him. She didn't *want* to want him. She was angry with him. She was so damn happy to see him. She never wanted to see him again.

When she didn't say anything, Kate huffed. "You never did tell me why he was here in the first place. Did he come to apologize? What?"

"His grandmother insisted he return the pin. But I can't take it. It . . ." She shook her head.

"Reminds you of Jared?" Kate prompted.

"Yes, and I don't ne—want any reminders of him."

"But you want him?"

Of course I do. "No, it's a recipe for disaster."

"It doesn't have to be. Just be sure you set the rules. The man wants you bad. He could have just given you the pin and left again but he couldn't resist you."

Kate made it sound so simple. And so easy. Still, the more she thought about it, the more she wanted him. Even with the risks . . .

"Don't think so hard, Annabelle. The man wants you. You want him. Just make him suffer before you let him rip off your clothes."

"You're right. You're absolutely right. I want him to crawl on the floor and beg me for it."

Kate's smile would have made a grown man run for his mother. "Then let's see what you're going to wear tonight."

* *

"What do you mean, you're not coming back right away? What the hell are you up to, Jed?"

"I'm not up to anything. I've just decided to stay a few more days. Miss me already, big brother?"

Tyler's derisive snort came through the cell clearly. "Yeah, right. I know you. There's no way you just decided to take a few days away from Philadelphia to spend it in some one-stoplight town."

"I'm not sure there's even one stoplight in town, as a matter of fact."

"All the more reason for you to come running home. What are you really doing? I assume you talked to Annabelle."

"Yes, I talked to Annabelle."

"And?"

And we had mind-blowing sex and I have this crazy idea that she might be the long-lost daughter of a famous dead painter. "I gave her the pin."

"So you've done your duty."

"We're going to dinner tonight."

Tyler paused so long, Jared wondered if they'd lost the connection. "Why?"

"Why what?"

Tyler's sigh sounded loud and clear through the phone line. "Don't be an ass. Why are you taking her to dinner?"

Because I want to see her again. "I've decided to offer her a business proposition."

"What kind of a proposition? Christ, Jed, what the hell are you talking about?"

"I think this area could be perfect for the spa we've been talking about."

The one Jared had been thinking about for the past few months. The hotel had been only the first step in their plans. Now that it was running smoothly, Jared needed something else to keep him occupied. The woman and the spa would do for now.

"And you decided that . . . when? In the space of a few hours?"

"Yes. Look, we can talk about it when I get home. I'm going to check out some land, maybe meet with a few Realtors while I'm here. It may not pan out but my nose is twitching, Ty."

"I bet that's not all that's twitching." His brother released another sigh and Jared knew Ty was pinching the bridge of his nose like he always did when he was frustrated with him. "Just keep in touch. And . . . if you run into Kate, tell her I said hello."

Jared grinned at his brother's attempted nonchalance. "You sure you don't want to come up here and help me look at property?"

"Yeah, fuck you, little brother. Just don't get too cozy up there or you'll find yourself out of a job."

"You can't fire me, bro. Fifty-fifty partnership, remember? I'll tell Kate you said hi."

* *

"The man won't know what hit him."

Annabelle glanced at the clock—six forty-five—then back into the mirror. "You don't think it's too much for dinner? I made reservations at The Boxcar."

Kate shook her head, her mouth curved in a satisfied smile. "No way. It's perfect."

Actually, Annabelle had to agree. She looked great in the straight wool skirt covered with bold geometric shapes of blue, rust, and green, and a deceptively simple V-neck sweater in the same green. The sweater showed just enough cleavage and she'd attached Jared's grandmother's pin to the V, drawing attention to the swells of her breasts. Not too dressy, not too revealing, yet clingy in all the right places. Luckily, she'd found the skirt stuffed in the very back of her armoire and, even luckier still, it fit and matched the turtleneck.

Paired with brown suede stiletto boots and a wide brown belt, her hair curling around her shoulders, she looked so very . . . feminine.

"And you don't think this is a huge disaster just waiting to happen?"

Kate's hands planted on her waist. "I think you'd be foolish if you don't go. And if we're going to have this conversation again, I'm going to go downstairs and smash your netsuke collection in a frustrated rage."

Yes, they'd been over this same material a hundred times already.

Kate had called her boss earlier and told him she wouldn't be back for the rest of the day. Surprisingly, he hadn't given her a hard time. They'd spent the time digging through Annabelle's closet for a suitable outfit for tonight. The activity had kept her mind off what had happened this morning while giving her something else to obsess over. She wanted Jared to take one look at her and have his tongue fall out.

And when she opened the door precisely at seven, she knew she'd achieved her goal.

While his mouth didn't hang open, she saw heat flare in his eyes, making her burn from her toes to the top of her head. And everywhere in between.

Jared recovered first but not before a telltale nerve in his cheek began to tick. "Hello again, Belle."

His gaze held hers for several seconds before he deliberately let it rake over the rest of her.

And she couldn't resist checking him out as well. Dressed in black pants, a tight cream sweater, and a black leather jacket, he looked devastatingly handsome. She didn't think she'd be able to eat a bite of dinner without wanting to have him for dessert.

And when he smiled, her mouth watered.

"You look beautiful." Jared glanced over her shoulder and his smile dialed down just the slightest bit to friendly warmth. "Kate, how are you?"

"Fine thanks. It's nice to see you again, Jared."

"And you. By the way, Tyler says hello."

Annabelle caught the blush that suffused Kate's face when she turned to take the coat Kate held. "Ah, that's, um, nice. Thanks." Kate turned an almost frantic look her way. "I'll lock up when I leave, Annabelle. Have a good time."

Poor Kate. Just the mention of Tyler's name—

"Are you ready to go, Belle?"

Of course, the sound of Jared's voice made her shiver.

She forced herself to meet his gaze and smile, just enough heat in her eyes to make him wonder.

Pulling on her coat, she stepped through the door. No need to tempt fate by inviting him in, even for a minute.

Then he took her arm and heat sizzled at the contact, even through the layers of clothes. As he led her to the BWM sedan sitting at the curb, she forced herself to speak.

"I made reservations at The Boxcar. It's only a couple of minutes away. I'm sure it's not up to the standards you're used to, but they have good food and it's a nice place."

He handed her into the car and shut the door, then walked around and settled into the driver's seat. "I'm sure anywhere you choose is fine, since I'm not familiar with the area."

After giving him directions, she leaned back in the plush leather seat and tried to keep from ogling him. The inside of the car felt toasty compared to the twenty-degree weather outside, but she couldn't be sure if that was due to his proximity or the car's climate control.

"Kate looks good," Jared said after she'd told him how to get to the restaurant. "Tyler asked about her when I called earlier. They seemed to hit it off at the party."

"Your *brother* seems like a nice guy."

Jared laughed at her slight emphasis. "You're going to make me work for everything, aren't you, Belle?"

She gave him wide eyes. "I don't know what you're talking about."

"Of course you don't. I don't mind. But there is something I'd like to talk to you about tonight."

Annabelle stiffened at the serious tone of his voice. What did he know? What had he found out?

"I've got a proposition I'd like to run by you."

Oh, God. Her heart pounded like she'd just run a five-minute mile but she forced a cool smile. "A proposition, huh?"

"Yeah." He grinned again, making her insides twist into knots. "I've been searching for a new location, somewhere for a spa. One out in the country, where there are no sirens, no cars. Somewhere isolated."

It was so not what she'd been expecting him to say that she sat in silence for at least half a minute before she said, "A spa? Out here?"

Those perfect eyebrows arched. "You sound doubtful."

"It's just not—When did you come up with the idea to build out here?"

"This morning, actually. It's close to the regional airport and minutes from the turnpike. The antiques trade in the area will be a draw and I'll hire you to furnish it. I'm thinking high-end English charm, Victorian without the clutter. Maybe a little Middle Eastern luxury mixed in. A sensualist's dream."

She opened her mouth to tell him no, but her imagination

turned traitor. Images of huge canopied beds, ornate furniture, and rich jewel-toned fabrics flashed in her mind.

Now her stomach tightened with anticipation. Damn the man. It wasn't fair how he could tie her in knots like this.

Still, she couldn't accept it. That would require spending way too much time with him. And the more time she spent with him, the more chance there was for him to discover her secret.

But, oh, the offer was tempting. The man, even more so.

"Budget wouldn't be an issue," Jared continued.

Of course it wouldn't. The man didn't play fair.

"And Tyler would agree with this?"

"We've been kicking the idea around for at least a year. We need something new to focus our energies on. A new challenge."

Had he glanced at her when he'd said that? Did he consider her a challenge? Someone to conquer before moving on?

"Sounds like you're bored, Jared."

He shrugged, drawing her gaze to his broad shoulders. "Maybe a little. Nothing a new project won't fix."

"And how long does a 'new project' usually keep you busy?"

His mouth curled up in one of his devastating grins. "As long as it takes to make sure everyone's satisfied."

Now she no longer needed the heater to keep her warm.

Luckily, he pulled into the restaurant parking lot and stopped the car. Call her a coward but she opened her door and got out before he could do something chivalrous like open it for her. She didn't need any help liking this man.

He caught up to her before she'd taken more than two steps away from the car and put his hand on her back. She barely felt his fingers through the layers but she knew they were there.

She straightened her back so she didn't sink into him like she wanted.

Jared stopped just before they entered. "Are they authentic?"

Turning, she found him staring at the structure with a contemplative look on his face. She couldn't help but smile at his expression. "Yes. They used to be dining cars on the line from Reading to Philadelphia sixty or so years ago. The owners bought the cars and opened the restaurant about twenty years ago. They've expanded the seating areas over the years but the cars are still intact. They have great food."

"Then I'm ready to eat. I seem to have worked up an appetite."

Oh, she was *so* not going to respond to that one.

As they stepped through the doors into the first car, Annabelle was reminded once again of just how small a town she lived in. Everyone in the restaurant turned to watch them and she recognized people at no less than four of the eight tables in this car.

Several actually stared, their mouths hanging open in surprise. Most of those were men.

The women gave her a once-over before their gazes locked on Jared.

And really, she couldn't blame them. The man would make a dead woman smile.

Of course, he didn't appear to notice.

Instead, he smiled at the approaching hostess, a sixty-five-year-old grandmother of three who ran this restaurant like a boot camp instructor. A former army nurse who'd served in Vietnam, Ginny Donaldson's eyes widened as she shook Jared's hand, barely glancing Annabelle's way as she led them to their table.

They passed through the first car, and people turned to watch them as they walked by. Annabelle stared straight ahead, trying to feign a composure she was fast losing.

Because she'd just remembered it was Monday.

And Monday night, Gary had a standing date at The Boxcar for dinner.

She froze just inside the door to the next car, causing Jared to almost bump into her. He placed a hand on her back and all thoughts of Gary fled at the heat of his body so close to hers. Images from this morning flashed through her head, making her draw in a sharp breath.

"Annabelle? Are you okay?"

Turning her head, she glanced up into Jared's eyes. Heat burned there, banked but visible. For her.

This gorgeous man wanted her.

She smiled, letting all the desire she felt for him shine in her own eyes. "Yes, I'm fine."

"Here you go, sweetie." Ginny waved them to the first table on the left, the one farthest from Gary, who sat at his usual table at the far end of the car, where he could check out everyone who entered.

His comically stunned expression made Annabelle swallow her own laughter. And when the bimbo secretary she'd found him messing around with only a few short weeks ago stuck her head out of the side of the booth to see what Gary was looking at, Annabelle slid into their booth so she wouldn't be tempted to stick out her tongue in sheer childish glee.

"Sorry, I didn't have a table in the other car." Ginny's lowered voice barely carried over the quiet conversations of the other diners, most of whom she didn't recognize. "We're a little busier than normal for a Monday."

"No problem, Ginny." Annabelle flashed the woman grin, suddenly feeling much better than she had all day. "This is just fine."

Jared's gaze narrowed on hers as he took his seat across from her.

The high, curved backs of the booths effectively hid them from the other diners and cocooned them in their own little space. She could no longer see Gary and, with hardly any effort, she put him out of her mind, focusing instead on Jared.

Who only had eyes for her. "So, what's good here, Belle?"

God, that voice. It made her shiver. And the intensity in his eyes filled her with heat. And fire.

"Depends on what you're hungry for." She allowed a small smile to kick up the sides of her mouth. "The menu's varied and the food's delicious."

Jared's eyes narrowed at her over the menu, as if he'd noticed her slight change in attitude. "What are you having?"

Kate's suggestion that she make the rules for their relationship and have Jared dance to her tune flitted through her mind.

He wanted her. And with Jared, she knew what she was getting. Great sex and no ties. She'd tried the relationship route. It hadn't agreed with her.

Kate was right about her history. Granddad had made sure no one could discover her secrets. And she'd taken the precaution of storing the rest of her dad's paintings, those hanging in her bedroom, in the temperature-controlled storage room in the shop.

Just in case Jared made it back to her bedroom.

Just in case.

"I haven't made up my mind yet," she said. "I'm still . . . debating."

He closed the menu, set it on the table, and stared straight at her. "I have the feeling you're talking about more than food."

Her mouth dried and images from New Year's Eve rushed through her mind. The things she'd allowed him to do. What she'd allowed another man to do . . .

Her cheeks heated and her lungs struggled to draw in air. His gaze burned hotter.

"We rushed things New Year's Eve, Jared—"

"Annabelle. You look . . . well tonight."

Gary's voice threw her for a moment, and she looked up to find her ex standing at the entrance to their booth.

His brown hair was perfectly combed to hide his receding hairline. He covered his thickening middle with well-cut clothes but he stood stiff and straight, as if he had a stick shoved up his ass.

The mental image made her glance back at Jared and smile.

Jared returned that smile for a brief second before he slid out of the booth and stood, holding out his hand. He towered over Gary, making Annabelle's smile widen.

Jared diminished Gary's presence.

"Jared Golden. And you are?"

Gary's expression vacillated between speculation and petty jealousy. Annabelle couldn't tell if he was jealous that another man was dating his ex-girlfriend or just of Jared in general. And Gary certainly had a lot to be jealous of. Jared was ten times the man he was.

"Gary Jarzakrak." Her ex looked between her and Jared and back again. Then his mouth kicked up in a faint sneer. "I see you've bounced back, Annabelle."

Jared's brows curved upward as he looked back at her. She knew Jared had picked up on the undercurrents between her and Gary, and Jared's smile turned deceptively bland.

"Were you sick, honey?" Jared's tone was all concerned innocence.

Gary snorted and her blood began a slow boil. "Didn't she tell you? We had a falling out a few weeks ago."

Jared stared into Gary's eyes and shrugged, his broad shoulders moving with an elegance Gary would kill for. "Sorry, she never mentioned you. No idea why that would be."

Gary's mouth opened and closed but no sound emerged.

And Annabelle was so ready to be done with the dramatics.

She reached for Jared's hand and laced her fingers through his before turning back to Gary. "I'm sure your date is wondering where you are. Don't let us keep you."

"No offense, Gary"—Jared's tone held a hard edge now—"but I don't want to waste my time with Belle shooting the breeze with you. Nice to meet you, though."

Jared dismissed the man without another look as he slid back into the booth. He looked into her eyes, the hint of a smile in his. "Have you decided?"

Heat lit through her, starting in her stomach and radiating out. Her smile softened and she only marginally noted as Gary slunk away.

"You're very sure of yourself, aren't you?"

His intense expression left her with no doubt about what he wanted. "About you, yes."

Sighing, she shook her head. "Why did you come here, Jared? You could have very easily FedExed the pin."

Leaning back into the booth, he let his head rest against the tufted seat as his gaze slid down, ostensibly to the pin. "I don't think I can make it any more obvious. I want to spend time with you."

Yes, but how much time? Was he looking for a relationship or just sex?

Well, the answer to that should be clear. Sex. A man like Jared could pick and choose his partners and for some reason he'd chosen her.

How long it lasted shouldn't even be a question. She wasn't looking for long-term. But short and hot certainly wouldn't hurt.

"Then let's enjoy dinner."

After they placed their order, Jared began to ask questions—about the area, traffic, construction, development, other businesses. He kept her occupied and entertained, his nimble mind always onto the next subject before an awkward silence could form.

Dinner was over before she realized she'd eaten her meal. Over coffee and crème brûlée she couldn't resist; she knew she was going to ask Jared to come home with her for a drink.

Maybe stay the night.

She went wet just thinking about it.

Their waitress laid the check on their table at that moment, and Jared turned to smile up at the woman, who couldn't help but look a little dazed.

Annabelle knew the feeling. "So, I guess you need to be going."

Jared's smile spread into a grin. "Trying to get rid of me?"

Her gaze dipped, unsure if she wanted him to know just how much she wanted him to stay. "No, I just figured you wouldn't want to drive back to Philly so late—"

"No worries there. I took a room at the Horse-and-Carriage for the next week, at least."

Jared watched Annabelle's gorgeous green eyes widen in surprise. He'd expected that. What he hadn't expected was the rush of other emotions that crossed her expression.

Desire. Hope. Heat.

She dropped her gaze, staring at the table for a few seconds before meeting his again. "I haven't had many relationships. They're time-consuming and most men don't appreciate the long hours I put into my work. When Granddad and I opened the shop, it was with the intention that I would take over and make it my own. I'm not about to give that up for a man."

Damn, he really liked this woman. She knew what she wanted and wasn't afraid to speak her mind. "I would never ask anyone to do that. Most of my life is consumed by the hotel. I want you, Belle. You're a beautiful, interesting woman."

Her chin jutted out and her gaze met his again. "I'm not looking for long-term, Jared."

He didn't know what she wanted him to say to that one. The phrase "long-term" wasn't even in his vocabulary.

She took a deep breath when he didn't speak.

"So . . . yes, to your offer. I'll help you look for a site for your spa but if either of us decides the situation's not working, we agree to let the other walk, no questions asked."

He dismantled his grin before it could start. "Agreed."

It was her turn to look surprised. "That was fast."

"I know a good deal when I hear it. Now, are you ready to leave?"

She stared at him for several seconds, contemplating. Then her lips curved in a sweet smile. "Would you like to come back to my place for a drink?"

Triumph had his own grin bursting out. "Absolutely."

Jared rose before she could change her mind and reached for her hand to help her from the booth. Her fingers curled around his, reminding him of how they'd curled around his cock earlier today.

He wanted her. And hopefully by the end of the night, he'd have her.

Ten

"So I thought you might want to consider featuring local products in your spa."

He took a sip of the wine she'd handed him and liked the idea almost as much as the wine.

"There are several wineries in the area and a world-famous microbrewery down the road. There are organic farms for fresh produce, dairy farms, and honey growers."

"Sounds like you and I are on the same wavelength. I've considered some of the same things. And I'm interested." Mostly in her, though her ideas were sound. Yes, he knew they'd have to talk business eventually but not tonight. Tonight, he wanted to talk about her. "How long have you lived here?"

She slid onto the couch next to him, which he took as a good sign, curling her legs under her and inching her skirt almost over her knees. Not enough skin to be indecent, just enough to tantalize.

"Granddad bought the property when I was in my second year

at college. He didn't want to travel as much as we had when I was growing up, and he finally decided to open the shop he'd been talking about for years. After I graduated from college, I came home to help run it. I've been here ever since."

"You don't miss traveling?"

She gave an indecisive shrug. "I still do when I need to. What I enjoy is finding treasure in someone's dusty attic. Tracking down the perfect piece for a client. I enjoy the hunt."

"Gets your blood flowing, does it?"

Her lips curled in a seductive smile, the look in her eyes smoldering. "I find it stimulating, yes."

Holy hell, his skin felt too tight for his body and his cock throbbed with desire. "What else do you find stimulating?

Her eyebrows gave a little shrug. "You."

The burn in his blood turned into a full-blown forest fire. "Then come here and let me stimulate you."

Instead, she leaned back against the arm of the couch and stretched her legs toward him. "Are sex and business all you think about?"

"Not just sex. Pleasure. There's a difference. Sometimes there's not much pleasure in sex. Sometimes sex is strictly business. But pleasure encompasses a whole spectrum of activities, not just sex."

"Sounds like you've put a lot of thought into this."

"You've seen the Salon. I personally chose every piece of furniture, every fabric, every piece of art and accessory. We didn't stay long enough for you to get the entire Salon experience."

Her eyes narrowed. "And what would that have entailed?"

"Sexual freedom. Whatever fantasy you could have dreamed up, I could have made come true."

"You didn't exactly give me that option."

"No, I was uncharacteristically selfish that night." And he

wasn't about to sit here and analyze his reasons for that now. "But I'm willing to make that up to you."

"Oh, really?"

"Absolutely. Tell me what you fantasize about, Belle."

Her smile faded as her gaze sharpened. "Is it all just fantasy with you?"

"No, it's about the pleasure. Fantasy is just a way to attain pleasure."

"And what do you fantasize about?"

"Right now, my fantasies involve you and whipped cream."

She laughed as he'd intended because he'd sensed her thoughts shifting away from the moment. "And if I told you I actually have a can in my fridge . . ."

"I'd say take off your clothes, sweetheart."

She drew in a deep breath, as if he'd shocked her. Or like he had reached between her legs and stroked her.

"And what if I want you to do the same?"

Now, that was an interesting question.

He was usually the one in control, the conductor, as such. He planned the games, and sometimes he even paired the players.

His life was all about control, professionally and personally. He knew exactly why he needed it. Made no excuses for it.

None of his friends and lovers thought any less of him for it. Hell, they expected it. He was the son of Glen and Helena Golden, the product of blue-blood old-money Philadelphia. He'd been born with the silver spoon in his mouth and a fortune in his bank account.

"I'd say I think we can work something out."

Her head tilted to the side, as if trying to get a different angle on him. "Do other women let you get away with this much control?"

Yes, actually, they did. "They know I'll deliver."

He let her think about that for a few seconds, watched her bite on that full bottom lip as she contemplated.

Then she sighed. "I live in a small town, Jared. People gossip. I don't want to be the subject of that."

The thought slid through his brain that maybe she'd had enough gossip earlier in her life. He was still considering putting Dane on the trail of that mystery. But that didn't have anything to do with now. "You're young and unmarried, Annabelle. Why shouldn't you be free to have a sex life?"

She didn't say anything in response to that but he saw her expression firm, as if she'd come to a decision.

Her chin tilted up. "I'm not looking for a relationship. I've got a business to run." She held up a hand as he opened his mouth. "Just hear me out. I want you. I can't deny that and I don't want to. The heat between us is something I've never experienced. So yes, I want to explore that. But I also don't want a sexual relationship to interfere with business."

"You won't have to worry about that. I'm capable of keeping the two separate."

She didn't hesitate. "Good to know. I want you to strip."

The command in her tone made his balls tighten with lust, his stomach clench in need.

He'd never let another woman control his arousal before. But there was something about this woman, something that made him want to relinquish the tight hold he had on his own desire. Something he'd never wanted to do for anyone else.

He reached for the top button on his shirt, and her gaze dropped to watch his hands as he slipped the tiny discs through their holes. He didn't rush but he didn't make a strip tease out of it either.

Just before he reached his waist, he pulled the tails out of his pants and released the last button. Shrugging the shirt off his shoulders, he tossed it at the nearest chair.

Then he let his gaze drop deliberately to her sweater.

Taking the hint, she reached for the hem of her top, pulling it free of her waistband, and exposing an inch of creamy flesh. His lungs tightened as she wiggled just the tiniest bit and revealed her slightly rounded stomach.

By the time she'd uncovered the black lace demi-bra cupped so lovingly around her breasts, his chest ached with the effort to draw in air. His gaze fastened onto those firm mounds, practically salivating at the slight jiggle as she pulled the sweater over her head. Her beautiful red curls bounced over her shoulders and spilled down to caress her curves.

Beneath the bra, her hard nipples peaked, nearly poking through the lace, tangible evidence of her desire.

He lifted his gaze back to hers and watched her eyebrows lift.

"Your T-shirt, too," she said.

With one hand, he reached behind him and pulled the white cotton over his head, dropping it on the floor.

Her gaze swept with blazing heat across his chest, searing him as if she'd reached out and touched him. He took a breath, trying to tamp down a little bit of his raging desire, just so he didn't go caveman on her and start ripping away her clothes.

But just the thought made him hotter still.

"Now your skirt."

She smiled as she reached for the zipper at her side. He heard each tiny tooth release with a metallic snick, every one causing his heart to trip heavier in his chest.

She had to lean back and lift her bottom off the cushion to get the skirt over her hips, wriggling a little and making his body temperature shoot up another ten degrees. When she got the skirt past her hips, his gaze locked onto her black garter belt and black lace panties.

Damn, he loved a woman who wore garters. They reminded him of the erotic art they both collected. Such a sensualist's touch. He wondered if she wore them all the time or if she'd deliberately worn them for him?

He wanted her to have worn them just for him.

By the time she'd drawn the skirt down her legs and let it fall to the floor, his hands had curled into fists at his sides. He wanted to reach for her, wanted to pull her over him so he could let his hands roam all over those soft curves.

Instead, he let his gaze trace the lacy straps that connected to the silky stockings then back up to the string bikini panties lying low on her hips. Beneath the lace, he saw the faint outline of the soft triangle of hair on her mound, knowing what he couldn't see was bare skin. His fingers remembered how soft she'd been between her legs, how silky.

"I want you to keep those garters and stockings on tonight, sweetheart."

"I think I can handle that. But you're not finished yet. Take them off, Jared."

He had to stop himself from tearing off his pants and reaching for her. Instead, he released his belt and the button on the waistband, then drew down the zipper. Her gaze had dropped to watch his hands and his cock throbbed as he pushed the pants down his legs, slipping off his shoes and socks and letting them fall in a pile by the couch.

"I absolutely love a man in boxer briefs." Her sexy voice reached out and stroked his libido, making his balls tighten and his cock throb.

Good to know but he was about two seconds away from ripping them off his body. The tip of his cock had already escaped the waistband of his briefs. The shaft felt like heated iron.

Reaching for some of his legendary control, he leaned back into the couch. "Why don't you come here and take them off me?"

Annabelle had never in her life seen anything as sexy as Jared Golden reclining on her couch in only his boxer briefs.

He should have been a Calvin Klein underwear model. He certainly had the body for it—broad shoulders and muscular chest, washboard abs, slim hips and powerful thighs. A swimmer's body.

When did the man find time to work out? And why did she care when he was spread out like a banquet just for her?

She wanted to climb onto him, feel every hot, hard inch of the man pressed against her. She wanted to let her hands roam over the sleek muscles of his biceps, then brush her fingers through the light covering of dark blond hair on his chest before sliding down to stroke along his abdomen until she reached the waistband of his boxer briefs.

His cock poked above the elastic, the ruddy red tip practically begging her to touch it. Or taste it.

She felt a momentary flash of hesitation as the little voice of reason in her brain started to nag.

This isn't you, Annabelle. What are you doing? You're not sexy, even if you are wearing fuck-me garters and stockings and a seethrough bra.

She'd chosen her undergarments specifically for Jared. And because they made her feel sexy. They gave her a boost of confidence she sorely needed.

And the look on Jared's face when he'd seen them had made

her want to stretch out in front of him and tease the hell out of him.

"Belle?"

She lifted her gaze from his groin to his face slowly, letting her desire for him blaze in her eyes. His expression tightened and a muscle in his jaw flexed. He looked so very sexy.

He swallowed, and her gaze dropped to his mouth. That mouth did wicked things to her body. Things she really liked.

Swinging her legs under her, she rose on her knees and put her hands low on his thighs, kneading her fingers into the taut muscles like a cat with a blanket. His gaze held hers as she moved her hands higher until she could slip her fingertips beneath his boxers. Curling her fingers, she let her nails scrape against his skin, making his muscles clench and bunch beneath her.

"I know somewhere else you can use those nails, sweetheart."

His voice rumbled, a sexy growl that made her sex clench with need and her blood thicken and heat.

"Come on, Belle. Take them off."

"I'm not sure I like your tone, Mr. Golden."

"Then I'll try again." He leaned forward until their lips were a hairsbreadth apart. "Please take my shorts off so you can wrap your hands around my cock."

Her fingers curled into the soft cotton of his boxers, but she didn't tug them down. "That sounds like another command."

"Do you want me to beg?"

Hell, yes. Her smile must have given him his answer because he leaned closer until his warm breath washed against her ear. "Please take them off, baby. Please. I'm dying for your touch."

She tugged on the material, slowly so she didn't hurt him, watching as every hard inch of him was uncovered. He leaned back and lifted his ass slightly so she could pull off the boxers, dropping them on the floor and moving until she knelt between his legs.

His cock reared up toward his stomach, and her mouth dried at his beauty. Perfectly straight, thick, and elegant, his balls drawn up tight against his body.

And so silky hot. She curled one hand around him, letting his heat soak into her skin as her other hand cupped his sac. She let her index finger straighten and scratched her nail lightly on his perineum.

He drew in a short breath, his cock throbbing in her hand, as she started a slow pump of his shaft. His gaze refused to release her as she caressed his cock.

He let her have her way for a few minutes before he reached for her. He brushed the mound of her breast then wound one red strand around his finger and tugged just enough to let her know what he wanted.

When she didn't comply, he moved, startling a gasp out of her as he sat forward, grabbed her around the waist, and shifted them until he sat on the couch the right way and she stood in front of him.

His mouth level with her breasts, she tensed with anticipation of his lips on her nipples. Instead he hooked his thumbs in the sides of her underwear and started to drag them off her hips.

Her stomach clenched as he watched the slow reveal of her mound and the wet flesh between her legs. This close, he had to be able to smell her desire. Hell, she could smell it and her need flared higher.

"So damn pretty." He let her panties fall to the floor and his hands reached behind to cup her ass, kneading them with strong fingers. She couldn't contain her moan and reached for his shoulders to steady herself when her knees wanted to buckle.

"Easy, baby," he murmured, the sound a caress against her clit.

"Jared."

His hands smoothed down her ass to her thighs, stroking all the way to her knees before making the return trip. When he slipped one hand between her legs and teased her lips, she clenched her thighs to keep his hand there.

"Spread your legs a little wider, sweetheart. And keep them open."

His tone brooked no disobedience, and she briefly wondered when she'd lost her share of control. Not that she really cared at the moment. All she could think of now was how to get him to please her.

She did exactly as he said, cool air caressing the hot flesh between her legs and making her burn even hotter.

"I'm going to put my mouth right here." His finger touched the bud of her clit, too lightly to give her any relief. "But first I want you to come on my fingers, Belle."

He stroked her lightly, back and forth, coating his fingers in her juices. Taking a deep breath, she looked down, his fair head almost touching her stomach, blocking her view.

She didn't need to see what he was doing to know he'd slipped two fingers into her channel and began to fuck her with them. Slow and steady, he pushed into her then withdrew. He provided enough thickness for her sheath to clench around him in need, and he stroked her clit with his thumb on each upward thrust.

She felt her orgasm building, felt it begin to fire deep in her belly, then cried out as it broke, her hands reaching for his shoulders to hold her steady.

"God damn, Belle. I can't wait to taste you. A little wider now, baby."

With her eyes closed, she only sensed that he was moving, but she did as he asked and the next sensation she felt was his mouth on her clit, sucking the little bud between his lips and teasing it.

Her body still tight from her first climax, the feel of his mouth on her threw her into sensual overload. His teeth and tongue worked her pussy with deliberate abandon—licking between the plump lips, nipping her clit. Fucking her with his tongue.

Her body felt energized and, at the same time, lethargic. She felt another orgasm building, but wasn't sure she wanted to come again so fast.

Her fingers slid into his hair, tugging at him to release her. She wanted to get her mouth on him, to torment him, but he wouldn't release her. His hands held her hips more firmly, and he continued his sensual assault until she felt lightning racing up her spine and bowing her forward with the force of this climax.

She barely heard his muttered curse but she felt his hurried movements as he rose from the floor, towering over her for a brief second before he lifted her off her feet.

Her eyes flew open but she only got a brief glance of his lust-hardened face before he turned back to the couch and set her on her knees on the cushions, facing away from him.

She put her hands on the backrest and arched her back, instinctively knowing what he wanted. And he didn't disappoint. After a brief moment of anticipation, when she vaguely realized he was donning a condom, she felt him cover her from behind and thrust his cock deep inside.

They both froze as he filled her completely, the heat of his shaft burning her, making her tighten around him. He groaned and his hips flexed, burying him even deeper.

One arm wrapped around her waist, immobilizing her hips

when she would have ground against him. His free hand cupped her breast, pinching the nipple and making her grind back against him.

"Don't move, Belle," he rasped in her ear. "If you move, this is gonna be over too damn fast."

She clenched around him, wanting to gain back a little bit of that control. "I've already come twice, Jared. It's your turn to burn."

He leaned forward just a little bit more, easing his cock out an inch or so before thrusting forward at a snail's pace. "I already am. I just want it to last."

She wiggled back against him as much as she could and was rewarded when he moaned and gave a sharp push forward.

"And I want you to let go, Jared."

She felt him freeze, as if the very notion of what she'd said was something he'd never contemplated.

But his next retreat and re-entry was even slower. "No, you don't. Just feel, Belle. Let yourself get lost in the pleasure."

She was. But she sensed the same wasn't true for him. Still she couldn't seem to wrap her brain around that when the friction created by each controlled thrust made her nerves flicker and snap with electricity, causing her sex to clamp around him.

His hand switched breasts, beginning another series of ripples straight to her womb.

"Jared. Please."

"I want to, Belle. Tell me what you want."

"Fuck me. Now."

She didn't know what it was that finally flicked his switch, whether her language or the command. His entire body tightened around her and he began to thrust hard and fast and with no mercy.

She didn't require any. Her body accepted everything he gave her and still craved more. Faster, harder.

Pleasure burst like fireworks in her blood, and her fingers clenched into the cushions as her pussy clenched around Jared's jerking shaft, milking him as he came with a shout.

Eleven

"Good morning, Belle. I hope you slept well."

Jared walked through the door of the shop just before noon Tuesday morning, dressed in jeans and a cream-colored fisherman knit sweater over a blue chamois shirt. He held two cups of coffee from the café down the street and she didn't know which to reach for first. Him or the coffee.

His blue eyes shone and his smile brightened an otherwise dreary January morning.

The man was just too good to be true. Handsome, smart, successful, and freaking awesome in bed.

What the *hell* was he doing here? With her?

"Morning, Jared."

She damn well was not going to tell him she'd slept like the dead, sated and exhausted, after he left. Or that she'd woken up reaching for him. Disappointed that he hadn't been there.

"I stopped at the café down the street for coffee." He held out a paper cup.

Because she needed the caffeine, she reached for it and felt the tingle of anticipation shoot through her as their fingers grazed. Trying not to show how much he affected her.

"I see you found the best coffee in town." And why didn't that surprise her? The man would never settle for less than the best.

She breathed in the rich aroma of Jamaican Me Crazy with a shot of cream. The coffee smelled great but Jared . . . Well, Jared held an appeal that was on another plane of existence.

Images from last night bombarded her, remembered sensations making her pussy go wet and soak her underwear.

"The woman behind the counter very kindly told me how you take yours."

In the dry tone of his voice, she heard exactly what he hadn't said.

Tracy Tate owned the coffee shop and made a mean pot of coffee and a wicked bear claw. She also dispensed gossip as fast as she could whip up two mocha lattes and an espresso to go.

Teddy had been busy yesterday. He'd probably hit every shop along the avenue. Hell, maybe he'd stood outside the chip factory with flyers so he didn't miss anyone.

She forced herself to hold his gaze. "And I'm sure Tracy attempted to pump you for information."

Unless Tracy fell under the Jared Golden charm and simply stood there with her mouth hanging open. Tracy's husband was a very adorable but overweight sweetheart of a guy who thought his wife walked on water. They loved each other but no woman in her right mind would not have drooled over Jared.

"Actually, we talked mostly about you."

She caught herself before she rolled her eyes. Terrific. Jared had gotten an earful about how weird Annabelle was, with her addiction to antique porn. How eccentric and strange. How much time she put into her business and how little time she spent with men, like her ex Gary, who'd had to go searching for comfort between another woman's legs.

She took a sip of her coffee and turned to walk to the counter, deciding she needed to recount the cash drawer.

"I'm sure that was enlightening." She didn't bother to look up to see if he'd followed her. She knew he had.

"It was more like a warning."

Her fingers froze for a second as a whip of pain licked through her. "Oh, really? Was she warning you away from me?"

"Actually, she seemed more concerned about you."

Her head shot up. "What do you mean?"

Jared leaned on the counter, coming close. "I got the distinct feeling I was being warned not to hurt you."

She snorted before she could stop herself. But since she didn't have a snappy comeback to that one, she simply ignored it and went back to counting the money.

"I like your little town," Jared said, filling the silence of the store. "It's . . . compact. So, you ready to get to work?"

Work, yes. But the look in his eyes didn't exactly say work. At least not the kind of work she needed to get done.

She did have a business to run, a business that took a lot of time. She did her own books and currently she had twenty-three searches for customer merchandise she needed to check on. The shop was open today and although she didn't get a lot of traffic during the week, she typically had at least one or two customers Tuesday through Thursday in the winter. Weekends were another story.

With a sigh, she closed the cash drawer, knowing the money total was correct because she'd counted it twice before he got here.

She leaned back against the opposite counter, farther away from him. "And where do you want to start?"

He barely hid his grin of triumph. "Here." He let his gaze roam the store before coming back to her. "Since you're going to be helping me, I thought maybe you'd like some professional advice on the layout of the shop."

"Excuse me." She plunked the coffee on the counter and put her hands on her hips. "What's wrong with my shop?"

Holding up his hands in mock surrender, he shook his head. "Nothing's wrong with it. I just noticed a few things that might set your shop apart from the others in the area."

Picking apart her business hadn't been part of the bargain. Her first instinct was to tell him where to stuff his opinion and she opened her mouth to do just that. But at the last second, she snapped her lips shut before the words could escape.

With a critical eye, she let her gaze roam.

It *had* been years since she or her grandfather had done anything more than move and replace furniture. She kept the place as clean as she could, which was pretty damn clean, if she did say so herself. But the paint had begun to show some wear, the wood floors needed to be refinished, and—maybe she didn't want to look at the ceiling.

Still, it was an antiques shop in Adamstown, not a trendy boutique in downtown Philadelphia.

She narrowed her gaze at him. "What kind of sprucing up are you talking about?"

"Why don't you show me around and we can talk as we go."

His smile nearly undid her and she clenched her thighs to try to ease the ache between them. She'd have to watch that. She refused to be one of his easy society women who fell at his feet. She'd seen them at the party on New Year's Eve, fawning all over him whenever he hadn't been with her.

Not that they'd had much opportunity. He had spent pretty much all of his time at her side.

Still, she'd traveled the world, knew four languages, and owned and operated her own business. People who knew her described her as steady, solid, and insightful. And boy, didn't that sound boring as all hell. No wonder she didn't have a man in her life. Not that she was looking for one . . .

Oh, for heaven's sake, she was only twenty-eight. Still plenty of time for her to find the man of her dreams and live happily ever after. And Jared was not happily-ever-after material. He was happily-right-now material. A playboy.

And she refused to fall for another playboy, even one as gorgeous as Jared.

She plopped onto the stool behind her and picked up her coffee. "Who made you king of the world this morning?"

The man must be made to stop smiling, she decided.

"Just in a good mood, I guess. What about you? Wake up on the wrong side of the bed?"

Yeah, the one without you in it. She took a sip. "No, just trying to figure you out."

He shook his head. "Nothing to figure out. We'll be spending a lot of time together for the next month. Since you're helping me with the spa, I just thought I'd give you a few observations. You want to hear what I have to say or not?"

Of course, she wanted to hear what he had to say. Jared and his brother owned and operated a successful hotel in a major metropolitan city. The man had brains as well as good looks and didn't that just make him too yummy for words?

However, Gary had seemed like a decent guy at first and look how that turned out.

But Gary was on a whole different plane of existence from Jared. Gary lived on the plane for assholes.

Jared, on the other hand . . .

"Hey, Belle. You still with me?"

Oh, yeah. She was still here. Held in place by blue eyes that reminded her of sunny days.

This man was nothing like Gary. He was so far from being like Gary they should have come from different planets.

She took a deep breath and nodded. "Alright, let me have it straight."

* *

After he'd left her bed last night, Jared had spent the rest of the night lying in the surprisingly comfortable bed at the inn, staring at the ceiling.

Thinking about this woman.

She'd fallen asleep on him, literally. He'd picked her up after that last round on the couch and she'd fallen asleep with her head on his shoulder.

After settling her into bed, he'd almost climbed in with her before he remembered what she'd said about gossip in a small town.

He knew how devastating gossip could be in a city like Philadelphia, but the city was big so you could always find a bolt-hole away from the snide comments and dirty looks. Or you could go to Europe to escape. His mother loved Europe.

In a small town, there weren't that many places to hide.

And if he'd stayed the night, the owner of the bed and breakfast would have told the owner of the café that he hadn't returned last night. And the owner of the café would have told the first twenty or thirty people who came through for their morning coffee. By noon, everyone in town would have known, or thought they'd known, that he'd slept in Annabelle's bed.

Not that he cared about his reputation. He didn't live here. But Annabelle did.

Even if he did find a property for the spa in the area, he wouldn't be dealing with the locals on a regular basis. He'd hire someone to do that.

So he'd forced himself to go back to the inn. And thought about her all night.

That didn't happen often. The women he dated were far from stupid, but their end goal usually involved a wedding ring and unlimited access to the Golden bank accounts. Which didn't rank high on Jared's list of things he admired in a woman.

The woman now staring at him with bright green eyes had neither of those goals in mind. If she'd had her way originally, he'd have been out of here yesterday.

Was that the appeal? Her seeming indifference to his social standing and his money? Or was she a better actress than he gave her credit for?

"Jared?"

He heard a question in her tone, saw it in the lift of her brows. And in the arms crossed over her beautiful breasts.

He smiled at her but she only lifted her eyebrows higher. "Why don't you show me around, tell me a little about this place and your goods. We can talk as we walk."

She didn't immediately snap to attention, and he had to admit he really liked that. After a few seconds she sighed but didn't come out from behind the counter. "What do you want to know?"

He wanted to know everything about her, but he'd take what

he could get for now. "Tell me about the shop. How long have you been here? Give me a little background."

"Well, Granddad bought the building about ten years ago. He decided to settle down while I was in college and this area seemed like a good one. Small town but it attracts a huge clientele in exactly what we sell. Granddad's specialty was furniture, French and English and a little Italian. I have a broader base in American furniture and art. I double majored in art history and business administration with a minor in American history at Gettysburg College."

Setting his coffee on the counter next to hers, he leaned closer to her. "Sounds like you were busy."

She shrugged but didn't move away. "I loved college, though I was pretty much an outcast. Both Kate and I were. I guess it's why we're such good friends now. But all I really wanted to do was get out and get back here."

"I know how that goes. I hated college, all that studying." He mock shuddered and was rewarded with one of her smiles. "But a college degree was included in the terms of my inheritance and we needed the inheritance to build Haven." She opened her mouth to ask another question, but he didn't want to talk about himself. "So you've been running the shop since your grandfather died?"

She nodded. "About a year ago."

He saw grief etched in the downturn of her lips and in the shadows of her eyes. He wanted to walk around the counter and take her in his arms, comfort her. But that was completely out of character for him so he stayed exactly where he was.

"And your parents?" he asked instead.

She shook her head, no hesitation in her answer. "I don't really remember them. They were killed in a boating accident when I was five. They were crewing a yacht in the Atlantic when a storm blew up. Witnesses say my father was blown overboard and my mother jumped in after him. Neither of them were seen again and their bodies were never recovered."

Jared heard something in her tone, something he couldn't put his finger on. He'd known about her parents because of Dane's investigation but it almost sounded rehearsed.

Or maybe he was just reading too much into something she must find painful.

"My grandfather raised me. He hired a tutor to educate me while we traveled around Europe. At that time, Granddad was an independent appraiser who worked for most of the major auction houses in Britain. Luckily for me, Granddad and my tutor, Isadore, fell in love and stayed together until Isadore died about four years ago."

"Her loss must have been tough for both of you."

"It was. And when Granddad died, I floundered for a little while. He was well known in the business and I was always riding his coattails."

"But you have the credentials?"

Her gaze snapped back to his, bright and determined. "Yes, and not just in years of experience. Granddad always said I had the eye."

"What does that mean?"

"I can tell quality, whether it's a piece of furniture or artwork. I learned from an early age how to tell a fake from an original. Granddad was a master. It would have been impossible not to pick up some of his wisdom."

She warmed to her subject as they meandered through the shop, telling him bits and pieces of information about each piece—where it'd been found, who'd made it, or who'd owned it. She had an incredible knowledge of each piece but lingered over the ones that had stories attached.

"The man who sold me this chair told me George Washington once sat on it while he was in Philadelphia for the Constitutional Convention of 1787. Of course, I can't prove it, but it is the right age and make, and I can trace its provenance back to the early 1800s in Philadelphia. I just can't place Washington in the chair." Her smile returned. "When I sit in it, though, I swear I feel presidential."

And she made him feel like a hormonally charged teenager when she smiled at him like that.

As she showed him around the rest of shop, he struggled to take mental notes. It was hard with her by his side, talking, laughing, and smiling. But he did manage some general impressions and he'd already had a few ideas from yesterday.

As they made their way back to the counter, Annabelle fell silent until she sat back down on her stool, the counter between them again.

"So?" She propped her elbow on the counter and placed her chin in her hand. "What do you think?"

He thought she looked damn good naked, and he wanted to spread her out on the counter and feast on her.

Of course, that wasn't what she wanted to hear, so he said, "Organization and presentation."

Tiny furrows grew between her eyes. "What do you mean?"

"I mean, you know your stuff. Now you just have to package it better."

He paused to see how she was taking this and was encouraged by the interest in her expression.

"And how do you think I should do that?"

He swallowed the smile that probably would have put her nose out of joint at his cockiness, but he knew he had her hooked.

"Well, that's going to cost you another dinner with me."

Her head tilted to the side, and she bit her bottom lip while weighing the pros and cons.

Most women he knew would have jumped at his offer. If Belle said no . . . Fine. No harm, no foul.

She looked to be seriously considering her options. And for the first time, he actually worried that he wouldn't measure up.

Finally she lifted her chin off her hand and sat up straight on the stool. "I can do dinner again. Here at my place, around seven tonight."

Her place? Not at a restaurant but here, which was more intimate. But was she worried about staying out of sight of prying eyes?

"Absolutely. Can I bring wine?"

"Sure. Are you okay with Italian?"

"Love it." And he did. Hell, she could make soup and sandwiches and he'd be there.

She hopped off her stool, rubbed her palms on her slightly baggy jeans, then put her hands in her pockets. "Great. So I'll see you tonight."

She wanted him gone. How was that for a kick in the ass?

With a true grin now, he acknowledged her unspoken demand with a slight nod of his head. "I should get to my meeting with the Realtor. I'll be back."

And she'd pay for kicking him out. And love every minute of it. He'd make sure she did.

* *

"Hello, girls. How are you today?"

"Hello, Mrs. Schell," Kate and Annabelle replied in perfect schoolgirl unison, causing them to exchange an eye roll.

Planted dead center in the first aisle of the grocery store, her hair in perfect blue-gray curls peeking from beneath her ball cap, Mrs. Schell held out a chocolate chip cookie in each blue-veined hand. "You young ladies can afford the calories. And"—she gave Annabelle a sly grin—"you need to keep up your strength, Annabelle. I heard he's a looker. Good for you, dear."

As Kate nearly choked on her cookie, Annabelle forced a pleasant smile for the great-grandmother of three who'd worked for this same store since the Vietnam War. She was half-blind and had a tendency to wander around talking to herself, but loyalty and longevity meant everything in a small town. "Thanks for the cookie, Mrs. Schell."

"Oh, you're very welcome. Have a good day, girls."

Annabelle pushed the cart into the produce aisle as fast as she could without running, Kate still trying to choke down her cookie through her laughter.

"Jesus, I swear I'm going to become a hermit." Annabelle stopped to pick up lettuce and shredded carrots, figuring she'd make a salad to start. She made a mental note to pick up walnuts in the next aisle. "The man is a menace."

"Right." Kate drew the word out to about five syllables. "So that's why you're making dinner for him. Because he's a menace."

"He wreaks havoc with my brain. Why else would I agree to make dinner for a man who only eats gourmet cuisine? Hell, I had a jar of unopened peanut butter and a box of stale crackers in my cabinet."

"But you can cook. You took cooking classes in Italy, for chrissake. And I know you enjoy it. Why *wouldn't* you ask him?"

Racing through the aisles, trying to figure out what to make, Annabelle stopped in the pasta aisle, picked up a box of linguine, and waved it at Kate. "Don't you start with me. You're supposed to nod and agree with everything I say."

Kate's smile reminded Annabelle of a lounging tiger who'd just spotted an easy lunch. "Sorry, but that only applies to discussions of boyfriends and fiancés. Jared didn't happen to cross over into that designation yet, did he?"

Annabelle huffed and put the linguine back on the shelf, reaching instead for the fettuccine. Fettuccine Alfredo with shrimp and broccoli. Simple, tasty, and basically foolproof.

"You know he didn't. We don't even really know each other. But . . . he offered me a job and now I'm cooking dinner for the man. How did that happen?"

Kate snorted. "I would assume you agreed to it."

Annabelle opened her mouth to swear at Kate until she noticed the Mennonite woman with three children headed down the aisle. So she settled instead for a death glare. "Yes, I did. But I swear that man puts a spell on me every time he smiles."

"He certainly does have a nice smile."

Groaning, Annabelle placed the pasta in the cart and headed for the meat and seafood counter. Thankfully, the store had decent fresh seafood. "I'm in over my head, Kate. He's so far out of my league, I feel like he's in the majors and I'm still in junior high. I don't want to fall for him. I can't let myself."

"And the harm in that would be . . . what?"

"He's a playboy. Just like Gary." After she placed her order for chicken and shrimp with the teenage boy behind the counter, she turned back to Kate. "And I certainly don't need another one of those in my life."

"Then what's wrong with having a little fun while he's here? It's not like you're going to marry the man, right?"

"Of course not."

Marriage and Jared Golden did not belong in the same sentence. He'd said as much New Year's Eve. And she had secrets to keep.

"So have a good time, enjoy the sex, and take the help with the business. And when everyone sees what amazing furniture you find for the spa, you won't need Carmen Moran's backing as an appraiser. You'll be turning away clients."

Annabelle took her packages and headed back to the produce aisle. She needed something for dessert and the strawberries had looked good.

"But why did I invite him for dinner? It's so . . . intimate."

Kate's smile turned apologetic. "Because you're already gone?"

"I can't be." Annabelle shook her head, sighed, then let her smile inch out. "So what am I going to wear tonight?"

Twelve

"So here's what I see." Jared pushed a piece of graph paper across the table at her. "You need to set yourself apart from the crowd."

The dinner plates had been cleared, and the strawberry tartlets she'd made for dessert sat in the center of the table along with the unopened bottle of wine Jared had brought.

"You need to come up with a distinct look that people will identify with you when they come into the store. You need to organize your collection and present it in a way that not only draws the customer in but makes it clear this isn't your grandfather's store."

Over dinner, they'd discussed the town, the economy, gas prices—anything but the shop. She'd begun to wonder if Jared had an actual plan, though she had to admit she'd enjoyed simply talking to the man. Articulate guys with a wry sense of humor completely did it for her.

And one glance at Jared made her hotter than hell. No other way to put it.

He'd pulled a sheet of paper from the breast pocket of the crisp white shirt he wore, unfolded it, and laid it on the table between them.

It looked like a floor plan for her shop but it was divided into distinct sections.

"Okay, that makes sense," she said. "But I don't think I understand your floor plan."

He tapped his long fingers on the paper, and her mouth dried as she remembered exactly what those fingers could do to her body. "I did some browsing up and down the strip today and, with the exception of one shop, none of the stores were shopper friendly. Frankly, they're a mess. They're cramped and hard to navigate. The lighting sucks. Small pieces are stuffed inside big pieces, paintings sit on the floor, the display cases are filled to overflowing. You don't get a real sense of each piece. It's just a huge jumble."

Intrigued, she tore her gaze away from his fingers and into his eyes, so blue she swore they sparkled even in the dim light. "And your answer to that would be . . ."

"Rooms."

She frowned. "You want me to put up walls in the shop, chop it up into smaller spaces?"

Shaking his head, he pointed to the floor plan, but she couldn't take her eyes off him. "No, I want you to create individual spaces without the walls. You have beautiful pieces, Belle, but you need to display them in a more coherent setting. Put the beds together, put a mattress on them, and dress them. Let people see each grouping as it might look in their house."

The man was absolutely gorgeous when he got passionate

about something, she realized. Of course, he didn't need much help but add in his enthusiasm and she needed a fan and new panties.

He seemed to have put a lot of thought into his ideas, which she was beginning to visualize.

"You've got lots of dishware but they're all stuck in boxes with one or two pieces on display," he continued. "Bring it out, set the tables. You're going to have to outlay some cash for linens and mattresses, maybe some rugs, but it shouldn't be enough to break you."

Yes, she saw exactly what he was talking about now. Still, there were some drawbacks. "What about the artwork?"

"Expand the gallery. Break into the back room you use for storage and combine the spaces. Do you have somewhere else you can use for storage?"

A true art gallery. She'd wanted one for years but had never wanted to ask Granddad for the space. He'd been much more interested in furniture and he'd already given her one room for her erotic collection. And though he'd encouraged her to develop her own tastes, there just hadn't been enough room for her art.

She nodded slowly. "Actually, I do. I can use the basement for storage. Granddad had a climate-control system put in when we first renovated the building, but it was a hassle getting the big pieces up and down. He'd used it as a workshop for a while, but not recently."

"Then make it easier to access with an outside entrance and a ramp. You could back the truck right up to it and transfer the furniture directly into the basement. Or you might want to build another room off the back. You have the space on the lot. I checked in at the borough offices today and made sure."

Sinking back into the chair, she couldn't believe he'd gone to so much trouble for her. "I don't know what to say, Jared. It sounds . . . wonderful."

He sat back as well and grinned at her. "Hey, I told you I was good."

And he knew it, too. But that confidence only added to his appeal. She returned his smile even as she shook her head. "I never had much interest in the business end of the shop. I'd rather be on the hunt for new material, though Granddad made sure I knew everything I needed to know to take over."

Jared refilled her wineglass and his then reached for a tartlet. "Tyler takes care of most of the business. I'm the idea guy. I think them up and implement them. Tyler finds the money to pay for it."

"Like the spa." She swallowed as he bit into the sweet. "I, ah, did some preliminary searches for furniture and found a few things I'd like you to look at."

He nodded, leaning farther back into the chair. "I set up a meeting with a local real estate agent for tomorrow morning to see if there are any properties in the area that might be suitable. You can show me the furniture tomorrow afternoon."

"And you really think this area will sustain the kind of business you're proposing?"

"I'm not looking for area residents to sustain it. I mean, I'll be glad if they come but I'm looking for this to be a destination. A place to get away from the fast pace of the big city. More like a resort."

Annabelle shook her head. "In Nowhere, Pennsylvania?"

"That will be part of the appeal. Middle of nowhere, no sirens, no helicopters. The spa will be all inclusive. The restaurant will be open to the public and so will the shops."

"What kind of shops?"

"Nothing extensive. Boutiques. Clothing, accessories, makeup."

"Lingerie?"

Jared's brows lifted. "Interesting. Why?"

"Kate designs some of the most beautiful lingerie I've ever seen. And some of the most exotic." She was wearing one of Kate's creations now. She'd worn it with the plan of showing it to him later. "She's never said anything about selling her designs but it was just a thought."

"And it's a good one. Have you given any more thought to the rooms? How to decorate them?"

Truthfully, not much because she'd spent most of her time thinking about him. "You said something about making it a sensualist's dream yesterday and that sparked some ideas. I've been thinking about themed rooms, possibly picking a piece of art for each room and building the theme around it."

And now that she was thinking about it, she couldn't stop. "Actually, let's go downstairs so I can show you a few ideas."

Jared watched Belle's gaze go unfocused as she stared at a spot just above his right shoulder.

He recognized that look. Tyler got that look when he had an idea he was chewing over. Usually a good idea.

Belle had completely dismissed him, her thoughts turned inward, as she rose from the table and headed for the stairs to the first floor. He followed along, curious to see what she wanted to show him. And he was completely enjoying the sway of her hips encased in tight jeans and the brush of her flame-colored hair against her purple sweater.

Though she wasn't wearing anything overtly sexy, the jeans and sweater hugged every luscious curve and made him lust for what he couldn't see.

In the shop, she flipped a switch and the lights in her erotic gallery cut through the dark. His cock gave a twitch as he remembered what they'd done the last time they were in there.

He followed more slowly and when he reached the gallery, she stood with her hands on her hips in front of a display case of shunga prints from the 1700s.

With a glance over her shoulder at him, she nodded toward the case. "How decadent do you want to go?"

He contained a snort of laughter. That was not a question she should be asking him because decadent was a word he took seriously. It was right up there with pleasure.

If he told her exactly how decadent he wanted to go with some of the rooms, he was worried he might scare her off.

With a deliberate gait, he walked to the chaise they'd christened yesterday and sat down, letting his legs stretch out in front of him as he propped himself on his arms.

Belle's gaze narrowed but he heard the slight catch in her breath when he smiled up at her. "How decadent can you make it without crossing the line into tasteless?"

"The shungas. Recreate some of the rooms depicted in the shungas from the wall coverings to the floorings. The colors are beautiful and the mood is right. I'm not saying we use the art itself in the rooms—"

"Why not use the art?" Jared started to see exactly where she was going with her idea and he loved it. "The more tasteful ones, yes. But we could go all-out debauchery with a few of the rooms. And why stop with the shungas?"

He looked at the two O'Malley pieces from the Passion series. He wanted those paintings for his own collection but unlike everything else in the store, they didn't have a price tag. He wanted to ask about them but didn't want to ruin the mood. He'd ask later.

So he pointed to the prints of the Carracci series, The Loves of the Gods. "Why not theme each room to a different painting?"

Belle turned to him, a small smile lighting her face. "I had thought of that, but I didn't know if you'd go for it. I mean, this is supposed to be a spa, right? Not a high-end brothel?"

He laughed. "No, not a brothel. Most of the rooms will be merely opulent. But I love your idea too much not to use it. And believe me, the crowd I'm targeting won't bat an eyelash at the décor."

"So you're going for the same crowd that you invite to the Salon?"

He shook his head. "The Salon is one of a kind and I only invite select people. I'm not planning to branch out to the spa."

Belle turned to face him now, crossing her arms over her chest and cocking her head to the side. "How *did* you come up with the idea for the Salon?"

He opened his mouth to give his answer. But he thought saying "Because I could" seemed like a cop-out. Spending time with Belle was becoming more and more hazardous to the façade he liked to cultivate with his friends and acquaintances.

And he'd have to examine that a little more closely. Later.

"The Salon actually had its beginnings my freshman year at college. A few friends with similar tastes, a few bottles of whiskey, and late-night bitching about a mandatory class in world cultures. The teacher was a bastard who delighted in tormenting freshmen. We decided to dig for dirt on the guy and embarrass the hell out of him. We figured there had to be something we could use against him."

"Sounds like the plot of a John Hughes movie."

He laughed, a completely natural sound he didn't hear that often. "Anyway, I hit pay dirt but it wasn't what we expected. Turns out old Professor Kohn had a lucrative side business as a writer and researcher for an underground Victorian erotica society."

Belle came closer until finally she eased onto the cushion next to him. Then she turned sideways until her back rested against the rolled armrest. Drawing her legs up, she rested her chin on her knee.

"How did you find out? And what is that exactly?"

"I had a friend hack his private email accounts. We found his links to this society, a private group like the Masons, but their organization met to discuss and reenact scenes from Victorian erotica."

Her mouth parted in shock before she let out a little laugh. "You hacked your professor's email and found out he was part of a sex club?"

"Not a sex club. Yes, they paid dues but they only went toward maintaining their meeting rooms. Actually, it ran a lot like the Salon. You had to be sponsored by at least three current members to get an invitation to be interviewed to join. Once you were in, you signed a confidentiality agreement. They had a required reading list and then they re-created scenes from books like *Fanny Hill* and *The Pearl*."

Belle shook her head. "That actually sounds really fascinating. Did you expose him?"

"Not me, no. It came out eventually, I think someone actually broke the confidentiality clause and got sued but I never told anyone. I was fascinated. I started to read all the Victorian erotica I could get my hands on. I already had a healthy interest in sex, but this was like nothing I'd ever seen. Porn is so . . . plebian."

She let out a hearty laugh, letting her head drop back and her hair spill down. She had such an erotic laugh, husky and deep and completely natural. "Jared, only you would use a word like plebian in relationship to sex."

"But you know what I mean, don't you?"

She rolled her eyes. "Of course. Reading Victorian erotica is like listening to someone with an English accent talk dirty to you for hours on end. Extremely arousing."

He was thinking the exact same thing about her. And her voice made his blood boil. "So are—"

His phone vibrated on his hip, intruding on the moment. He'd set it so that only his brother's calls would come through and if his brother was calling, it only meant two things.

"Jared?"

He pulled the phone off his hip and looked at the number just to make sure.

"Damn, I'm sorry. I have to take this, Belle. It's Tyler."

He expected to have to soothe her. Most women he knew would pout if he interrupted their flirtation to take a call.

Belle smiled and rose. "No problem. I'll be in the main shop."

No snark, no snit.

He answered the phone, shaking his head. "Dude, you're killing me. What's so im—"

"You need to get home. Now." Tyler's tired sigh echoed through the phone line, making a cold shiver run though Jared's body. "Mom's having an episode and we can't get her calmed down. She keeps asking for you and I'm afraid we're going to have to hospitalize her if we can't get her to take the meds. Damn it, Jed, you know how she gets when she's like this."

Yeah, he knew. And he knew why she usually got like this. "What'd the bastard do this time?"

Tyler sighed again, his frustration coming through loud and clear. "Jed, she needs you."

And that was really all that mattered, wasn't it? No matter what he wanted. "I'll be there in an hour. Can she hold it together until then?"

"If I tell her you're coming, I think so, yeah."

"I'm leaving now."

He disconnected the call and shoved the phone back on his hip. Emotion lay heavy in his gut. Fear and concern for his mom. Rage . . .

His goddamn father. Fury began to overtake the fear and concern. Anger at whatever it was he'd done to make his mom have an attack bad enough for Tyler to have to call him home.

It didn't happen often and she hadn't had an episode like this for years.

He had to leave. Right now. Just get in his car and go.

He couldn't stop to think about Belle. Not now. He'd be back tomorrow. It wasn't like they were married. Or even that they had an emotional attachment. Sure, the sex was great. But that's all it was.

Just sex.

He walked out into the main shop, where Belle sat on the counter, watching him approach.

"Jared, are you okay?"

He forced a smile. "I'm fine. But I need to head back to Philly. Something's come up at the hotel and Tyler needs me."

He stopped in front of her, knowing his smile didn't reach his eyes. Not caring if she noticed.

Her eyes narrowed as her head tilted to the side.

He stepped in close and kissed her with a finesse he'd never used on her. A slickness that always served him well with women. Most couldn't tell it was all technique and no emotion.

He stepped back and knew Belle had noticed.

He smiled again, but he knew this time it was more like a grimace. He needed to get out of here. Now.

"I'll call you, Belle. Good night. And thanks for dinner."

He turned and walked out the door.

* *

"So he just walked out? Without any explanation?"

On Wednesday morning, Annabelle had a copy of Jared's layout in front of her on the kitchen table while she drank hot chocolate and waited for the pan of Pillsbury cinnamon rolls to hurry and bake already.

Sometimes a girl needed more than Special K with Red Berries in the morning. This qualified as one of those mornings.

Kate sat at the other end of the table, both hands around her mug. She didn't start work until noon on Wednesdays and they had a standing date for breakfast.

Except Kate had called this morning to make sure she wouldn't be interrupting anything. Annabelle had assured her she wouldn't be and Kate had rushed over.

Now, Annabelle figured Kate's shocked expression echoed hers from last night.

"He said he had to get back to the hotel. That something had come up."

And she was trying really hard to believe that. But the look on his face . . .

"But you don't believe him?"

Finally, Annabelle looked up at Kate. "No, I think something happened but . . . he just didn't want to tell me about it. He shut me out like he'd slammed a door in my face."

"That doesn't sound like Jared." Kate's frown narrowed her eyes to slits of glittering black.

Annabelle huffed as she dropped her gaze back to the layout in front of her. "Really? Because we know him so well, right?"

Kate paused. "Hey, did something else happen last night?"

Annabelle sighed and shook her head. "Not a blessed thing. Except he gave me this nice little layout for my shop. Needs some work but at least he gave it a little effort before he skipped town."

"Oh, Annabelle. I'm sorry."

Shit. She hadn't wanted to sound that . . . hurt. Because she wasn't. "No, forget I said that. We had an agreement, not a relationship. Hell, we had three nights of sex, Kate. I didn't fall for the guy."

She forced a smile as the oven timer dinged. Getting up, she pushed Jared's rough draft and her own more detailed sketch toward Kate. "So tell me what you think."

Annabelle got the pan out of the oven and dropped the rolls onto a plate. She considered just scooping out the icing with her finger and lathering it on the rolls but that might smack of desperation. And hurt. She grabbed a knife instead.

Kate was still staring at her when she turned back to the table. "Annabelle . . ."

She dropped the plate on the table with a clatter and held up her hand to stop anything else Kate may have said. She didn't want to talk about him anymore.

"I have plans to make, a carpenter to contact, and a shop to run. I really like his ideas and I'm going to move ahead. I'm going to call Henry today, see if I can get him out here to at least look over the space sometime this week."

Kate snorted. "I'm sure he'll be able to fit you in. Henry's been crushing on you for years."

"Shit, I forgot about that." Christ, just what she needed. Sweet, handsome Henry Schmidt hitting on her all day. Maybe she should contact another carpenter.

"You know," Kate said, "Henry is a real sweetheart."

Annabelle nearly stuck her fingers in her ears like a two-year-old and stomped her feet. "Oh, no. Don't even go there. Guys are no longer on my to-do list. Hell, I'll date Teddy before I get wrapped up with anyone else."

Kate nearly choked on her roll dripping with two hundred calories of icing. "And if you ever date Teddy, I'll know it's time to put you out of your misery."

Misery? She was not miserable. Jared hadn't broken up with her. Hell, they hadn't had a relationship to break up. Just sex. Hot sex. Great sex.

But *just* sex.

"Jared had said he'd be back. And if he doesn't return . . . Well, then that's fine too."

* *

"Jared, are you leaving?"

With his hand on the front door knob of his parents' home, Jared paused for a moment to wipe his face of all emotion before turning to face his father.

It was just after three in the afternoon. He'd caught a few hours of sleep after his mother had finally closed her eyes this morning.

"I have a business to run. I'm needed there."

His father nodded, his mouth twisting into a slight grimace. As if he couldn't be allowed a full one. "Then I appreciate you coming. I know how difficult this is for you and Tyler."

Jared felt the rage start to bubble like lava in his stomach. His hand clenched around the cut-glass knob, so tightly he felt the fine edges nearly pierce his skin. If he didn't get out of here soon . . . "Yes, it is."

He didn't say anything else, just waited for his father to say whatever it was he wanted to say.

"I just want you to know . . . how much we especially appreciate your time."

Staring into his father's eyes, the exact same shade of blue as his own, Jared had a momentary flash of the man as Jared had seen him fifteen years ago—gleaming smile, hearty laugh, and carefree attitude. With his hand on another woman's breast and his mouth on her neck.

Only minutes before he'd caught his father in that affair, Jared hadn't known how much of a farce his parents' marriage had become.

He'd known they no longer shared the same room and barely spoke to each other. He'd also known, since he'd been at least eight and maybe even before, that his mom was mentally unstable.

She'd have incredible highs, days when she'd keep him and Tyler home from school to go skiing in the Poconos or to New York for a show. A few times they'd flown to Florida to spend time on the beach.

Of course, the incredible lows had followed with screaming fits, crying jags, and a trashed bedroom.

She'd had a "personal assistant" since Tyler's birth. Jared had realized sometime in his teens that the "personal assistant" was really a registered nurse. He remembered three. He also remembered how each time there'd been a new one, the transition had been difficult. Especially when Jared knew his father had had an affair with the last one, which was what had caused her to leave.

Jared's eyes narrowed. "She's my mother and I love her." He tried hard not to emphasize the "I" in that statement. His father knew how he felt. "Do you know what triggered this one?"

His father's back straightened, as if preparing for battle. "No. She's been fine. She hasn't had an episode like that for more than a year. The medication has made a marked improvement in her control." His father's gaze unfocused. "Things have almost been back to the way they were when we first met."

Jared heard something in his father's tone, something that sounded almost wistful, and he had to work hard to keep the sneer off his lips. He didn't want to get into a potential knock-down drag-out with his dad. Not now.

Last night had been exhausting. He'd sat with his mom all night. For some reason, she hadn't wanted Tyler. Sometimes that happened. They had no idea why. And when Helena started to come down, when the meds did their job, no one wanted to talk about it, much less ask questions.

She had a psychiatrist for that. Jared was no psychiatrist.

And though he wasn't a doctor, he'd done more than enough reading to know his mother's bipolar disorder would never be cured. She could only manage it with treatment and drugs.

Some days were better than others. Sometimes she went for months without an episode like last night. But then she'd think she was getting better and would forget to take her meds. Or refuse to take them.

It was a vicious cycle, one they were all trapped in.

She was his mother and he loved her. He'd do anything for her.

But now he wanted to get the hell back to Annabelle.

He owed her an explanation for his abrupt departure last night. He'd promised her his assistance and he wasn't going to leave her high and dry.

"Then I'm glad I could help." He turned the knob after giving his father a nod. "I'll see you later."

Thirteen

"I want floating walls and I've got the paint color already picked out. On the ceiling, I want a track lighting system that can be adjusted depending on the number of pieces I have on the walls at any given time."

As he'd done Monday, when this had all started, Jared entered the shop unnoticed. This time, though, the passionate dancer had transformed into a focused business woman.

"I'm also going to need you to install a ramp at the outside entrance into the basement to offload furniture."

From the front room, he saw her consulting with a lanky man who towered over her inside the storage room where she was going to expand her gallery.

Standing with her back to the front room, she couldn't see him and he could only see the back of her. She had her beautiful hair pulled back into a severe braid and wore baggy jeans and an oversize white shirt that hit her mid-thigh, covering what he knew to be a perfect ass.

Desire made his skin heat and his hands clench with the urge to touch her.

He watched her hands move as she described how she wanted the gallery to look. He wanted those hands on his body. He wanted his hands on her breasts, on her ass, on her thighs, holding her open—

Well, shit. Now he had a hard-on.

Tearing his gaze away from Belle, he looked at the man standing with her, hanging on her every word. Jared didn't think the guy would notice if a bomb dropped next to him. From the expression on his face, Jared could tell the guy had the serious hots for Belle.

And his blood began a slow boil.

He caught himself before he barged in and laid claim to her, like a goddamn caveman. Put his arm around her shoulders and draw her into his side. Better yet, press a kiss to her delicate, sensitive nape. She'd shiver and her eyes would flutter closed.

The other man, standing with his hands shoved in his pockets, would know she was off-limits. *His.*

Which was ridiculous. He didn't do possessive jealousy. Hell, he actually liked to share.

Delayed reaction to last night. That's all.

Taking a deep breath, he merely watched.

She was a woman with a mission, and it was the sexiest thing Jared had ever seen. He could stand here and listen to her talk all day.

"So, you'll have an estimate for me by the end of next week, Henry?"

"Absolutely, Annie. I'll bring it by myself. Should have one worked up for you in about three days."

Jared barely bit back a snort. Of course Henry would return with the estimate himself. He'd do anything to get in Belle's good graces and her baggy jeans. The fool would probably work it up tonight and bring it by tomorrow.

Belle gave the obviously smitten Henry a huge grin and a squeeze on the arm. "Thanks so much. I knew I could count on you for this. Tell your mom and dad I said hi and that I'm still looking for that missing piece to your mom's china pattern. I've finally got a lead. I'm hoping this one pans out."

"Well now, I know Mom'll be glad to hear that. She'll want you to come to dinner, you know, so she can show it off."

"I look forward to it. Your mom makes the best *schnitz und knepp.*" With one more smile for the smitten contractor, Belle turned to walk the man out but froze as soon as she caught sight of Jared.

Her eyes widened and her lips parted like she was going to say something. Then she gave him a bland smile and led Henry to the door.

The contractor gave him a once-over before Belle thanked him again for coming over on short notice and closed the door behind him.

Then she flicked the lock on the door and leaned back against it, watching him.

"I take it you're moving ahead with plans for the gallery."

She nodded. "It's a good idea. I'm surprised to see you back so soon."

"The problem was resolved faster than I anticipated. Are you finished for the night? Would you like to go to dinner?"

Damn, he really hoped that didn't sound as desperate as he

thought it had. A pain he'd thought was heartburn had been building in his chest since he'd left his parents' home. But he hadn't eaten anything in hours.

And the feeling was more like something cracking apart. He clamped down on the urge to rub at his sternum.

"Actually, I made plans to meet Kate and her fiancé for dinner." She paused again, just long enough for that ache to crank up the intensity a notch, before she continued. "Would you like to join us?"

No, he wanted her all to himself. He wanted to crook his finger and have her come to him. Wanted to tear the shirt over her head, put his mouth on hers, and lose himself in the sweetness of her, in the heat he knew he could elicit from her. The heat that would ease the tight knot in his chest.

He wanted her spread out beneath him, screaming his name as he made her come.

He forced a natural-looking smile. "I'd love to, if you think your friends won't mind."

Annabelle's smile certainly looked more natural than his felt. "Kate will be happy to see you again and Arnie wants whatever Kate wants."

"Sounds like true love." Which really sucked for Tyler. His brother had asked about Kate again this morning.

Annabelle finally pushed away from the door and walked over to him. "I'm sure he loves her. I just . . ." She shook her head. "Anyway, I hope you don't mind pizza."

He couldn't care less what they ate as long as they did it together. "Love pizza." Then because he couldn't help himself, he said, "That man has a thing for you."

Belle's brows lifted in surprise and she smiled, just a slight tilt of her lips. "Henry? He's a nice guy and a good friend. He and his father helped Granddad with the original renovation of the building. When Bud, Henry's dad, had a heart attack last year, Henry took over the business."

He let his gaze roam over her features, the wide eyes and mouth, the freckles sprinkled on her adorable nose and cheeks. He wanted to lick them. "Do you know everyone in town?"

When she shrugged, he followed the movement of her shoulders, barely visible beneath that oversize shirt. For a man used to women who dressed in designer clothes to walk their yappy little dogs, he shouldn't be as turned on by a man's white button-down dress shirt and a pair of baggy carpenter jeans, the pockets filled with pencils, business cards, and at least two small objects he figured were tape measures.

"It's a small town. Everyone knows everyone else. I take it the problem at the hotel wasn't too severe?"

The tone of her voice was steady but her gaze searched his. "No, not too severe."

The need to talk to Belle about his home situation, about his mom, shocked the hell out of him. He never talked about that, not to anyone but Tyler.

He'd never had any desire to talk to his friends about it. Most had known his mother all their lives. They'd treat her differently if they knew how severe her problem was.

They'd want to pity him. And he couldn't stand that. He didn't need pity.

Belle's eyes narrowed, as if trying to read between the lines. Then she sighed, as if giving trying to figure him out. He couldn't decide if that was good or bad.

"You know, I don't expect you to stay here continuously." She tilted her head to the side. "I understand you have other, more important obligations in your life."

Other? Yes. More important? He couldn't think of any. His

mother's episode had passed. And now he just wanted to forget everything else for a few hours and spend time with her. "I have the time to spare. You're open Sunday, right? I'd like to see what weekend traffic is like around here."

"Doesn't Tyler need your help with the hotel?"

"The hotel can manage without me for a week. Tyler's a big boy. He doesn't need me to hold his hand."

But Jared needed to touch her. He reached for her hand, now resting on the counter, and laced their fingers together. After a few seconds, hers curled around his.

And that tight knot in his chest eased a little more.

She let her gaze drop to their hands, let her fingers tighten for just a second, then released him and picked up the old-fashioned hard-wired phone on the counter.

"I'll give Kate a call and let her know you're here. Anything you don't like on your pizza?"

He shook his head, fighting the urge to bend her over the counter and take her right here and now.

Where the hell was this seemingly uncontrollable lust coming from?

Christ, he wasn't a sex fiend. Yeah, he enjoyed it but he didn't let it run his life.

He needed to keep himself under control before Belle thought that's all he wanted.

Of course, what the hell else did he want with her? Yes, they were attracted to each other. And he knew exactly why he was attracted to her—brains and beauty were a lethal combination in his book. So why the need to act like a caveman with her?

Because she wasn't like the other women he knew? Those fell into two groups: Those who wanted him for his bank account and name and those who wanted him for sex.

Belle enjoyed the sex. She wasn't the most experienced partner he'd had but she . . . What was so different about Belle?

"Hey, Kate. Just wanted to let you know Jared's back. Would you mind if I bring him along tonight?" After a slight pause, Belle gave a little laugh, sending his heart into a pounding rhythm. "Uh, no." She glanced his way for a brief second. "Don't think I have to worry about that. Yeah. Okay. We'll be there in a half hour."

She hung up, gave him a smile, and headed for the stairs. "I'm going to change. Give me a few minutes. Make yourself at home."

Images of her naked flashed through his brain and he moved to follow her up the stairs.

"I'll just come up with you, if you don't mind."

She gave him a quick, startled glance over her shoulder as they made their way upstairs and when she turned, he let his gaze drop to her beautiful rear end swaying in front of him.

"No problem," she said. "I won't take too long."

Lust swept over him, made it hard for him to breathe. Belle appeared absolutely oblivious as she headed for her bedroom.

"Kate's house is just up the street," she said. "It's not far to walk."

"Good to know."

She hesitated for a second as she realized he hadn't stopped in the living room but had followed her to her room.

He wanted her, the need a growing ache in his balls. He recognized the fact that he'd never wanted anyone with the single-minded purpose with which he wanted Belle.

Now she stared at him like he'd grown another head. What the hell was wrong with him?

"Jared?"

He continued forward until he could touch her, lifting his

hand to run a finger along one perfect cheekbone. With a fierce and almost savage elation, he felt her shiver and her lids lowered to half-mast until only a slit of those pale green eyes showed.

He bent his head slowly, wanting her to know exactly what was coming and giving her more than enough time to tell him no. Though he hoped like hell she didn't.

He *needed* her.

When her eyes drifted shut and she tilted her lips up to him, Jared released the restraint he'd been holding on to by his fingernails.

She gasped as he pressed his mouth to hers with little finesse and slid his tongue into her mouth. He kissed her, pressing hard so she couldn't block him. His lips slanted, wanting more, and she opened further, giving it to him. Her hands latched onto his shoulders as if she needed the support and his moved to cup her ass and pull her tight against his erection.

Moaning, she arched into him and something snapped in Jared's head. Some final remnant of control.

Lifting his hands to her shirt, he went to work on the buttons, fingers clumsy as he forced the tiny discs through their holes. Her hands slid into his hair, her nails scratching lightly at his scalp, shivers of pleasure shooting down his back, straight to his balls.

When he had the shirt unbuttoned, he went for the bra, groaning in approval when he found the front catch. With a flick of his fingers, her breasts spilled into his hands. He cupped her, kneaded the warm, soft flesh, and rubbed his thumbs over the pointed tips.

Moaning into his mouth, she thrust hard against his hips, pushing her breasts more fully into his hands.

The need to take her right here and now, to make her scream his name as he came inside her became his only reason for being. Letting one hand drop to her waistband, he undid her jeans and slipped his hand into her panties. Her heat seeped into him as his fingers slid into the silky wetness of her sex.

Her moans and attempts to get him to sink deeper fueled his own lust, the deep, pounding need for her. His cock felt like heated iron against his stomach.

Pulling his hands free, he grabbed her waist and lifted her off her feet, turning toward the wall of her bedroom. It was closer than the bed and every second counted.

Her back hit the wall and she gasped into his mouth. Freezing, he pulled away to look down at her, afraid he'd hurt her.

"Belle . . ."

Her passion-glazed expression made his balls tighten to the point of pain and her hands gripped his hair hard. "Don't stop. I'll kill you if you stop, Jared."

Her raspy voice hit his system like a powerful aphrodisiac, and he bent to devour her mouth as her hands reached for the button on his jeans and his went to push hers down.

He couldn't take the time to strip her. He had to be in her now. With a growl, he ripped his lips from hers and spun her to face the wall. "Brace your hands and don't move, Belle."

"Faster, Jared."

He tried. Jesus, he tried. He stripped her pants down to her ankles and moved her legs as far apart as they could go. Her shirt tails covered her beautiful ass, and he pushed them out of the way so he could pet her with one hand while he ripped his own jeans open and pushed them down far enough to release his cock.

The cool air of the room barely registered against his heated skin. When he slipped his cock between her legs to coat himself in her juices, sensation shivered through him.

He had the vague notion that he should slow down, that he

was out of control, but the pure ecstasy of her slick lower lips sliding along his shaft short-circuited every synapse in his brain.

Pulling her hips just far enough away from the wall so that he
could get a better angle, he thrust into her and started a fast, hard
rhythm that made her moan his name.

Pleasure fired in every cell of his body as his bare flesh pierced
her, creating an intense friction. Already so close to orgasm, he
moved faster, going as deep as he could get, one hand on her back
to keep her bent, the other arm around her waist to immobilize her.

She was his, completely under his control. Every action in response to his.

His.

When he slowed down, she cried out his name and begged
him for more. When he sped up, she panted and told him how
much she loved it.

Her slick essence bathed his cock in warmth and moisture,
and her channel gripped him tight, each thrust and retreat filled
with friction.

Mine, mine, mine kept running through his mind.

He had a millisecond to realize he was going to come before
his cock jerked and shot his seed deep into her body. Barely conscious of what he was doing, he flicked his thumb over her hard
little clit and felt her clamp around him in her own climax.

He heard her moan, felt her shudder against him as she ground
back into him. For several seconds, they stood silently, their heavy
breathing the only sound in the room.

Bending over her, he pressed his mouth to her nape, trying to
calm his racing heart, which sped up the second he realized he'd
screwed up in a big way.

"Annabelle."

"Hmm?"

Her sexy murmur made desire twist in his stomach but he forced himself to ignore it. Considering what he'd forgotten, he should've had an easier time of it.

"Annabelle, I'm not wearing a condom."

She didn't flinch, didn't tense, didn't do any of the things he'd imagined she would.

"I'm on the Pill, have been for years." She paused. "Unless . . . you have something you need to tell me."

Something twinged in his chest and he assumed it was relief. Still, he held her a little closer as he slid from her body. "No, I'm clean. In fact, I can't remember the last time I didn't use a condom. I don't think I've ever gone without one before."

As she straightened, his arms tightened instinctively but she only stood there and let him hold her.

"Gee, almost like I was your first, huh?"

Her teasing tone struck a chord in him, loosened something that had tightened into a knot in his chest. "My first time was probably just as fast but definitely not as much fun."

"Glad to hear it. But even though it was quick, we still only have fifteen minutes to get to Kate's. And I'm going to need to change."

With reluctance, he let her go, suppressing a groan as she bent over to hike up her jeans, giving him another look at her beautiful ass.

He caught himself before he smoothed his hand over that soft white skin. Instead, he reached for his own jeans.

"Give me a few minutes to clean up and change and I'll be ready to go. I'll get you a washcloth, too."

"Belle."

From the door of the attached bath, she stopped and looked back at him with a smile.

He had no idea why he'd called to her, only that he wanted her again. Hard and fast and a little dirty.

For a man who prided himself on his finesse, that last one caught him off guard.

"I'm glad I'm back."

Her head tilted and she got that look on her face, the one that he swore looked into his psyche. "Me too."

Fourteen

Sitting on the wooden chairs around Kate's kitchen table, Annabelle still tingled from head to toe.

Hell, tingle didn't come anywhere close to describing what happened every time she thought about Jared nailing her to the wall of her bedroom.

It'd been the closest he'd come to losing control since she'd known him.

She had to admit she liked knowing she could do that to him. But she also knew he hadn't liked the loss of control. And she knew something had happened in Philadelphia to affect him like that.

Jared had something weighing on his mind.

And she wished he'd confide in her. Wanted him to *want* to tell her.

Which was ridiculous. She had secrets to keep.

And they had a business arrangement. With benefits.

She pressed her thighs together. Damn good benefits.

Now, though, he was being his normal charming self. He kept the conversation moving like a master. He made Arnie comfortable, even though she knew Kate's fiancé had felt completely out of his depth from the moment he'd met Jared.

She knew the feeling.

"So your family owns hotels?" Arnie said after a sip of beer to wash down the pizza. "Must be tough right now with the economy?"

"My family's been in the business for years," Jared said in a complete understatement. "We haven't been hit as hard as the chains since we don't rely as much on the vacation crowd. We get a lot of business people."

"Kate said you threw a pretty decent party on New Year's Eve." Arnie smiled at his fiancée, who managed a fairly credible smile for him. Only Annabelle seemed to notice it didn't reach her friend's eyes.

Jared's grin, when he sliced it her way for a few brief seconds, burned. "I'm glad Kate had a good time. That's what we strive for. What good's a party if you don't have fun?"

Heat burned through Annabelle's body, hot and enticing as she remembered the secondary party Kate hadn't attended. She wondered what Arnie would think of her if she told him about that. Arnie was by no means a prude, but having sex in front of a room full of people might just make him keel over.

Arnie was a sweetheart of a guy. He worked as a truck driver for the potato chip company in town and helped out as a mechanic at his parents' gas station down the road. Steady, solid, hardworking.

Annabelle knew he'd make some woman a great husband.

Just not Kate.

Her sarcastic, brilliant best friend with the wicked sense of humor became a wet dishrag around Arnie.

Kate didn't say much during dinner and dessert, and by the time Annabelle and Jared got up to leave, Annabelle saw stress starting to take its toll on her friend.

Stress that seemed just a little more pronounced lately.

Annabelle held on to Kate a little longer as they hugged good-bye, while Jared and Arnie shook hands by the door.

"Kate, are you—"

Kate shook her head, cutting her off. "Thanks for coming, Annabelle. I'll call you tomorrow, okay?"

Annabelle took the hint and smiled. "Sure. Thanks for having us over."

With one more thank you, they left, beginning the short walk back to the shop down the town's deserted sidewalks.

"I like your friends, but you're right about Arnie," Jared said after a few minutes. "He's not the right guy for Kate."

Belle let her head drop back as she sighed. "Thank you! Finally, someone agrees with me. Oh, don't get me wrong. I like Arnie. He really is a nice guy. But they just seem so . . . uninspired when they're together."

Jared nodded, his expression thoughtful as he placed an arm around her shoulders, drawing her closer. Before she could stop herself, she melted into his side. The cold night air seeped through her clothing but pressed against him, she began to warm.

Was it possible to overheat in thirty degree weather?

"That's a good word to describe them. Uninspired. And you haven't been able to make Kate see the error of her ways?"

"I tried, several times, to tell her she's marrying the wrong man. But she won't listen. She's decided Arnie will make a good husband and never leave her. Kate's parents didn't have the best marriage. Bad scene. She doesn't talk about it much, but I think she believes Arnie will never treat her like her dad did her mom so she's determined to keep him."

"Sounds like desperation."

She nodded. "Yeah, it does. It's sad, really. It's not something you ever want to be, is it?"

Something passed over his expression, but he quickly cleared it and smiled. "No, it isn't."

He didn't say anything else and they walked in silence until they arrived at her home.

As she shed her coat, she noticed Jared didn't. He remained by the door, as if unsure whether he was staying.

"Jared, is everything okay? You seem a little . . . distracted tonight. Is everything alright at the hotel?"

He nodded, leaning back against the wall, staring at her. "Everything's fine. Now."

She took notice of his slight emphasis. As if there had been something wrong but it'd been taken care of.

Turning away from his intense stare, she headed for the fridge. "Would you like some wine?"

"Sure. Thanks."

As she poured, he pushed away from the wall and removed his black leather jacket. Hanging it on the coat rack by the door, he walked to the breakfast bar and leaned against the counter, watching her every move with those beautiful blue eyes. She pushed his glass across to him, then sipped at her own.

Since he didn't seem inclined to start a conversation, and since she couldn't stand the silence, she said, "Will you need to get back to the hotel this weekend? I do understand that you have a business to run."

One golden brown brow arched as he tasted his wine. "Trying to get rid of me, Belle?"

She wanted to laugh out loud. No, unfortunately, that was the furthest thing from her mind. God help her, but she wanted him to stay. For a very long time.

Forcing a playful smile, she shook her head. "Not at all. There's still a lot of furniture to move."

Her tone was deliberately teasing and she knew he knew it. Still, his gaze sharpened as if she'd said something enlightening. "So you find me useful?"

She heard something in his tone, something she just couldn't figure out. "You've been very helpful, Jared. Why wouldn't I want to keep you around?"

His expression turned thoughtful. "Glad to hear it. So, are you planning on rewarding me for my effort?"

That heated gleam had returned to his eyes. The one she couldn't refuse. When he stood and held out his hand, she gave up all thought of refusing him anything. She placed her hand in his and let him draw her against him.

When he pulled her close to his body and began swaying in time to the music, Annabelle closed her eyes and tried to let her mind drift.

But his scent tantalized her with remembrances of the New Year's Eve ball.

That night she'd wished for some fun, a way to forget about her two-timing ex-boyfriend and the rut her life seemed to have fallen into.

She'd wanted to experience just a little bit of the lust for life her parents had had.

She'd experienced more excitement than she'd dreamed possible. And her fun had followed her home.

But the ties she'd wanted to avoid were beginning to wrap around her heart.

And that could be dangerous to a woman with secrets.

Annabelle felt Jared's every exhale against her hair and the warmth of his body against her cheek. Each shift of muscle fanned the flames of her rapidly rising desire.

As if he'd read her mind, he lifted her hand to his shoulder so she could wrap both arms around him. His free hand drifted to her hair, twining into the curls and holding her to him.

The song ended but he seemed in no hurry to release her. In fact, she knew his desire was rising along with hers. She felt his erection lengthen and harden against her lower belly, and his chest rose and fell in an ever-increasing rhythm.

But he didn't move his hands, didn't let them wander. And that merely built the anticipation until her skin ached for his touch.

As they swayed, she pressed closer and closer until she swore she could feel the heat of his stiff cock through their clothes.

"Belle?"

God, she loved the way he said her name. Her nerve endings tingled and her pussy pulsed with need. "Yes?"

He deliberately ignored the question in her voice and instead tugged on her hair until she tilted her head back. Then he kissed her with the most devastating desire she'd ever experienced.

His lips moved over hers, eliciting a swift response she couldn't control. And didn't want to.

Her body buzzed with desire from her curled toes to her tight nipples. Her mind went blank and only sensation processed. The heat pouring off his body, the tension building between her legs, the pressure on her lungs that made it hard to breathe.

He kissed her with a dominating force that made every cell in her body melt in surrender and she opened to him. Her lips parted for his tongue to slide in and tangle with hers.

Her hands clutched at his shoulders, fingers sinking into sleek muscles, wishing he was naked so she could get her hands on his warm skin. His hands moved to her waist, where they slid under her T-shirt to stroke along her sensitized flesh.

He splayed his hands on her back, each finger a hot brand. Arching into him, she rubbed her aching breasts against his chest, silently begging him to ease her. Or make her burn hotter.

He chose the latter, his hands sliding up to cup her breasts for a brief second before sliding back down. She moaned in protest but he'd already begun to lift her shirt over her head.

Pulling back, he tugged the T-shirt up, having her lift her arms over her head so he could pull it off. His gaze dropped to the pink lace bra Kate had designed and his lips curved in a smile.

"Very nice, sweetheart. You're going to be leaving that on."

His husky voice made her sex pulse, and a flood of juices seeped into her already-wet panties.

"I'm going to lay you out on the counter and have you for dessert. I'm going to make you scream my name and then I'm going to make you beg."

Annabelle couldn't breathe. The air in the room had been replaced with a drugging haze that she couldn't seem to draw into her lungs. She barely noticed when his hands moved to her jeans and pushed them over her hips.

As she watched, he went to his knees in front of her, dragging her jeans down her legs, lifting her feet to get rid of her sneakers, and tossing her jeans to the side.

Panting, she swore she felt his breath against the sheer lace panel of her pink thong. Her knees nearly buckled when he placed a kiss on her stomach directly below her belly button.

Her hands slid into his hair, grasping the strands so tightly he couldn't get away. Not that he seemed in any hurry to do so.

His mouth and teeth blazed a path from one hip to the other, nipping and sucking and kissing. His hands reached around to caress her buttocks before filling his palms with them and pressing her closer.

As he spread her thighs wider, she was truly afraid her legs wouldn't hold her upright any longer. Reaching behind, she braced herself on the breakfast bar just as he pressed his mouth over her clit, causing her body to arch.

He tongued her through the lace, the slightly rough texture of the material making her clit throb with each swipe of his tongue. Teased her until her body felt like one tight ball of sensation, nerves popping and flaring, muscles clenching, her brain about to overload.

And when he nipped her, a short, sharp orgasm lit through her with the intensity of a flash fire.

Her mouth parted to gasp in air as she sagged, only to have Jared stand and lift her onto the counter.

"Lay back, Belle." His voice had dropped to almost a growl. "Lay back and hold on, honey."

Without conscious thought, she did as he asked, her eyes closing as her head came to rest on the counter.

The surface felt cool against her naked flesh, but she only had a second to notice before Jared grabbed the strings of her thong and drew it off. He wasn't gentle about it, and the wet material didn't want to separate from her flesh. So the flash of almost painful sensation that flashed through her nearly made her come again.

Overstimulated and starting to ache, her back arched and she spread her thighs until she knew her sex was completely exposed.

"Oh, sweetheart." Jared's voice came from somewhere above her. "You are so beautiful."

Practically panting with desire, she cried out when one hand molded to her breast, pinching the hard tip between his fingers and sending lightning flashes straight to her womb. It tightened in response as did her pussy, and she opened her eyes to find Jared.

The glow of the light over the sink gave off just enough illumination for her to see the hard planes of desire on his face. His mouth had drawn into a straight line that made her sex pulse with the promise of satisfaction.

But not before she danced to his every command.

His other hand began a slow, forceful caress from her knee to her hip and down again. He repeated the motion until his hands worked in a rhythm that made her body respond. He stroked and she lifted into his hand, her flesh molding to his.

Switching hands, he paid attention to her neglected breast and leg until she thought she might sink into a blissful stupor.

Just as she felt her body tighten for what she hoped would be a climax, he released her.

Her eyes flew open and she tried to speak, to beg, but before she could, he put his hands under her ass and lifted her sex to his mouth.

He flicked his tongue over her clit before plunging it between her plump lips and into her sensitive sheath. After a few seconds, he retreated to nip her clit with his teeth, testing her limits with sharp bites and gentle squeezes.

Her body moved as if she had no control over it, completely under his domain.

And he played her like a grand master.

By the time he lifted his head and opened his jeans, she would have thought it couldn't get better.

But it did.

When the broad head of his cock pierced her, she felt an entirely new set of emotions and sensations shift through her.

She'd moved from pleasure to complete abandonment. She wanted him to fuck her, begged him to fuck her, hard and fast, as he worked his cock into her in controlled thrusts.

Her hands reached for his wrists to hold herself steady as he rocked against her, vaguely noticing how his thrusts began to lose their smoothness.

He was losing his control with every thrust, every retreat.

She loved it. She tilted her pelvis and took him even deeper on his next plunge. He groaned as he thrust and held for several seconds before she rotated her hips and caused a shower of sparks to ignite low in her body.

Her sheath tightened around him just before her orgasm detonated.

She cried out, her body caught in the throes of her climax, and she vaguely registered the fact that he was pumping his release into her body seconds later.

Minutes later, when she'd regained enough energy to move, she opened her eyes and looked straight into Jared's. Dark with some emotion she couldn't fathom, his eyes stayed glued to hers as he pulled away from her body. Then he reached for her hands to pull her up into a seated position, lifted her into his arms, and carried her to the bathroom.

"Can you stand?"

She lifted her eyebrows. "Think that highly of yourself, do you?"

There, that made him smile. "I only ask because you look . . . a little tired." He set her feet on the ground but kept an arm around her shoulders as he nuzzled a kiss into her neck. "Shower?"

Part of her wanted to just curl up in bed with him and pass out. But the other didn't want the night to end, knowing he wouldn't be there when she woke. And that— No, she didn't want to think about that now.

"Only if you promise to wash my back."

"Baby, that's not all I'll wash."

In the bathroom, Jared turned on the water and waited for it to get to the desired temperature before he stripped off her bra and waved her in. Then he shed his clothes before following.

As the water fell around them, she let him wash her from head to toe, falling more and more under his spell with every stroke of his hands.

He poured her body wash into his hands, then slicked it all over her body, paying careful attention to her breasts and between her legs.

She felt arousal flare low in her belly and stepped closer to wrap her arms around his shoulders.

"Will you stay tonight?" She barely whispered the words in his ear but his hands faltered for a second.

"Absolutely."

* *

Jared couldn't get his brain to shut off.

Annabelle had fallen asleep right away, which made him want to beat his chest like a caveman. He'd fucked her so good, she'd passed out.

And yeah, he knew that sounded crude but damn . . .

So why was he still awake when normally he'd be passed out too?

Because he loved lying here, holding her. That was part of it. The other part was the phone call he'd made earlier today. He hadn't told Dane the whole truth about why he wanted him to come up here, and Dane had inferred that his visit would involve sex.

Yes, that was part of the reason. And no, he couldn't completely explain his rationale for inviting another man into her bed. Except for the fact that she'd enjoyed the hell out of their play at the Salon and he wanted to give her more of that pleasure.

Hell, he wanted to give her a lot more than simply pleasure. Which made the second part of why he wanted to talk to Dane tricky.

But he had to know.

Fifteen

The bell over the door rang only minutes after she'd unlocked the shop.

Annabelle still wore the smile she'd had since waking up with Jared's bigger, harder body curled around her. He'd tried to convince her to stay in bed with him and had almost succeeded.

But she did have a business to run.

Jared had kissed her one last time and ran his hand over her ass in a hot caress before he got up, pulled on his pants, and called his brother. She'd left to give him some privacy, since they seemed to be talking hotel business.

She didn't recognize the man who walked through the door but there was something about him that seemed familiar.

First, she noticed how absolutely gorgeous he was. Straight, dark hair hung around a face full of sharp planes, cheekbones to die for, a straight slash of a nose. Only his full mouth . . .

She knew that mouth.

She felt a frown crinkle her brow. Why would she know him?

Her gaze shot back to his pale green eyes. She drew in a quick breath, her pulse kicking into a staccato pace as goose bumps covered her entire body.

Oh, shit.

She took a deep breath, trying not to let her recognition show. What the hell was he doing here? Maybe he didn't remember her.

Oh, God, please let him not remember me.

She forced a friendly smile, hoping he couldn't see the sheer panic rushing through her like adrenaline. "Can I help you?"

He didn't answer immediately, just let his own smile build.

"Nice shop," he finally said.

Her smile wanted to slip but she shored it up. "Thank you. Can I help you with something?"

Was that smile of his supposed to mean something, or was she reading too much into a simple expression?

"I was told you have a decent collection of erotic art."

She swallowed hard and forced her mouth to hold its pleasant curve. "Are you looking for something in particular?"

"As a matter of fact . . ."

"Hey, Dane. I see you found your way here."

Annabelle whipped around at the sound of Jared's voice. His expression was carefully neutral as he caught her gaze, but she knew he was cataloguing her every conflicting emotion.

"Annabelle, this is Dane Connelly. A friend of mind for a very long time."

Her heart beating a mile a minute, Annabelle forced herself to turn back to Dane and put out her hand as she tried to swallow down her rising . . . confusion? Fear?

No, it wasn't fear.

Anticipation?

Had Jared asked Dane to come? Why? To join them in bed?

Heat flashed through her body, hard and fast. Her nipples peaked beneath her cotton T-shirt and she went wet between her thighs.

She should be embarrassed, should want to crawl in a hole somewhere and hide.

But this was definitely *not* embarrassment.

This was lust, pure and simple.

And both men could probably read it all over her face though Dane's smile was nothing but pleasant.

Damn them.

Fighting back the urge to gape at the man, Annabelle forced her lips to curve in a smile. She could do nothing at all about the blush she knew stained her cheeks.

"Nice to meet you, Dane."

Again.

Jesus, did Jared actually think she wouldn't know who this man was? That she wouldn't recognize that mouth and those eyes?

Did he expect her to just fall into bed with both of them?

And would that be such a bad thing? The first time was amazing.

Dane released her hand as she pulled hers back, successfully quashing the impulse to rub her sweaty palms on the thighs of her jeans.

Damn it, she was *not* into playing games. She wanted to know what was going on. Her arms crossed over her chest as she looked directly into Dane's eyes. "So, what brings you all the way to Adamstown?"

Dane's lips curved in a devastating grin. "You're right, Jed. I do like her. She cuts to the chase."

What the hell was that supposed to mean?

She opened her mouth to ask but Jared touched her elbow, effectively cutting her off and drawing her attention. "I asked him to give me his opinion on a few of the properties since Tyler's tied up at the hotel."

Blinking, she tried to get her brain to function enough to ask rational questions. "Oh. Are you in the hotel business too?"

Dane shook his head. "I'm in information retrieval."

She gave him a confused frown. "And what does that mean?"

"It means when Jed needs information, I track it down for him."

Her breath caught in her chest, but she shoved down the trepidation threatening to choke her as she flashed a quick glance at Jared. "And what information are you tracking for Jared now?"

Dane shrugged. "Mainly boring stuff. Local zoning laws, tax structures, things like that."

Okay, that sounded innocuous enough. But she still couldn't shake the feeling that that's not all Dane was investigating.

The way he looked at her, like he was dissecting her . . .

Was she reading too much into this?

Or had Jared invited Dane here to join them in bed?

Her heart pounded as Dane's expression gave nothing away, and her gaze flipped back to Jared.

Hunger started to show in the darkening of his eyes and the line of his mouth. That gorgeous mouth that gave her so much pleasure.

"Are you wondering if he's going to join us in bed, Belle?"

All the air left the room and her lungs collapsed in on themselves. "Jared . . ."

He took a step forward, their bodies almost touching. "Are you thinking about New Year's Eve? You remember him, don't you?"

God, yes, now she could think of nothing else. Her mouth

went dry and her hands clenched into fists, practically aching with the desire to touch him. To be touched.

By both of them.

Jared's features had sharpened with lust. He had to have seen her thoughts in her eyes, read it in her body language. He took another step closer and this time she took a step back. Right into Dane.

Dane's hands settled on her shoulders, light and unconfining. But her reaction to his touch was anything but. She began to burn.

Oh, holy hell, this was screwed up.

"No, don't start to analyze it." Jared cupped her chin in one hand, forcing her to hold his gaze. "Pleasure isn't bad. If no one gets hurt, there's no need for embarrassment or regret. I asked Dane here to help me out but yes, I specifically asked him to come *here*. To stay the night."

Jared didn't ask her permission for Dane to stay. But she didn't feel like he was forcing her to agree to take Dane into her bed.

And if she had to admit it, if only to herself . . . she wanted to explore that passion again, that sense of freedom.

"Belle, do you want Dane to leave?"

She took a deep breath and shook her head. "No. He can stay. But traffic may be heavy today. The weekends always pick up and the shop's open until eight tonight. I won't have time to *talk* until later."

Jared controlled the smile that might have made Annabelle run for the hills. Or kick him and Dane to the curb.

"Then Dane and I will get out of your hair for awhile."

He bent to kiss her, forceful enough that he pressed her even more fully against Dane. She didn't flinch. And when he knew she was about to open her mouth and let him in, he pulled away.

Belle's cheeks blushed a very pretty pink before she carefully stepped out from between him and Dane.

"I've got work to do."

She walked away and he turned to watch, her fiery braid twitching down the back of her dark green T-shirt and that luscious ass swaying in her tight jeans.

Christ, he'd be hard all day.

When he'd called Dane yesterday, he'd wondered if he would be pushing her too far, too fast.

Yes, she'd enjoyed the party on New Year's Eve, but that had been a moment out of time for her. She'd never told him otherwise, but he knew the moment Dane had touched her that night, that she'd never had two men make love to her at the same time. It wasn't a situation most women found themselves in. It wasn't a situation most men would be comfortable with.

He wasn't most men. And neither was Dane.

Her agreement to let Dane stay made Jared feel like swinging from a vine.

Because Jared knew, with Dane's help, he could make Belle burn hotter than she ever had. He could take her to a whole new level of pleasure.

"I thought I was about to be shown the door." Dane's voice drew his attention and Jared turned to see his friend watching him closely. "You sure this is what *she* wants?"

"Believe me, Annabelle will let you know exactly what she's thinking. If she doesn't want you in her bed, she'll tell you to get the hell out."

Dane paused, as if thinking that one over. "You want to tell me why I'm here now? I mean, besides the sex? I know you, Jed. There's something else going on."

* *

"You're serious?"

"Yes."

Dane took a sip of coffee as they sat at a table at the diner down the road, their booth far enough removed from anyone who might overhear them. "You really think she could be O'Malley's daughter?"

"Yes."

Jared watched Dane think about that for a few seconds.

"Based on the fact that she has two O'Malleys in her collection?"

"Three. I told you about the portrait I saw in her hall. No way that wasn't an O'Malley. And I noticed tonight she's moved it. No idea where. Like she hid it."

Dane paused again. "So what if she is? Are you planning to expose her?"

Jared grimaced. "Hell, no. Christ, the tabloids and the national media brutalized this story when it happened. The girl was fourteen and pictures of her parents' dead bodies were everywhere. I hope whoever leaked those photos goes to hell and fast. No, I just . . . I need to know."

"Then why not ask her?"

Because if she lied . . .

He shook his head. "Just do it, okay? And make sure no one else finds out what you're up to."

Dane rolled his eyes. "You know, if this *doesn't* turn out to be a wild goose chase, and she really is who you think, she's going to be pissed as hell that you pried into her background."

"I know that. Which is why I never want her to know. I don't want her to be hurt by this."

"Then what difference will it make?"

"It won't make any difference. Just do it, Dane. Get me the information. Now, about those property taxes . . ."

* *

Jared set up at one of the tables in the farthest corner from the door of the shop. He'd opened an area real estate site with the intention of browsing available properties but found himself watching Annabelle instead.

Since he'd returned after meeting with Dane, who'd gone upstairs to start digging into Annabelle's background, a steady stream of customers flowed through the shop.

Annabelle spoke to each one, even if only to say hello and let them know to ask if they needed any help. Most were browsers with no intention to buy. They strolled through the aisles, stopped to run their hands over a chest or pick up a plate but moved on to the next shop empty-handed.

A few were seriously looking for specific pieces. Annabelle helped them take measurements, wrote the figures on the back of one of her business cards, and spent as much time with the customers as they needed. She didn't push but she asked questions about where they were going to use the piece and how, what the rest of the décor looked like. She took a genuine interest in what they were looking for and those customers, even if they didn't buy anything, ended their visits by promising to return and to bring friends, all of whom would "love this place."

The two customers who did buy something left with huge grins on their faces, completely satisfied.

The first sale had been to a previous customer who'd returned to buy the sideboard he'd been looking at for at least two months.

Annabelle remembered the man by name, asked about his

family, then got down to business. They bargained for five minutes, and when they agreed on a price that even Jared might not have paid for the piece, they smiled, shook hands, and made arrangements for it to be delivered to his home next week.

The second sale . . . Well, that one boggled his mind.

The couple was well dressed but not ostentatious. They'd walked around the store not stopping at anything until the woman spied the painting.

Hell, even Jared could see it was love at first sight.

She stopped and stared, went to move on but stopped again. She checked the price, her mouth pursing and eyes narrowing before she'd moved on. But not far before she returned to stand in front of it again. Her husband returned in a few minutes.

They'd held a short, hushed conversation, which consisted mainly of the woman speaking and the man shaking his head.

Annabelle had said hello when they'd first walked in but she'd been answering questions from another couple. Now, Annabelle made her move.

"It's lovely, isn't it?"

The woman turned to her with an almost apologetic smile. "Yes, it is. It reminds me of my granddaughter."

Jared took another look at the portrait and hoped like hell the woman's granddaughter was cuter than the artwork.

Then again, there was no accounting for taste. He didn't think much of the painting but he wasn't into primitive Americana, which was definitely what that painting looked like.

He turned out to be right as Belle told the woman its pedigree—the artist, when it was painted, where it came from.

"I'm not much of a collector," the woman said with a small laugh. "I just think it's such a beautiful piece."

"That's what you said about the last three you bought," her

husband teased. "Got to admit, that one does look like Christie, though."

For the next five minutes, Belle talked to the couple about their grandchildren, all five of them. She found out they were both retired schoolteachers who enjoyed antiquing.

Belle never turned on the hard sell. She didn't have to. She knew the woman wanted the piece but she also knew she couldn't justify paying the price.

If the woman was working Belle, Jared caught no whiff of it. She seemed apologetic for taking up Belle's time when she knew she wouldn't be buying anything.

But Belle knew how much the woman wanted the painting.

"I know what the sticker says, but let's forget that for a moment," Belle said. "Tell me how much you'd be willing to pay for the piece."

The woman's eyes widened in surprise and she quickly looked at her husband, who put up his hands in surrender. "Sweetheart, I'm not the one who watches *Antiques Roadshow* religiously."

"How's this," Belle said. "Let me tell you what I paid for it and we'll see if we can come to an agreement."

Jared had absolutely no doubt that the number Belle quoted the woman was exactly what she'd paid for it. The markup was high but, as Belle explained, she'd done some restoration work to the piece. Then she told the woman exactly how much that had cost.

Shaking his head ten minutes later, he watched as the woman and her husband walked off with the painting, thanking Belle profusely for allowing them to give her their money.

Hell, she'd made a small profit. Not much, but probably more than if the painting had sat for another couple of weeks. Or months.

He was still shaking his head when she finally locked the front door at eight, a few minutes after the couple left.

She didn't join him. Instead, she went to the cash register, removed the cash and checks and stashed them in the safe built into the floor beneath the front desk.

Only after she'd set the alarms and made one last trip through the store, straightening things and making sure the windows and doors were locked, did she finally approach him. She looked nervous.

And then he remembered Dane upstairs.

His cock throbbed and his muscles tightened with anticipation.

Images from New Year's Eve ran through his head: the way she'd responded, how she'd let herself embrace the pleasure. He'd been waiting to see that woman again.

Not that the sex hadn't been great with just the two of them. It had. But she'd enjoyed that touch of the forbidden, the thrill of the exotic.

He could give her that with Dane's help. He *wanted* to give her that.

Wanted to give her whatever she wanted.

"Jared . . ." she said, seeming to think twice about what she wanted to say next.

He stood, closing his laptop and hopefully covering the lust building every second. "I thought we could send out for food, have dinner in. Any place you would recommend?"

She opened her mouth then closed it. He saw uncertainty in her eyes, confusion, anxiety. But beyond that, he saw desire in the flush of her cheeks and the faster pace of her breathing.

If she told him to send Dane home, he'd do it in a heartbeat. He didn't want her to be uncomfortable.

But, damn it, he wanted her to say yes. Without worry, without fear. He wanted her to want the pleasure as much as he did. And she'd been so damn hot that night at the Salon when Dane had touched her while he fucked her.

Maybe he was asking too much.

She took a deep breath and he could practically see her back straighten. "You have three choices: Chinese, pizza, or sandwiches," she said. "Take your pick."

It looked like she'd made hers.

He tried to contain the satisfied grin, tried not to let her see how hot her unstated acquiescence made him.

"Sandwiches sound great."

She nodded toward the stairs. "I have the menu upstairs. We should order soon. They get busy on a Saturday night." A slight pause. "I'll ask Dane what he wants before I order."

The heat in her gaze practically melted his bones. His balls tightened and his cock throbbed. *Yes.*

"Sounds good."

It took her a second but she finally nodded and turned to head upstairs.

Jared couldn't believe the amount of control it took him not to throw her over his shoulder and race for the bedroom.

* *

Annabelle tried very hard to keep her mind from wandering further than what to have for dinner as she made her way up the stairs.

Because if she let herself get beyond dinner to dessert . . . Hell, she couldn't even think about dessert because she certainly wasn't thinking about chocolate.

Unless it was smeared all over two male bodies.

Oh, God, was she really going to do this?

New Year's Eve had been a step out of time.

Did she really mean to go through with . . . this?

She took the last step and immediately sensed Dane in the room. She sucked in a sharp breath when she found him seated at her dining table, typing on his laptop. He hadn't turned on any lights other than the one in the kitchen over the sink. Come to think of it, maybe she'd left that on this morning.

He seemed engrossed in what he was doing, his expression intense as he studied something on the screen.

She felt like a rabbit who realized the hawk hadn't seen her yet.

Then Jared came up beside her and her entire body went weak with lust. She tingled from her scalp to her toes and everywhere in between, a tingle that soon turned into an achy burn.

God, she really was crazy to even be considering a repeat of New Year's Eve.

But you have to admit you want it.

She did want it. More than she ever thought she would.

For months after her parents' murders, the debate about what constituted a family had raged. Her granddad had tried to shield her from most of the American news machine and its hideously invasive, and mostly exaggerated, coverage of her parents' lives.

But even the move to Europe hadn't shielded her from everything.

And when the discussion had turned from the horror of what had happened to the more controversial aspect of the ménage and the fact that the three of them had raised a child in that atmosphere of sexual freedom, her parents had been called perverts.

And worse.

Hell, there'd even been a documentary on CNN about the mental health of children raised in alternative households that focused mainly on Annabelle. Not that they'd bothered to talk to her, to find out how very well-adjusted she'd been until a crazy woman had blown apart her life.

No, they just assumed she'd grow up completely screwed in the head.

Wouldn't all those talking heads be shocked to hear she was questioning whether she should indulge in a ménage herself?

Or was she merely letting the past interfere with what she did want here and now?

Damn it, she was young, unmarried, and healthy. And the man she was sleeping with was all for it.

So are you just doing this to please him?

Jared moved by her, heading for the drawer where she kept the take-out menus, as if he lived there.

His movement caught Dane's attention and his gaze went to Jared first and then to Annabelle. She expected to see cocky self-assurance there or at least a leering desire.

Instead, he gave her a breathtaking smile.

"We're going to order sandwiches," she said. "What would you like?"

God, the man was almost as beautiful as Jared, maybe a little broader and a few inches shorter but gorgeous just the same. He had pale skin that made his green eyes that much more striking, especially set against his dark hair.

"Anything dripping with fat and grease. And fries. I'm dying for decent fries."

He could certainly afford the calories. Neither guy had an ounce of fat on him.

And you get to see that firsthand.

Her mouth started to water and not for food.

"Hey, Belle. What do you want, hon?"

She wanted Jared to strip her naked and lay her on the dining table so he and Dane could make her come. So they could put their hands and their mouths all over her body until she couldn't take the pleasure any more. She wanted them to fuck her until she couldn't see straight.

Biting her tongue so she didn't accidently blurt that out, she took another deep breath, trying to hide her quickening pulse and the fact that she wanted to squeeze her thighs together to ease some of the burning ache.

"Just put me in for a grilled chicken salad."

"Two burgers and fries for me." Dane handed the menu back to Jared then looked at her. "Menu says they make the best chocolate cake around. That true?"

Jared snorted in amusement. "Dane's got a hell of a sweet tooth, Belle. You're gonna be old and fat one day, buddy. Just remember that."

"Then I better enjoy life while I can, right? Don't bust my ass just because you never touch the stuff."

"Oh, I have a sweet tooth," Jared said, his gaze transferring to her. "Just not for chocolate."

If there was such a thing as spontaneous combustion, she'd be igniting right now.

"The cake lives up to the hype, Dane," she forced herself to answer, tearing her attention away from Jared before she told him to forget dinner and move onto activities that would surely burn a few calories. "I'm sure you'll enjoy it."

Dane's smile seemed to burn a little hotter as well. "I'm sure I will."

He wasn't talking about the cake. She knew that as surely as she knew her own name.

She needed to cool down, collect herself. "I'm going to go take a shower. I'm sure you two can entertain yourselves until I get back."

She saw Jared nod as she turned toward her bedroom, and she swore she felt two hot male gazes follow her all the way.

Without looking back, she closed the door behind her, shutting her in her room, where she collapsed back against the door and took a deep breath that she released with a sigh.

Are you really going to do this? And are you only doing this because Jared wants it?

She pondered that question as she stripped off her jeans and sweater and turned on the water for the shower. Her stomach had tightened into a knot and her hands shook as she washed her hair and body. As she drew her washcloth across her breasts, she bit her lip at the sharp pleasure that zinged through her.

Oh, God, yes, I want this. I want it for me.

And that was the bottom line.

She wanted them. Jared because her heart demanded him.

And she wanted Dane because . . . Well, the man was gorgeous. What red-blooded woman wouldn't want him?

The fact that Jared wanted him in bed with them only made her that much hotter.

Okay, maybe you are *a pervert.*

No, enjoying sex did not make her a pervert. Not even when there'd be two men in bed with her instead of one.

After drying off, she walked into her bedroom and pulled open her underwear drawer, staring down at the colorful jumble, most of it courtesy of Kate. She hadn't been exaggerating her friend's abilities. Kate truly had a gift for creating breathtaking lingerie.

What would Jared and Dane do if she walked out there dressed only in a pink satin-and-lace thong and a pink satin demi bra?

Part her of her wanted to do it, just to prove she could. And to see the looks on their faces when she did.

Another part knew that wouldn't happen.

Still, she'd get to see their faces when they took off her clothes later.

And they *would* take off her clothes. She had no doubt about that.

Anticipation made her dress quickly. Over the lingerie she pulled on a clean pair of form-fitting jeans and a tight, long-sleeved black T-shirt with a rounded neckline. The shirt showed off a good amount of cleavage, the mounds of her breasts pushed up and out. She thought about pulling out her red-heeled stilettos but that might be pushing it so she went instead for bare feet.

Makeup?

No. It'd just get smudged . . . later.

Now, she just had to leave the bedroom.

Come on, Annabelle. You want this.

Yeah, she really did. After a deep breath, she opened the door and walked out.

* *

Dinner was surprisingly laid back. Not nearly as awkward as Annabelle had thought it'd be.

The sexual tension . . . Now that was off the chart. She swore she felt it rubbing against her skin, keeping her in a constant state of arousal.

Yet, as the night went on, the more relaxed she was. The more confident she became.

She felt feminine and sexy. Desired by two of the most handsome men she'd ever known.

The guys had kept up most of the conversation, talking about property values and tax rates, though they listened intently whenever she had anything to say.

Which wasn't often because she was fascinated by the interplay between them. They obviously knew each other well and their masculine ribbing made her hot.

When Dane smiled, she was struck by the man's sheer beauty. Then her gaze shifted to Jared and a whole different set of feelings hit her. She wanted to melt under Jared's steady gaze.

And the lust she'd kept banked through dinner made a roaring comeback.

She made no attempt to hide it from Jared and knew he'd gotten the message when he started to smile.

"I think we've had enough shop talk for the night," Jared said to Dane, never looking away from her.

At this particular moment, she cared about nothing other than what pleasure these two men were going to give her.

"Belle . . ." Jared didn't move, and instead let her name hang between them.

"Yes."

Absolutely yes. She was sick of waiting.

Jared took her at her word.

He stood and she let her gaze travel the length of him as he did. She knew the body hidden by his tight T-shirt and faded jeans. She'd explored every inch of it and couldn't wait to again. And tonight there'd be another . . .

She didn't know how she was going to get her brain to function on any level as Jared reached for her hands to draw her to her feet. She had no time to think as Jared bent over her and kissed her.

And this was no light, teasing touch. This was flat-out arousal. Her breath caught in her chest at the heat that drenched her as his lips ravaged hers. His tongue swept into her mouth and claimed hers, exploring, tantalizing, while his hands reached unerringly for her breasts.

He molded them in his palms, rubbing his thumbs over the sensitive tips and making her arch her back. She pressed herself further into his palms as her arms circled his shoulders.

Her fingers sliding into his hair, she tilted her head, deepening the kiss. As she tried to breathe, his scent hit her low in the gut, making her thighs clench.

Her blood heated and her sex moistened. A deep-seated craving built until she thought she'd have to beg Jared to hurry.

But Jared had no intention of cooperating. He kissed her with a slow, languid ease that only inflamed her that much more. Even his hands refused to move any faster.

She moaned, but the sound was cut off when Dane put his mouth on her neck.

Her body stilled as Dane's hands gripped her around the waist then slid upward, under her shirt and against her bare skin.

She drew in a deep breath through her nose because Jared continued to kiss her, refused to release her.

Submerged in sensation, she didn't want to swim out of it.

Synapses popped and fired and pleasure ran through her like adrenaline.

Dane's hands spread across her stomach as he moved closer to her back, close enough to feel his heat soak into her, just as Jared's warmth blasted her from the front. She felt cocooned between them and knew if her knees gave out now, she'd never hit the floor. These men would catch her.

She gave herself completely over to the pleasure at that moment.

And the men must have sensed it because the vibe changed.

Jared's mouth became more demanding and Dane's hands worked to open the button on her jeans.

Behind her, she felt Dane move and realized he'd gone to his knees behind her, his hands pulling her jeans down her legs. Cooler air brushed her barely covered ass cheeks as Dane lifted her left foot then her right to take off her jeans.

She bucked against Jared as Dane's hands cupped her ass, petting her before sliding between her thighs.

"Damn, Jed, I think I'm gonna leave the panties on. Just looking at them might get me off."

She shuddered at the lust in Dane's voice, and Jared finally broke their kiss to stare down at her. Into her eyes first then down further to take in her undies. "Do those match the bra, sweetheart?"

She wanted to smile seductively up at him but could only stare at him in pleasure-dazed lethargy. "Of course."

Jared's smile hardened. "Then you're leaving them both on."

Her sex tightened and she thought she might've come just from the sound of his voice and the feel of another man's hands stroking her skin.

"Lift your arms, Belle."

She automatically obeyed Jared, stretching her arms up so he could pull her T-shirt over her head.

She felt no awkwardness standing in front of them nearly naked while they were fully dressed. It was decadent, like one of her paintings come to life.

Jared dropped her shirt and let his gaze roam over her. Her lips puffy from his kiss. Her breasts nearly falling out of her bra as she tried to catch her breath. Then Dane's hands brushed against the satin covering her mound.

She hissed in a breath as his fingers traced over her clit but never settled to stroke her like she needed.

And she cried out when Dane brushed his lips against a fleshy part of her posterior and bit down.

"That's right, sweetheart," Jared rasped in her ear as he bent toward her, his own mouth capturing her earlobe and nipping. "We want to hear you."

Hell, if Dane continued to move his hands like that, the entire town would be able to hear her.

"I want you to touch me."

"Tell us where, sweetheart," Jared breathed against her cheek. "I want to hear you say it."

"My nipples, Jared. Tweak them. And I want Dane to finger my clit."

Jared's hands moved to cup her breasts, his fingers brushing against her nipples. His light touch made her sex tighten and moisture spill. Dane had to be able to feel the wetness against his fingers as he continued to stroke between her legs, conveniently avoiding her clit.

"More." She needed more.

"You'll get it, Belle. We've got all night. Don't want to wear you out right away."

She hadn't realized she'd spoken, she was so caught up in the wild and wonderful sensation of having two men touch her at the same time.

"I'm going to hold you to that," she said.

"There's two of us and only one of you, hon." Dane's voice held an edge of amusement. "I think we may have the advantage there."

"Then be men," she said, "and take advantage."

In the next second, she was gasping as Jared swung her into his arms and headed straight for her bedroom.

The hard edge of anticipation rode her as Jared laid her out on her bed and stripped off his clothes in seconds. He followed her down and covered her body with his. He took her lips again as he played his hands over her body, touching, stroking. Everywhere he touched, she burned.

She writhed against his hard body, wanting more skin-to-skin contact. Her thighs rubbed against his, spreading willingly as his knees worked between them. The heated silk of his erection pressed against her mound and she arched closer, trying to get him to give her what she wanted.

She wanted to be filled, to ease the ache in her body with his hard shaft.

Wanted . . .

Turning her on her side, Jared eased down her body to nip at her breasts, still covered in satin, as Dane molded himself against her back.

"Jared."

His name emerged on a gasp as Dane swept her hair to the side and settled his mouth on the sensitive skin where her neck met her shoulder. His naked cock nestled between the cheeks of her ass, the hard shaft burning hot against her skin.

Her brain conjured up an image of what the three of them must look like and she shuddered.

"Feel good, baby?" Jared's voice sounded muffled as he moved his mouth from breast to breast, pulling down the satin cups of her bra until they bared her nipples. "Hang tight 'cause it's gonna feel a hell of a lot better."

She'd be crazy by that time, she decided. But she couldn't get her mouth to form the words to tell him.

Jared latched onto one nipple, sucking hard on the tip and making her arch into his mouth. At the same time, Dane's fingers slid between her legs, brushing against her clit in a teasing caress before pulling back to stroke at the moisture gathering between her lips.

Her hands slid into Jared's hair, kneading like a cat, holding him close to make sure he never stopped.

She fell into a state of almost delirious pleasure, a place where she allowed herself only to feel the two pairs of hands and mouths that caressed her.

Jared and Dane petted, stroked, and drove her wild. The darkness added to the decadence of the act because she wasn't completely sure whose hands were where at any given moment.

She did know it was Jared who slid down her body and finally pulled the tiny panties from her waist so he could put his mouth between her legs.

Easing her onto her back, Dane moved to her breasts as Jared licked at her pussy as if she were a delectable treat. His tongue sent shocks of lightning deep into her body while Dane's mouth made her breasts swell, her nipples tighten and ache.

She tensed only seconds before her orgasm broke, sharp and short and definitely not enough. She wanted more.

Jared gave her clit one last lick before he moved up her pliant body, rolling her back on her side with Dane's help.

She tasted herself on his lips when he kissed her, and she moaned into his mouth.

"Are you ready, Belle?" Jared asked, his voice nothing more than a harsh whisper.

God, yes. She was ready. She needed them.

Behind her, Dane lifted her leg, holding her open as his cock, now sheathed in a condom, slid against her sensitive lips. She gasped at the aching need that seized her and wriggled her ass back against him, silently pleading.

When Jared rose to his knees in front of her, she reached for him, laying one hand on his waist and wrapping the other around his cock.

As Dane began to sink the head of his cock into her channel, Jared slipped the head of his cock into her mouth.

She took them both in eagerly, moaning at the silky glide of Jared's shaft against her tongue and the fullness of Dane's possession between her legs.

Drowning in a state of pleasure, she couldn't concentrate on any one sensation.

Jared fucked her mouth with slow, deliberate strokes while Dane set a hard and fast pace below. She drew hard on Jared, wanting to give him as much pleasure as she was getting, needing to push him over the edge she was fast approaching.

Orgasm lurked just out of reach, the men fueling the fire but never letting it burn out of control. They stretched her already frayed control to the breaking point but left her hanging on the edge.

She took Jared in as far as she could, his hands cupping her chin, stroking her cheeks and her lips as he slipped back and forth.

Dane reached around to tweak her clit, his pace quickening.

"Fuck, Jared, she's tight."

Dane's voice made her burn even brighter but it was Jared's that finally pushed her over the edge.

"That's right, baby. You feel so good. Come now, Belle. Do it."

And since she couldn't refuse him anything, she did. She cried out, her pussy bearing down around Dane as Jared pulled out of her mouth. Caught in the throes of the most powerful orgasm she'd ever had, she opened her eyes to see the fierce lust on Jared's face as she came around another man's cock, who twitched and pulsed inside her.

"Was it good, baby?" Jared asked as she finally regained her senses. "Because we're not done."

As Dane pulled out, Jared wasted no time lowering himself

over her. He'd pulled a condom on and slid into her still-spasming channel.

"Put your legs around me, Belle. I want you to come again."

Just the sound of his voice had her clenching around him. If she'd made a bet that she wouldn't be able to come again, she would've lost it.

Jared's thicker cock stretched her, lit her on fire. And Jared seemed determined to make her crazy. She thrashed beneath him as he pounded into her and she felt the moment he lost control.

He shuddered over her, grabbed her tight, and thrust once more, high and tight. She felt every pulse of his cock as he came into the condom, and it took only the slightest grind of his pelvis against hers to make her cry out and come all over again.

* *

When his eyes opened the next morning, Jared registered the warm weight of Annabelle draped over him.

She was still asleep. With a glance at the clock, he knew he'd have to wake her soon. Almost six on a Saturday morning, one of her biggest days of the week, and she opened at seven. He didn't think she'd set an alarm last night.

Dane slept in the spare room, and Annabelle had fallen asleep right after so they hadn't had time to talk.

Which might have been a good thing.

Would she regret last night?

Some women, after they had a chance to think about what they'd done, weren't too keen on repeating the experience. They let the doubt and the guilt destroy the pleasure until all they could think about was wiping the night from their memory.

Others couldn't get enough. They became addicted to the rush and embraced the lifestyle with a passion.

Much like he and Dane. They'd been perfecting the mechanics of ménage for years. Though they dated different women separately, they rarely dated the same women for long, and a ménage worked for them in ways a normal male/female relationship never had.

He and Dane had grown up in the same world of money, privilege, and family dysfunction. They'd been friends since grade school and had managed to maintain that friendship through high school and college.

They enjoyed the same music, sports, entertainment. Hell, they actually enjoyed each other's company. If they were gay, they'd be disgustingly monogamous.

His lips curved at the thought. A female acquaintance had actually thrown that in their faces after Dane had broken off their relationship.

They'd laughed but both of them realized they maintained their friendship through sex. Just not with each other.

The ménage also allowed them to keep a certain distance from the women they shared. Neither he nor Dane was looking for a permanent attachment.

At least, Jared hadn't been before last night.

Last night, more than any other time in his life, he'd been focused almost solely on giving pleasure. On Annabelle's response. He'd wanted her wild and burning with passion.

"I can practically hear you thinking."

Annabelle's husky voice brushed his chest as she shifted against him, repositioning until she rested her chin on her hands that laid across his chest. She stared up at him with clear green eyes, her rumpled curls inviting him to sink his hands into them. He wanted to kiss her and wondered why the hell he was even thinking twice about it.

He bent to capture her lips for a brief second before going back in for seconds. "Good morning."

As he pulled back, he saw her lips curl up at the corners. "Morning. What are you thinking about?"

He figured he might as well just get it out in the open. "Did you have a good time last night?"

His cock hardened as her cheeks blushed a very pretty pink but she didn't lower her gaze. "Yes, I did." She paused. "Where's Dane?"

"The spare room."

Her expression held no shame, only curiosity. And heat. "Is it always you and Dane?"

"Yes."

"Will Dane always be here with us?"

"No." He wondered if the flicker of reaction in her eyes was relief. Or disappointment. "He has to go back to Philly today. He has his own business to run."

"So . . . he's a fuck buddy?"

His eyes narrowed at the crude term but he could see Belle was trying to figure out the new parameters of their relationship.

And he wondered if he'd screwed up by bringing Dane here.

"Think of him more like a friend with benefits."

Her gaze grew sharper. "So what does that make you?"

Yours.

That one word hung in his brain, tantalizing him with possibilities. And confusing the hell out of him. Something had changed, something he didn't want to examine too closely right now because if he did . . .

"The man who would like you to accompany him to the Arts and Artists benefit ball next Saturday, if you're free. My mother chairs the committee every year and Tyler and I are required to make command performances."

He saw surprise in the lift of her eyebrows before a bemused smile curved her lips. "I've heard of it. I understand the organization funds some great programs for children and adults in the city."

"Yes, and it's been my mother's pet project for years so there's no getting out of it for me. Afterward, we could stay the night at the hotel, unless . . . Do you have someone who can cover the store for you?"

She shook her head then paused, as if considering her options. Finally, she said, "But I can close early that day."

He refused to examine the urge to beat his chest. "I would appreciate that."

Christ, why did that feel like one hell of an understatement?

She tilted her head to the side, looking as if she wanted to ask him something. He waited, wondering what was putting that look on her face.

"So I'm going to meet your parents, as your date?"

The utter seriousness of her question made him pause before answering. Did she not want to meet his parents? He couldn't blame her but he didn't think she knew how much of a dick his father was. "Yes, as my date."

"And you're okay with that?"

He smoothed out a frown. "I wouldn't have asked if I didn't want you there, Annabelle."

She paused. "So . . . we're dating?"

Well, when she put it that way, with that hesitant tone of voice . . . "Maybe you'd like to tell me how I should answer that question because I'm really not sure what you're asking."

He wanted to grab for her when she moved to sit up, pulling the sheets around her upper body. "I thought we had a business arrangement. Dating and business don't usually mix. I mean, sex is great but it's still not dating. I'm not certain I—we're ready to cross that line."

Jared tried to hide his shock at her reasoning. Not because he disagreed but because he'd used this same argument in the past with other women.

Wow, when had he become the clingy one?

A reluctant grin curved his lips. "You're absolutely right. But that doesn't change the fact that I'd like you to come. I enjoy spending time with you, Belle. Think of the event as a necessary evil before a night at Haven. Besides, my grandmother would like to meet you."

And now he was using his grandmother as a way to get Belle to spend time with him.

What the fuck was going on with him?

Belle hesitated and he forced himself to breathe while waiting for her answer.

Finally, she nodded. "Okay. Sure, I'd love to go."

Sixteen

"Jared, I don't know about this. This is more of a family thing. I feel like I'm intruding."

As Jared pulled the car to a stop at the curb, Annabelle tried not to fidget and possibly crush the beading on her dress. She looked like a million bucks but that didn't calm the butterflies in her stomach.

"This is definitely not a family thing." Jared turned to smile at her, that devastating grin that always made her want to run the other way, but only so he'd chase her.

The butterflies had started last Saturday morning. After he'd asked her to accompany him here. After that amazing night with Dane.

Just thinking about it still had the power to make her thighs clench.

And even though it hadn't happened again—Dane had returned to the city last Saturday—Annabelle wondered if maybe, tonight . . . Jared told her they'd be staying at Haven tonight. Would the Salon be open?

Jesus, where the hell had her common sense gone? Had it been blasted away by the great sex?

Or had she fallen for the man who'd introduced her to the best sex of her life?

"You're not intruding," Jared continued. "You look beautiful. But here's the deal. Don't let Nana get you alone for too long. She'll monopolize you because she's good at it. Ignore my father at all costs. My mom will be too busy to interrogate you, but she'll be too curious not to give you a few rounds. And you're only allowed one dance with my brother. He's almost as bad as my nana when he gets going."

She opened her mouth to speak, but he leaned over to whisper in her ear. "Don't make me kiss you to shut you up, Belle. I'll mess up your makeup. Besides, I've had a hard-on all week because all I could do was think about you. So if you don't get your pretty ass out of my car, we won't make it to the ball. We'll go straight to Haven."

When he drew back, she could barely breathe.

As she stared into his beautiful blue eyes, she couldn't believe how much she'd missed him this past week. He'd left last Sunday to return to Haven. He hadn't seemed happy about it but she understood he had responsibilities. He owned a hotel, for heaven's sake. Of course, he had business to take care of.

Besides, it's not like they had pledged themselves to each other. They had a business arrangement. With benefits. Really freaking good benefits.

And how much better would it be if it was all pleasure and no business?

When he finally released her gaze and got out of the car, she used the few seconds before her door opened to pull herself together. She flipped down the visor to check her makeup, satisfied that her lipstick wasn't smudged and her mascara hadn't run.

When her door opened and Jared stuck out his hand to help her out of the car, she gave her dress a shake to make sure everything was in place. Kate really had outdone herself with this one.

It was a good thing Kate used her as a model for her designs. It meant Kate had a workshop full of dresses for Annabelle to choose from. She'd promised to never again complain about standing for hours while being stuck by pins.

The beaded scarlet dress made the most of her fair complexion and, with her hair piled on her head in a seemingly random mass of curls, Annabelle knew she looked damn good.

Good enough to be seen with Jared Golden, who looked like he just stepped off the cover of *GQ* in a perfectly fitted tuxedo.

But as good as he looked in the tux, he looked even better naked.

No, can't think about that now. You'll embarrass yourself by drooling.

And she was about to meet his parents.

As they entered the GoldenStar, Annabelle considered how perfect the name was for Jared's father's hotel. The flagship of the Golden chain of luxury hotels, the Old City Philadelphia hotel had an expansive lobby and a grand staircase leading up to the second-floor ballroom that sparkled and glittered with candles and crystal.

The ball already seemed to be in full swing when they entered. A quartet played dinner music in the far corner while the stage was set for the youth orchestra to play after dinner.

And all around the room, easels displayed the works to be auctioned later. Jared had told her all the money raised went back into Arts and Artists to fund the programs.

Some pieces had obviously been done by children, but there were others that were stunningly good.

"Jared, would it be okay if we looked around a little before we met your parents?"

Not that she didn't want to meet them but she just had to get a closer look at one of the paintings on the opposite side of the room. The bold colors and design had caught her eye from the moment she'd walked in.

Jared's soft snort of laughter drew her attention away from the painting.

"I'll be lucky to have a minute with you to myself tonight."

She frowned up at him. "What do you mean?"

"I mean, my mom and nana are going to want to monopolize you. Come on, let me do the introductions quickly so you can scope out the paintings."

Warmth suffused her but she pushed it away. Why should it matter what his family thought of her? It wasn't like they were getting married. They were business partners, though, and she wanted to make the right impression.

She looked down to make sure her dress covered all the right places.

"You look beautiful, Belle," Jared said, no trace of exasperation or amusement in his tone. "Are you really that nervous?"

No. But she didn't know what she was feeling right now. "I don't typically attend charity events for a thousand dollars a plate. Give me rare Staffordshire and I can sell the plate for a thousand. But this . . ."

"Honey, looking like that, you could sell a load of reproductions to the Smithsonian, and they'd never know. I'm going to talk to Kate about having her own boutique in the hotel. She's got phenomenal talent."

Annabelle couldn't agree more. "Yes, she does. But I think you might have a hard sell getting her to take you up on the offer. I don't think her fiancé even knows she does this kind of work."

"Then I guess it'll be up to you to convince her."

Jared couldn't tear his gaze away from Belle. She was absolutely stunning, looking like a lick of flame in the scarlet sheath. He'd be beating away other men all night.

Already, he wished they could skip this part and head back to Haven. He didn't want to share her attention.

But he knew he couldn't do that. His mom lived for tonight. He needed to be here for her. And Annabelle was eyeing the paintings on display with a collector's eye.

No, he'd have to suck it up and stick this out for a few hours.

No matter how much he wanted Belle. The past week away from her, he'd needed a cold shower every night.

And had absolutely no desire to fill his bed with anyone but her.

The thought should have rocked him to his bachelor's soul. But then he'd never met anyone like Belle before.

And she had found the pin . . .

He smiled at the thought, though he didn't believe Nana's story about the pin pairing off soul mates. How could he? It was a legend created by an artist to sell his jewelry.

As he steered her toward the front of the room, where he knew his mom would be holding court, he barely noticed the glittering crowd moving around them. Most of the usual Main Line suspects were here, in addition to anyone who was anyone in the city.

Many of them stared back at him. He saw contemplation on the women's faces, some of them women he'd been involved with. But he knew they weren't looking at him. They were sizing up Annabelle. So were the men, but for different reasons. His hand tightened on her shoulder until she shot him a concerned look, which he soothed with a smile.

Maybe this wasn't such a good idea after all. He sent a quick glance around the room and found Tyler sitting at a table with his grandmother. Better the devil he knew.

"Come meet my grandmother, Belle."

* *

Tension pounded in Annabelle's temples, threatening to burst into a full-blown headache.

Tonight had been more stressful than she'd expected.

Not that anyone had been mean to her. On the contrary, everyone had been wonderful and Jared had stuck to her side like glue for the past two hours.

Until a second ago when he'd gotten up to dance with his mother.

"Time to do my duty," he sighed. "I'll be right back, Belle."

Then he'd slid a glance at Tyler.

"Would you like a drink, Annabelle?" Tyler asked, leaning forward slightly to speak over the din of the large crowd. "I need something a little more fortifying than champagne."

Annabelle liked Tyler, who was so different from Jared. Quiet and intense, Tyler looked into you with his dark brown eyes, almost as if he could see what you were thinking. He'd been polite and kind all evening, saying just enough to keep up with the conversation.

But that intensity had flared when he'd asked about Kate. She'd been ready to bring up the subject herself when he'd asked how she was doing. But other than his question, she couldn't tell how he felt.

"How about a glass of orange juice, with a lot of ice, please. I think I've already had a few too many glasses of champagne."

And she didn't want to fall asleep too early tonight.

Tyler nodded and moved away, leaving her alone with Beatrice Golden. Somehow she'd dodged that particular bullet all night. But when Beatrice turned to her with a knowing smile, Annabelle knew her time was up.

"So, dear. Alone at last." The tiny-featured, frail-looking woman patted one thin hand on the seat next to hers. A royal summons, if Annabelle had ever seen one.

She couldn't very well say no, so she smiled and shifted over two seats to sit next to Beatrice.

Out of the corner of her eye, she saw Jared on the dance floor with his mother, Helena, who'd been overcome with emotion when she'd been honored earlier by the charity's board of directors. From what little Annabelle had seen of her tonight, she seemed like a nice woman.

Glen Golden also seemed pleasant. She hadn't been able to figure out why Jared didn't want her anywhere near his dad.

"How are you enjoying the party?" Beatrice asked.

"Jared's mother has done a wonderful job," she answered truthfully.

Everything had gone off without a hitch. Though personally, she'd rather be at one of Jared's parties at Haven. Here, she felt like she needed to watch her posture and smile all the time, as if she were on display.

"Yes, Helena loves this kind of thing." Beatrice sighed. "Me, I'd rather be over at Haven, sitting at the bar, having a gin and tonic."

Annabelle's tension headache lightened a little at Beatrice's forlorn tone.

"Now, tell me, young lady, how did you come to find my pin?"

Ah, the pin. She'd been wondering when Beatrice would get around to asking about it. Annabelle curved her lips in what she hoped was a convincing smile even as her temples throbbed as if someone had tightened a vise on them. "Actually, my grandfather did, about thirty years ago at a flea market. I don't really know that much about how he found it. All I know is that he found it in a box of costume jewelry. He didn't know it was there until he emptied the box and realized the stones were authentic. I'm so sorry I can't tell you anything more. I understand it was stolen?"

Beatrice placed one hand over Annabelle's. "Yes, yes, many years ago. I want you to know I don't suspect your grandfather of having anything to do with its disappearance. We long suspected that it was a maid who took it. She disappeared at the same time as the jewelry and we never were able to find her or the pieces."

"I really wish you'd let me give the piece back to you."

Beatrice wrinkled her nose. "Absolutely not. I want you to have it, dear. It's yours now, has been for years. It is a beautiful piece, isn't it?"

"Yes, it is. I've always loved it. But, Beatrice, I'm a firm believer in reuniting families with their treasures. The pin is yours."

With a quick look to see that Jared still danced with his mother, Annabelle opened the small velvet satchel tied to her wrist, another of Kate's creations, and drew out the pin.

"I just don't feel right keeping it."

Beatrice dropped her gaze to the pin, the smile on her face spreading. She reached for the pin and Annabelle thought she was going to take it. But Beatrice closed Annabelle's fingers over it. "The pin's in the right hands. It was originally part of a set of seven that had been in my family for years until a few were sold off in the Great Depression. My grandfather managed to keep the pin and a blue sapphire ring in the family. The set was given to my parents on their wedding, and I inherited the pin on my eighteenth birthday, when I met Jared's grandfather." Beatrice sighed. "When my mother passed, I inherited the ring as well. Both were stolen before I could pass them to Jared's father."

Beatrice looked out over the dance floor, and Annabelle followed her gaze. Glen and Helena danced together now. She didn't see Jared.

Her stomach dipped as she looked for him.

There he was, dancing with another woman. A slim, gorgeous creature with jet-black hair and a bearing only acquired through years of functions like this. Someone Jared seemed to know very well.

The woman's hand caressed his shoulder as they danced so closely she couldn't see a centimeter of space between them. They moved together as if they'd been doing it for years.

Her stomach rolled at the look on Jared's face—calm, in control, flirtatious. It was that last one that made her stomach tighten.

She'd known all along that he was a flirt, a playboy.

And hadn't she been the one who'd insisted on keeping their relationship strictly about business and sex? Isn't that what she'd told him last weekend?

Maybe he'd been seeing that woman this week while he'd been in Philadelphia.

Damn it, what was wrong with her? Why did she feel . . . What? Possessive? Jealous?

After the whole debacle with Gary, she'd sworn off men.

Then what does she go and do? She falls for the first millionaire playboy she meets.

She wanted to laugh at the absurdity of it, but she was afraid Beatrice would think she was crazy.

Slipping one hand to her temple, she rubbed at the expanding ache there and dragged her gaze away from Jared and the other woman.

Maybe she'd send Tyler back to the bar for a bottle of vodka to add to her orange juice.

Beatrice patted her on the hand, drawing her attention back to the older woman, smiling at her in a way that made Annabelle's brows lift.

"Annabelle, my dear, I would like to employ your services."

* *

Jared's head ached.

It had started with a dull throb at the base of his neck and spread throughout his skull to compress his sinuses into oblivion.

And Katherine Sinclair's incessant sexual innuendo wasn't helping.

He'd known he wouldn't be able to ignore everyone all night. He'd known eventually he'd have to make the rounds. There were too many people he knew here. He couldn't just sit by Annabelle's side. He shot a quick glance her way and breathed a little easier when he saw her engaged in conversation with his grandmother. Nana would take care of her until he could return to the table.

"So, Jared." Katherine ran one slim finger around the collar of his shirt, failing to raise more than his ire. "David's out of town until the end of the month and—"

Jared cut her off before she could finish the thought. "I'm afraid I'm leaving tonight."

Katherine smiled, and Jared had learned that when a woman smiled like that, fur was about to fly. "She's pretty, but not your usual type. I don't recognize her."

He stifled a sigh. "You wouldn't. So I understand your mother's surgery went well."

Katherine flashed him a look that spoke volumes. She knew what he was up to. "Mom's fine, the knee replacement went well and, of course, Daddy promised her a shopping trip to Paris as soon as she's up and about again. Why don't you give me a call next week? I'll plan a day at the spa at Haven and then we could get some dinner?"

With his headache starting to take on gargantuan proportions, Jared fended off Katherine for the rest of the song. But as the band swung into the next number, Darcy Adams took Katherine's place.

Why hadn't he remembered that these events were basically meat markets?

He turned down another proposal. Discreetly, of course. None of them interested him.

He only wanted to return to his table where a certain green-eyed woman waited for him. He looked that way to see what Belle was up to and discovered her gone.

His gut tightened with some emotion he couldn't place. Without trying to be obvious, he swung a quick glance around the dance floor and sighed with relief when he found her dancing with Tyler. Her smile brightened his night from halfway across the room. And, by God, his brother had a smile on his face, too.

Amazing.

Well, maybe not so amazing. Belle was starting to give him ideas he'd never thought possible.

Somehow he got through the rest of the dance without stepping on Darcy's feet or making a complete idiot out of himself. The game of seduction he typically thrived on held no thrill tonight.

Maybe he wasn't as much like his father as he'd thought.

He missed a step and apologized to Darcy.

That topic was obviously not a good one to think about now. He'd only been out of the loop for a few weeks and already he thought himself above it all. That might've been the most dangerous thought he'd had all night.

Hell, look at his parents. His father claimed to love his mother, but he'd still cheated on her.

He vividly remembered his father trying to explain his adultery to a sixteen-year-old. How the relationship he had with his wife forced him to seek "comfort" outside the home. That Helena's condition made it difficult for them to have a true relationship.

It was the first time either of his parents had ever touched on the subject that there was something wrong with Helena.

Shit, that really wasn't what he wanted to be thinking about now.

Thankfully, the song ended, and he untangled himself from his dance partner. It took longer than it should have. The woman had wanted to continue their discussion but he managed to get away without drawing attention to himself. Goldens never made a scene.

Finally, he made his last regret and, on his way to reclaim Annabelle from his brother, he passed close enough to his parents that Helena stopped him.

He leaned down to kiss her on the cheek. "Great shindig, as always, Mom. Guess we know where I got it from, hmm?"

"Thank you for coming, sweetheart. The recognition was such a surprise and to have you all here was a real treat. I just wanted you to know I'm glad you came."

Jared heard a note in his mom's voice that made him take a

second look at her. Her color was high, though that could be attributed to the warmth in the ballroom and the excitement of the event.

Then he noticed how hard she clutched Glen's arm, her knuckles nearly white.

He smiled, tried not to let her see it was forced, and slid a glance at his father. "I wouldn't have missed this. So, are you staying much longer?"

"Well, of course we can't leave yet," Helena said. "I feel like I could dance all night."

Now Jared looked straight at his father and saw strain in the lines of his face.

Shit. Shit.

The tension in his head spread through his body as every muscle tensed.

"Are you leaving soon, sweetheart?" His mom smiled up at him, her eyes just the tiniest bit glassy. "Taking your date back to the hotel for the night?"

Jared exchanged another glance with his father. "I think we'll hang for a little while, dance a little."

"Well, you have a good time, dear." She turned to Glen. "I'd like to dance some more myself actually. I feel like I could dance all night."

"Mom—"

"Jared, we don't need a chaperone." Glen smiled at him but it never reached his eyes. "Go on back to your date. Your mom and I'll be fine."

Jared felt helpless as his parents walked away back into the thinning crowd on the ballroom floor.

For a few seconds he merely watched them, watched his father maintain his hold on his mother's elbow, then take her in his arms and move to the music.

They laughed and talked, smiled at each other.

Jared's eyes narrowed. Okay, maybe he'd been wrong. Maybe his mom was just excited by the party, the recognition. Maybe . . .

He turned back to the table where Belle was once again sitting with Nana and Tyler. She looked tired, her skin a little more pale than normal.

He quickened his pace, wondering if she thought he'd deserted her.

Maybe—

A commotion behind him made him stop and turn.

Just in time to see his father carry his mother off the dance floor.

* *

"You're welcome to take a room for the night," Jared said. "But I don't think I'll be back. I'll probably stay at the hospital."

Annabelle nodded, seconds from a clean getaway. She gripped the door handle, ready to jump out of the car and go back to her home.

Jared's mother had been taken to the hospital. Helena's doctor, who had been at the benefit, had believed she was having a reaction to a new medication.

She understood Jared's need to go with his mother. But something else was going on here.

The man she'd arrived at the ball with had been replaced with a block of cold stone. There was no way she'd misinterpreted the wave of frigid cold coming from Jared.

He hadn't said a word since he'd told her he'd take her back to the hotel before he went to the hospital.

Something else was happening here, something she didn't understand going on in the background.

And Jared had no intention of telling her what it was.

He couldn't seem to be rid of her fast enough.

It was as if he was done with her. As if he couldn't care one way or the other what she did.

It hurt more than she'd thought possible.

Forcing a smile, which he never saw, she said, "I think I'll head home, that way I can open the shop tomorrow."

Jared nodded, staring out the front window. "Thank you for coming with me tonight. I'll give you a call later this week."

Right. Sure you will. Annabelle got out of the car. "Good-bye, Jared."

He nodded again, sparing her a quick glance. "Have a safe trip home."

By the time she got her car started, all she saw was his brake lights as he pulled out of the parking garage.

* *

"It just doesn't make any sense. That doesn't sound like Jared."

Kate lifted her whiskey sour to her mouth, nearly missing her lips as she shook her head.

Or it could be that Annabelle had double vision. She'd lost track of the number of whiskey sours she'd consumed in the past couple of hours after she'd closed the shop Sunday at five. Probably more than she wanted to count.

Her brain was a little—No, her brain was a *lot* fuzzy and the alcohol was doing a hell of a job on that throbbing ache in the middle of her chest. It had loosened considerably in the past few minutes. And so had her mouth.

"Well, maybe I didn't know him as well as I thought I did."

Annabelle took another swig, no longer grimacing at the burn of the whiskey. "Hell, I don't even know what I'm bitching about. I was only in it for the sex."

Kate snorted. "Yeah, right. If you think I believe that, tell me about the bridge you want to sell me."

"No, really. The sex was great but I knew he was never gonna be around long term. Hell, I might as well have pushed him away. After that night with Dane and Jared—"

Oops. *Way* too many whiskey sours. Annabelle snapped her lips shut as Kate's eyes rounded like dinner plates.

"*What* did you just say?" Kate's glass and the table collided at high speed. "Did you just say Dane *and* Jared? Do you mean . . . *Both?*"

Oh, shit. She'd let the bag out of the—No, wait, she'd let the cat out of the bag.

Definitely no more whiskey sours.

But now that she'd opened her big mouth, she didn't want to lie to her best friend. In the past week since it'd happened, she'd wanted so badly to talk to Kate about it.

"Yes. Both." She drew in a deep breath. "Oh, God, do you think I'm a slut?"

Kate continued to stare at her. "Holy *crap*. Wait, who's Dane? When was this? Was it good?"

Annabelle closed her eyes and let her head fall back. "Dane is Jared's friend. Last weekend. And if I say yes, will you ever talk to me again?"

Kate's face broke out into a smile so wide it had to hurt. "Hell, yes, I'll talk to you again. Damn, I can't even get decent sex from one guy and here you are, getting it good from two."

Relief at Kate's response made her suck in much-needed air. "Oh, thank God. It was amazing. I mean, really freaking amazing. I thought maybe it was just that it was naughty, you know? Forbidden. I thought that's why it was so freaking good. But . . ."

Kate leaned forward. "But what?"

"But I think it was because of Jared. I think I really liked the guy."

"Oh, Annabelle." Kate's expression fell into despair. "That's so . . . so . . . sad. And you wanna know why? Because I don't think I ever felt that way about Arnie."

Annabelle bit her bottom lip. *Damn, maybe whiskey sours were good for something other than getting shit-faced. Maybe they were the key to unlocking whatever was stuck inside.* "What do you mean?"

Kate's mouth twisted. "Oh, please, you know what I mean. You never really liked Arnie—"

"No, that's not true—"

"And I know now I don't love him enough to marry him."

Annabelle shut her mouth tight before she could say anything else. Even as drunk as she was, she still had enough brain cells left to know Kate had to come to this decision on her own.

Kate took a deep breath, tears shining in her eyes. "Oh, my God. I can't believe I said that out loud. I mean, I've thought about it but I never came out and said it. It sounds . . . so final."

Annabelle reached across the table to take Kate's hand. "Kate . . ."

"No." Kate shook her head, as if trying to clear her thoughts. "No, I don't want to talk about it. Not now. Right now, I want to know more about this wild side of yours."

Wild side? Was she really as passionate as her mom? Did she *have* a wild side? Or had it all been about her trying to please Jared?

No, that wasn't right. He hadn't coerced her. She'd been a more than willing participant. "I don't think it matters much anymore. I think . . . I think I probably won't be seeing Jared again. At least not in a personal way. I don't think he'll back out of our business arrangement. He's not like that. And it's an amazing opportunity for me to work on the spa. But I'm afraid if we continue to have a sexual relationship while we work together, it's going to be messy when it ends. At least for me."

And despite all her protestations that she wasn't looking for a relationship, that she didn't want a guy in her life, that what she and Jared had shared was lust and a business relationship, she finally realized she'd been lying to herself.

* *

"Jared, honey, why don't you go home and get some rest? I'm pretty sure you didn't sleep at all last night and I'm in no danger of expiring at this moment."

Standing by the window in his mother's bedroom, Jared turned to find her staring at him with a faint smile on her pale face.

He reached for a smile and found one hard to dredge up. He'd been running on adrenaline since last night and was starting to crash.

"I'll go in a little while. You'll start to complain of the stench soon anyway."

His mom actually laughed at that. "You would never stink, dear. Besides, I lived with you as a teenager, remember?" Then she sighed. "I really did a number on you, didn't I?"

He frowned as he walked back to the bed, checking her eyes to make sure they were clear and not glassy. He knew the doctor had said she hadn't had a manic episode last night. That she'd had a reaction to the new drugs she'd just started taking. A new regimen Jared had known nothing about. That had been something of a shock.

Even more of a shock was that his father had known. He'd been going to the doctor with her, had known what symptoms to look for to know if she was having an episode or a reaction to the meds.

Still, for so many years Jared had been assessing her condition and her mood, it was now second nature.

"What are you talking about?"

She shook her head, her lips twisted in a slight grimace. "You lived your childhood wondering what mommy was going to show up that day. The manic or the depressive. Not a good way to raise a child, is it?"

"Hey, Mom—"

"We never talked about it back then, your father and I. My parents never suspected anything was wrong. I was merely high strung. And the worst of the episodes only started after we married."

Yeah, because his father was a lying sack of—

"And you can stop with that line of thinking right now, Jared." Her voice held a note of command he didn't hear from her often. "No, your father is not perfect but what you never knew was that I told him flat out to take a mistress. That I no longer wanted a sexual relationship with him."

Whoa. His head snapped back in shock. "Mom—"

"No, let me finish, Jared." She took a deep breath, then continued. "We had two sons who meant more to me than anything in the world. And everyone knows your father and I didn't marry for love. We united two fortunes. But your father got more than he bargained for with me. Honey, you and your brother were the lights of my life but your dad . . . Your dad took the brunt of my depression. And it wasn't pretty."

She stopped to shake her head, her smile becoming bittersweet. "I don't blame him for seeking comfort elsewhere. But you do your dad a disservice by treating him like the bad guy. He could've divorced me years ago. Hell, he should have. But—"

"When you love someone, it's not that easy to let go."

Jared turned at the sound of his father's voice. Glen leaned against the doorjamb, dressed in faded jeans and an old Temple sweatshirt. The man looked damn good for fifty-eight. Jared knew he still worked out and swam to keep in shape.

When Glen started toward the bed, Jared noticed the smile he wore for his wife. Jared barely recognized it because he hadn't seen it for years.

Or maybe he just hadn't been looking.

"You really should get some rest." Glen bent down to kiss Helena on the lips, a rare display of open affection. Another shocker. He could probably count on his fingers the number of times he'd seen his parents kiss like that. "The doctor said you'd have no lasting effects but you need to rest. Jared can visit tomorrow."

"Only if Jared wants to visit." Helena's gaze came back to him. "I'm fine, honey, really. You don't need to hover. No one," she said, looking at Glen, "needs to hover."

His father just patted her hand and smiled.

And Jared realized maybe she was right. "Actually, I need to be out of town tomorrow. There's someone I need to see."

"A female someone?" Helena lifted of her eyebrows. "Maybe a certain pretty redhead?"

He nodded slowly. "Yeah, though I'm not sure she's going to want to see me. I may have been a little . . . brusque with her."

More like rude, cold. An idiot.

"Oh, you might be surprised at what a woman will do for a man she wants," Helena said. "Just be prepared to grovel a little."

"Yes, groveling goes a long way," Glen agreed, his gaze steady on Jared's. "So does just being there."

The conversation had turned surreal. His father was giving him relationship advice . . . that sounded almost reasonable.

Yeah, he was *so* not ready to deal with his dad and their issues. Not yet. Maybe soon . . .

But first, he needed to brush up on his groveling.

Seventeen

The doorbell was a torture device from hell, Annabelle decided around ten Monday morning.

Its only purpose in life was to make her head feel like she'd pounded it against the wall for a few hours last night. Of course, the only thing she'd been pounding had been whiskey sours.

Luckily for whoever was laying on her bell, she'd just taken a shower and was feeling slightly more human than when she'd rolled out of bed an hour ago. And the three acetaminophen she'd taken had brought her hangover down from traumatic to merely mind-splitting.

As she stumbled to the door, she really, really, *really* hoped it wasn't someone she had to be pleasant to. In fact, she almost wished it was Gary. She would love to be able to just slam the door in his face.

She didn't think she could manage pleasant. Upright was about as good as it got.

What she definitely couldn't handle was the man standing on her doorstep, holding two cups of fragrant, steaming coffee.

Jared Golden looked good enough to eat. She swore she could actually taste him on her tongue.

Damn, who would have thought her libido would still work this morning?

She couldn't stop her eyes from eating him up, from the top of his golden-brown head to his luscious lips to the broad shoulders she'd clung to not so very long ago in the throes of passion.

Her mouth dried and her lungs caught on a hitch. *Okay, that was not a good thing to think about now.*

She had to stop herself from grabbing for the coffee. She knew a bribe when she smelled one. She should just say "Thank you very much" and close the door in his face. Gently. Definitely no slamming.

Instead, here she stood, staring at him like a fool, wondering if he'd drop the coffee if she threw herself at him. Probably not. He was that good.

And even though she was still smarting from Saturday night's treatment, she wanted to throw herself at him.

Damn, have I no self-respect?

"Good morning, Belle. May I come in?"

A sharp gust of cold air made her catch her breath, and she took an automatic step away from the door, which Jared took as permission to enter.

And really, it wasn't like she would have refused him anyway.

Not when he made her stomach flutter when he smiled at her with that wry grin. He almost looked apologetic.

No, stay strong. The guy practically told you to get lost.

After his mother had been rushed to the hospital.

Jesus, of course I should cut him some slack.

"How's your mom, Jared? Is she okay?"

As he handed her the coffee, he nodded. "Much better, thank you. She had a bad reaction to a new medication. She told me to tell you she's sorry we had to cut our night short." He took a deep breath. "And I'm very sorry too. Please forgive my attitude. It was unconscionable and I have no other excuse than that I was worried about my mother."

He looked so sincere, her pique with him dissolved in a puddle at her feet. It just shouldn't be that easy, she thought. He should have to work for it, right? Maybe grovel a bit more. Or at least bring doughnuts with the coffee.

"The medication she's taking is for bipolar disorder. She's been dealing with it since I was a kid."

Her eyes widened with shock. "I'm so sorry. That must be difficult."

"It is, yeah. But even more difficult to handle was my dad's infidelity. He cheated on her and I hated him."

She didn't know what to say to that. "What I didn't realize was that she knew the whole time. She actually *encouraged* him to do it. I've hated my father for years because I thought he was lying to my mom. That he was making a fool out of her by cheating on her. But she knew. I guess I'm still having a hard time processing everything because I feel like they've both lied to me."

She had a hard time swallowing, knowing she was lying to him every day she didn't tell him who she really was. "That's a lot for a teenager to process. I can't imagine your dad would hold your attitude against you."

"Yeah, that's the thing. He doesn't. And I've treated him like shit for so long, I don't know any other way to treat him. I don't know how to fix this."

"Maybe you don't have to fix it. Maybe you just have to accept him for who he is, put it all aside, and move on. Forgive him and forgive yourself at the same time."

There was that smile again, the one that made her knees melt. "Beautiful and smart. Do you know how sexy that is?"

Her own smile broke free, even though the little voice in her head kept battering at her, telling her over and over that she, too, was lying to him.

"I'm glad your mom's feeling better."

"So am I. Now, what did you have planned today?"

* *

"Where are we off to?" Annabelle asked as Jared slipped into the driver's seat of his car.

Jared twisted the key and the car hummed to life. "I thought we'd just drive around so I can get the lay of the land. There're a couple of properties I'd like to look at but mainly I just want to look around."

"Then you might want to head out Route 568," she suggested. "There's some nice country out there."

As they drove off, Annabelle let her mind drift. She'd planned to spend the day digging through the Internet for Beatrice's missing ring. She'd start her search by contacting auction houses and antique jewelry dealers in the tri-state area to see if they remembered seeing or selling the ring at any point.

Beatrice had said the police made a thorough investigation at the time of the robbery. She'd also hired someone to search for the pieces every five years after they'd been stolen until about fifteen years ago, when she'd given up on ever seeing them again.

If the ring was out there, it could be hiding in another box of costume jewelry or buried in someone's jewelry box. Or safe deposit box.

She'd have to go through her grandfather's records and see if she could come up with a name or a receipt for the pin, though she didn't hold out much hope there. If her grandfather had bought a box full of what he'd thought was costume jewelry, he'd probably paid cash and hadn't gotten a receipt.

Beatrice had promised to email a picture of the ring this morning, though she hadn't had time to check. Jared's grandmother had asked her not to say anything to Jared about their arrangement and Annabelle had agreed, mostly because it'd seemed an innocuous request. Maybe Beatrice wanted to surprise her grandsons with the pieces. Annabelle was determined to give the pin back to her as well, even if she didn't find the ring. It really did belong with her family.

She let her gaze land on Jared. Beatrice had said the pieces united soul mates.

Which was pure fairy tale.

Jared was *not* her soul mate.

Neither of them was looking for happily ever after. Nothing had changed since she'd first met him.

Just because her pulse leaped in anticipation every time he touched her, it didn't mean it was love. It wasn't love. Just pure old-fashioned lust. It could never be more. She couldn't imagine the scrutiny she'd be under if she and Jared . . . What? Got married?

She huffed. Was she crazy? She wasn't thinking about marriage. She'd flat out told him she wasn't in the market for marriage. And she'd told Kate she was going to break off their personal relationship.

Look how well that worked out.

So had she changed her mind?

No, of course not. They could work together but mind-blowing sex did not make for a stable marriage.

No, but great passion did.

"Hey, you're not falling asleep on me over there, are you?"

Jared laid a hand on her knee, and even through a layer of denim, she could feel his body heat. His touch wasn't sexual, just a light squeeze. But electricity jolted through her body, sparking her ever-present desire for him.

As casually as she could, she shifted so she was facing him more fully, but he had to remove his hand because her knee was now too far for him to reach. He slid a glance her way and she smiled at him.

"So, what exactly are you looking for?" she asked. "Was there a property you had in mind? Did you see something in the news-paper?"

He shook his head. "Not really. I'll know it when I see it. I don't like to do a lot of prep work for something like this. I like to go with my gut. I knew the moment I saw the building in Phila-delphia that it'd be perfect for Haven."

"And you really think you're going to find what you're looking for around here?"

His mouth turned up in a sexy grin, and he reached over to run a hand along her cheek, making her skin tingle. "This past month has been full of surprises. I'm sure there'll be more."

Okay, the man didn't even have to touch her and lust threat-ened to burn her up from the inside out. Her cheeks flamed and she silently cursed her fair skin.

Luckily, his attention was focused on the road at the moment. They drove the next few miles in silence as Annabelle tried to stuff her desire back into the little box she'd nailed shut Saturday night.

She wasn't having much luck with that.

Instead, she focused on the scenery, on the rolling farmland abruptly interrupted by sprawling, cookie-cutter housing developments and the occasional thick stands of trees. The closer they got to Reading, the more developments and less open land. So they ended up back on Annabelle's side of the highway, heading into the hills.

The homes were farther apart up here, the trees more dense, hiding buildings at the end of the unmarked lanes shooting off from the two-lane road.

Jared had punched a couple of buttons on the dashboard and music filtered through the speakers. Etta James, early Elvis Presley, and several blues musicians she couldn't place enveloped them in a warm cocoon that soon had Annabelle fighting to keep her eyes open.

She must have lost the battle because when the car came to a halt, she woke with a start.

"Hey, Belle, what do you think?"

The intensity in Jared's voice caught her attention right away. His eyes were narrowed as he stared out the driver's-side window. She had to lean toward him to see what he was looking at. With him this close, she caught the clean, dark scent of him, which made her stomach clench.

She really had to get a grip.

Following Jared's gaze, she found herself staring at a castle.

She blinked. No, that couldn't be right. She shook her head, trying to make things come into focus, but that castle wouldn't budge.

She looked around, trying to get her bearings. She wasn't exactly sure where they were but she knew they couldn't be too far from home.

"What is this place? How did you find it?" she asked.

"I have no idea. We're about fifteen miles or so north of Adamstown. I just happened to see a 'For Sale' sign on the road and followed an unmarked lane up here. It doesn't even show up on the GPS."

Annabelle felt Jared's excitement like a physical force. It infected her, made her heart beat a little faster. She swore she could actually see his brain working.

Jared slid out of the car and she did the same. He walked forward to lean on a short stone wall encircling what looked to be a garden laid out in front of the building.

The stone in the wall matched the stone of the building, which had all the characteristics of a castle. Twin towers jutted from either end and a multitude of windows and balconies dotted the façade. A huge arched wooden door beckoned.

It nestled into the forest like it had been there for centuries. All the building needed was a princess in the tower to look as if it had been transplanted from Germany or England. Though it was not as huge, it was still pretty impressive.

"I never knew this place existed. I've lived here for years and no one's ever said anything about it."

"Jesus, this is perfect."

Striding to the garden gate, Jared flung it open and walked through like he already owned the place, his gaze taking everything in.

She approached cautiously, not wanting to get in his way. He looked intense. He wore that same expression when he made love to her.

Unreasonable jealousy curled through her. Which was just too ridiculous.

"Look at the lines," he said, though she wasn't sure if he was talking to her or himself. "Three floors and maybe ten or twelve rooms on the second and third floors if the number of windows is any indication. It's gonna need a hell of a lot of work but still . . . I'm gonna take a walk around the back. I'll be right back."

He strode off around the side of the building and disappeared. Annabelle decided to get comfortable and found a marble bench in the overgrown garden. As she settled onto it, the cold seeped into her thighs and she welcomed the clarity it brought.

What would she do if he actually found a site for his spa retreat so close to her home? Would they continue their relationship? Meet every couple of weeks for sex? Would it be enough?

She'd known from the beginning that this relationship wasn't going to last. But if Jared actually bought this place, she'd already committed to furnishing it. Could she continue their sexual relationship as long as they did business together? Without falling in love with him?

Did she *want* to continue the relationship?

It was a stupid question. Of course she did. Because no matter how many times she told herself she wasn't looking for the man of her dreams, she had to admit Jared would fill the bill.

She was afraid and . . . Well, she should just leave it at that. She was afraid.

She'd spent so many years hiding her identity, terrified of igniting a media frenzy that would make her life a living hell again. Could she trust him with her secret? And what if they actually took their relationship further? Jared occasionally made the gossip rags. Would they dig into her background? Would some reporter get lucky and figure out who she was?

She didn't think she'd be able to live through that scandal again.

Maybe you're getting way ahead of yourself.

Yes, he'd asked her to the fundraiser but it wasn't like he'd asked her to move in with him.

And then there was the question of his lifestyle . . .

Which, she had to admit, thrilled her. No question about it.

Shaking her head, she sighed. So many questions. Not enough answers.

Jared reappeared around the other side of the building then, heading toward her with a smile that could devastate the entire female population in a three-county area. When he reached her, he swept her into his arms and kissed her hard and fast, his taste fleeting but heady.

"I think you must be my good luck charm." He smiled into her eyes, making her thighs clench. "This place is perfect."

But she thought he was the perfect one, with his gorgeous smile and devastating personality.

Releasing her, he pulled his cell phone from the pocket of his jacket and dialed a number. "I'm betting the real estate agent will drop off the key. The place looks like it's been on the market for a while. There're a few structural problems but— Yes, hi. I'd like to speak to Danielle West, please."

Thinking she'd give him some room, she started to move away, but he caught her and pulled her back against him. He kept one arm around her shoulders, and she allowed herself to rest her head on his chest, hearing his heart beat through his warm cotton sweater. She breathed deeply, letting his scent envelop her.

His voice rumbled in his chest as he charmed the person on the other end into dropping off the key. She enjoyed watching him in action. He knew exactly what he wanted and he got it.

"So what do you think?" he asked when he hung up. He stared down at her with an expectant expression, as if he really cared what she thought.

She forced a smile. "It's gorgeous. How long will it take for the real estate agent to get here?"

Jared looked at his watch. "She said it'd take her a few minutes to finish what she was doing and then about twenty minutes to get out here. Are you cold? Do you want to sit in the car?"

She shook her head, not wanting to leave his side. "Why don't you show me around?"

They walked the perimeter of the building hand-in-hand as he pointed out attributes and faults, picking up on things she never would have noticed. He talked about where more rooms could be added while maintaining the charm of the building.

He was pointing out loose roof slates to be replaced when the sound of a car driving up the lane caught their attention.

They hurried around to the front of the building and caught sight of a young woman arriving at the front door. Her eyes widened when she caught sight of Jared. No surprise there, Annabelle thought.

After introducing herself, the real estate agent handed over keys and a thin folder.

"I spoke to our branch manager in Philadelphia who's done some work for you," she said. "She said it would be okay to leave the keys with you. I'm so sorry I can't stay. I have another showing in just a few minutes, but I'll be back in about an hour. We can talk then. A few of the rooms had been decorated for a recent designer showcase in a magazine but none of the furniture is included with the asking price. Of course, if you like it, I'm sure we could work something out. Anything else, just let me know what you need."

Giving her a patented Jared smile, he agreed, but Annabelle could tell he was anxious to get rid of the woman. When she'd

left, he set off like a kid with the key to the candy shop, pulling
her along after him with a tight hold on her hand.

Opening the front door, he walked into the foyer. "Damn, it's
even better than I thought."

"Oh, Jared." Annabelle felt her mouth drop open in surprise.
"It's like a fairy tale."

The circular foyer led to a sunken area that was twice the size
of the entire first floor of the shop. A grand staircase with a balus-
trade of dark wood to the right of the door led to the second floor.

Wandering through the first floor, Jared noted broken windows, some water damage. Looking through the materials from
the agent, he said there were eighteen bedrooms on the second
and third floors, but only three had separate baths.

"Have to add baths," he mumbled under his breath. "Lose a
couple rooms there. The kitchen's huge but that'll need a total
update."

After exploring the first floor, they headed up the staircase. The
first few rooms lacked anything other than wallpaper and trim.

Jared stopped in one room to check out the bathroom, but
Annabelle continued on to the end of the hall, her curiosity piqued
by a large intricately carved panel of wood on the wall. Flowers
and vines writhed over the surface in a pattern reminiscent of
Arabic script. She moved closer to have a better look and realized
the panel was a door.

She looked for a knob but found none. After a few minutes of
pressing her fingers into any and all indentations, she found a hidden latch in one of the carved flowers.

The door glided open on silent hinges to reveal a curved stairwell. Up the stairs, she gasped in delight as the tower room came
into view.

Rose moiré silk draped curved walls, inset with windows every few feet and a door she assumed led to a bathroom next to the entry. This room was bare, but an intricate metal spiral staircase near the back led to a loft. Climbing up, she came face-to-face with a scene out of *Arabian Nights*.

Panels of gold, silver, and purple fabric hung from a ring on the ceiling, creating a tent-like effect over a large circular bed dead center in the loft.

Wandering over to the bed, she ran her fingers down the drapery, marveling at the quality of the silk. Golden tassels held the panels together at the sides, and a purple comforter covered midnight-blue silk sheets.

Wow. She'd love to meet the designer of this room.

What a bed! Annabelle couldn't help but kick off her shoes and stretch out. She closed her eyes and let the sensuous silk surround her, soothe her, seduce her into relaxing.

A small sound made her eyes fly open, and she saw Jared at the top of the stairs.

"You look like you belong there." His voice caressed her, the intense heat in his eyes scorching. "I want to tie you to that bed and never let you leave."

Her heart began to race and she couldn't catch her breath. His desire was a palpable force, holding her in place as if he'd tied her hands to those silken panels with the tassels.

Just thinking about that made her body heat and moisten.

As she stared, Jared shrugged out of his coat and dropped it to the floor. She raised herself onto her elbows and watched as he walked toward the bed and stopped in front of her.

Reaching for her jeans, he popped the button, then released the zipper, the metallic rasp echoing through the room. The cool air seemed to heat around them, and she swore she'd be able to see steam rising from their bodies soon.

Instead of pulling down his own jeans, though, he grabbed the sides of hers and yanked them to her bent knees hanging over the side of the mattress.

She drew in a sharp breath as her underwear caught and followed, leaving her exposed to his hot, searching gaze. And her legs trapped.

Wanting him to touch her, she arched her hips but he reached instead for the buttons on her sweater. The little discs didn't give him any hassle, but she felt each pluck and release between her legs.

He didn't remove the sweater, just parted the sides so the pretty pink bra that matched her underwear was exposed. His fingers drew white-hot lines of fire over her skin, drawing her nipples into aching points that throbbed under his gaze.

She reached for him, but he caught her hands before she made contact and held them at her sides. When she murmured a protest, he just smiled.

"This bed was made for sex, wasn't it, Belle?"

Instead of being turned off by his language, Belle's body tightened, desire drenching her like a downpour. Her nipples tightened into unbearably hard peaks, the muscles of her pussy clenching in anticipation.

"Will you let me fuck you on this bed? Clothes on, fast and hard, down and dirty."

Jared released one of her hands so he could run a finger down her torso starting at her chin, carefully avoiding her breasts until he reached the soft curls between her legs. He drew a few strands between his fingers, curling them around the tips, before he withdrew, causing her to groan.

"Do you trust me, Belle?"

She couldn't speak so she nodded.

He moved then, reaching above her head.

When he untied the tasseled cords from the posts and left them dangling, she thought she might hyperventilate from excitement. He released her right hand, then brought her left one up and wrapped the cords gently around her wrist, laying the ends in her hands.

When he'd done the same to the right, he just stared, his breathing a harsh rasp in the silence.

When he reached for her again, he brushed against the sides of her breasts, sweeping down to her hips and her outer thighs. Sensation followed, pulsing over her like a wave. He touched every inch of her body but the throbbing flesh between her thighs, until she strained against the cords so hard she was afraid she'd bring the bed down on them.

At the precise moment she couldn't take it any longer, he groaned and froze, his fingers shaking as his control began to implode.

Then his fingers moved again, arrowing straight between her thighs. He slipped two fingers between her legs and felt the wetness seeping from her. Because of her jeans at her knees, she could barely open her legs, and his fingers felt huge as he worked her.

When she was panting and nearly ready to climax, he withdrew, making her cry out. But in the next second, he found her clitoris and rubbed the moisture around it until she sobbed.

"Jared, please."

Her eyes closed, she banged her head against the mattress and pulled on the cords, wanting to release her wrists so she could reach for him.

The sound of foil tearing made her pause and her eyes opened to find him rolling a condom onto his engorged shaft.

"Hurry."

He didn't answer. Instead, he stepped back, but only far enough so he could grab her ankles and lift them to his right shoulder. He lifted her until he was perfectly aligned to thrust into her. The tip of his cock pierced her, and he gave one shallow thrust before he slammed home and slid deep.

The pace he set was hard and fast and just this side of dirty. The position allowed him to watch her, his eyes slitted and intense, a dark, dark blue. He reached out to caress her breasts in time with his thrusts. Raising her hips to meet each thrust, she encouraged him to go faster, to fuck her harder.

She couldn't look away. He had her pinned with his eyes. He forced her to stay with him, to match his every thrust with her own.

"Like it, Belle?"

She didn't have the breath to answer. She could only tighten around him, making him groan.

"I know you do. Jesus, Belle, you are so fucking tight. I love being inside you."

His words tugged on that invisible string inside her, making her body tighten almost to the point of pain.

Her orgasm built low in her body, her blood beating in her veins. She drew the scent of him into her lungs with each breath and let that trigger her final descent into bliss.

Her orgasm ripped through her, arching her body and taking him even deeper.

With a groan, he froze for a second before he began to piston his cock in and out, each stroke a sensual delight, until finally he came with a flood of warmth.

With her eyes closed, she felt every inch of him buried inside her, felt every twitch and pulse. Only the sound of their heavy breathing filled the air for several minutes.

Jared lay unmoving on top of her, the heat of his body like a blast furnace.

Finally, he pressed his lips to the side of her neck for an open-mouthed kiss that roused her desire once more before he slid out of her and reached for the cords around her wrists. With a few flicks, he released her, staring down at her with lust-darkened eyes and a wry smile on those gorgeous, talented lips.

"You're going to be the death of me."

"I think that's my line," she said, running her hands up and down his sweaty, but quickly cooling arms. They'd been too hot for each other to notice the cold before. "Are you cold?"

His chuckle sent a tingle down her spine. "Yeah, not so much. But I'm sure you're freezing."

Jared pulled her up and into his arms, holding her against his naked chest. For several seconds she listened to him breathe, felt the steady rise and fall of his chest beneath her cheek.

Now, this is what I want. Forever.

Everything stilled in that second of realization, which wasn't really that much of a shock. She'd been falling for him since the first moment she saw him. Her heart had made up its mind days ago. Her brain had been slower to catch up.

Well, crap. What the hell did she do now?

Jared took that second to sit back, his gaze dropping to her sweater to watch his fingers slide each button back into place.

When he'd finished, he stood and gathered the rest of her clothes and placed them on the bed next to her.

His blue eyes glittered and his smile made her want to pull him back down onto the bed with her.

"I'm just gonna see if the bathrooms are working. Stay put. I'll be right back." He bent down to kiss her softly on the lips before pulling up his pants and heading down the stairs.

Annabelle couldn't move, her emotions roiling from more than just sex. Swallowing past the lump in her throat, she took a deep breath and tried not to panic.

She loved Jared.

She loved his tenderness and his wit, his laugh and his sexy smile. She loved the way he held her after they made love and she loved to see him asleep in her bed, sprawled on more than his half, but always touching her.

He made her adventurous and she loved feeling that way about herself.

She finally felt like she was coming alive after being in limbo for so many years since her parents had died.

She realized she needed to tell him about her parents. About who she really was. He deserved to know the truth.

And when he knew the truth, would that change how he felt about her?

As a kid, she'd encountered two kinds of reaction to who she was. Horrified outrage from those who thought her parents were degenerates. Or sly, innuendo-filled curiosity.

That last had been the worst. She could shrug off the outrage because those people didn't have a clue. They hadn't known her parents, hadn't known how loving their relationship had been. How adored she'd been by three parents, who'd loved one another.

But the curiosity . . . That had been the toughest to deal with. The cruel questions from the press, even some of the cops and social workers who'd taken custody of her until her grandfather had taken her away.

How would Jared react when she told him?

And she had to tell him. She couldn't love him then continue to lie to him about who she really was. What if someone in the press figured it out before she told him? He might not forgive her and he had a reputation to protect.

Jared was Philadelphia blueblood royalty. The gossip rags would have a field day.

If she told him, maybe . . . Maybe what?

Maybe when they got married, her cover story would hold up to the press?

Christ, was she really considering marriage?

Shaking her head, she grabbed the rest of her clothes.

No, she was getting way ahead of herself. Jared hadn't said anything about marriage. Hell, he'd basically told her he wasn't looking to get married. And she'd told him the same.

She heard footsteps below and hurried to pull on her clothes, working to clear her expression of any and all signs of her thoughts.

She needed a little more time to think about this.

* *

Jared couldn't believe his luck as he hurried down the steps from the loft.

This place was almost too good to be true.

And then there was Annabelle.

She was perfect.

For the first time in his life, Jared thought he might actually be in love.

It should have scared the crap out of him. Should have made him want to head back to Philadelphia like there was a gun aimed at his head.

Instead, all he wanted to do was run back to Belle and tie her to him. Forever.

There, that brought the fear back. Not a fear of commitment, though.

The fear she'd say no.

Latching onto the basin in front of him, feeling the cold porcelain beneath his hands, Jared tried to sort through an avalanche of feelings threatening to bury him.

Annabelle rapped on the door. "Jared, are you okay?"

Staring into his reflection, noting his disheveled hair and sated expression, he knew he was more than okay.

"Yeah, I'll be right out."

Turned out only the cold water worked, but it helped. And when he opened the door a few minutes later, Belle still waited on the other side.

She smiled at him, and he couldn't resist. He wrapped her in his arms and pressed a kiss to her lips that left her gasping.

"Come on," he said when he could breathe, "we've got work to do."

For the next hour, they wandered through the house, Jared making all sorts of notes as he placed phone call after phone call—to his brother, his lawyer, a contractor. It seemed like he was planning a siege, and maybe he was.

Stopping in what would be the reception area just inside the front door, while Jared continued into the kitchen, Annabelle took a closer look, trying to see what he saw.

Yes, the building had a great shape and large rooms, several fireplaces and the grand staircase. But it didn't have enough bathrooms, the kitchen wasn't equipped to handle a multitude of guests, and the entire place had been plastered, which meant there were thousands of cracks all over the walls.

Jared saw beyond the surface. From what she'd picked up in his conversation with the contractor, he already had an image in his head of what he wanted. He explained in detail the building's attributes and its faults. Crown molding and paint colors were already fixed in his mind's eye.

He was fascinated and, as she watched, she became fascinated with his vision. The more she listened to his plans, the more it took shape in her mind. She saw how to furnish Jared's dream.

"Hey, Belle, you ready to head out? We've gotta get to the agent's office by six."

"Yes," she said. "I'm ready."

Eighteen

"Annabelle, someone's been digging into your background."

With the cell phone caught between her shoulder and her ear as she carted a rug out of storage to the shop Friday afternoon, she had to stop to catch her breath. Though not from exertion.

Dropping the rug where she stood, she took the phone away from her ear and blew out a deep breath. She wanted to be surprised. Really, she did.

She wasn't.

"Annabelle, are you there?"

Was it Jared? Was her background something he had Dane looking into? Had she said something to tip him off?

She put the cell back to her ear. "Yeah, I'm here, Reggie. Were they able to get enough info to piece it together?"

The man who'd been entrusted by her grandfather to keep her secrets gave a frustrated sigh and Annabelle knew Reginald Kauffman was running one hand over his bald head as if shining it.

"That's the thing, Annie. I'm not sure. Whoever was nosing around was damn good. My IT guy wouldn't have caught it except for the fact that he was actually in the system at the same time as whoever was attempting to access the files. He's not even sure if the guy got in or not."

"And when was that?"

"Last Saturday afternoon."

The day Dane had been there.

"Thanks for letting me know, Reggie."

"Would you like me to look into it?"

If Dane was as good as Jared claimed, Reggie wouldn't find anything. And if it hadn't been Dane, then maybe she'd be forewarned about some journalist's interest.

"Sure. That'd be great."

Reggie paused. "You sound . . . unsure. Is something going on, Annabelle? Is everything alright?"

"Yes, everything's fine. I've just . . . I've been thinking about revealing my identity, Reggie. I've met a man . . ."

"Ah."

So much said in one word.

"Annabelle, are you sure that's wise?"

"No, I'm not."

Another pause. "Would you like me to have him checked out?"

The thought had occurred to her, though she couldn't imagine Reggie would be able to discover anything about Jared she didn't already know or couldn't find out by asking.

And maybe she was being incredibly naïve.

If Dane had been the one digging into her background for Jared, what was he looking for? Did Jared suspect who she was? And if he did, was he only interested in her because of who she was? And the paintings she owned?

What should she do?

"Listen, can I call you back, Reggie? I need . . . I'll let you know."

"Of course you can. And you know I'll do whatever I can for you, Annabelle."

After saying good-bye, she hung up the phone and silence filled the shop.

Jared had left Tuesday morning for Philadelphia to deal with hotel stuff. And put an offer together for the property, which looked like it was a go.

He'd called every night but hadn't been able to return yet. Hotel business, he'd claimed.

She tried to take a deep breath but it kept getting stuck on the lump in her throat.

Was he playing her?

Yesterday, she might have said no. Today . . . she didn't have a clue. It made her feel like an idiot.

He'd said he'd call tonight. Should she confront him? What if it turned out Jared had nothing to do with this and she revealed her most closely kept secret without cause?

Would it be bad if he knew who she really was?

And what if someone else was hunting her? What if someone exposed her before she got the chance to tell Jared who she was? Would he be angry she'd lied to him?

Hell, maybe her true identity didn't even matter anymore. The tragedy that had destroyed her world more than a decade ago was old news. She'd survived. She'd built a life and a career.

And she'd fallen for a guy who deserved to know who she was. Because if the past blew up in her face, she wanted him to know what he was in for. But did she want to continue a relationship with a man who was having her investigated behind her back?

There were too many damn questions.

The bell over the door rang, startling a gasp out of her.

"Hey, you ready to head—Whoa, Annabelle." Kate held out her hands, as if declaring surrender. "I didn't mean to scare you. I . . ." Kate's gaze flashed over her, concern showing in her narrowed eyes. "What's wrong? What happened?"

She sighed. "Someone's digging into my past."

Kate frowned. "Oh. That's not good. Who do you . . ." She paused. "Wait, you think it's Jared, don't you?"

"It makes sense. He's seen the painting of my mom and he's a smart guy."

Annabelle abandoned the rug in the middle of the floor to sit on the stool behind the main desk, resting her elbows on the counter.

Kate followed, mirroring her pose on the other side of the desk. "Assuming you're right, and that's a big assumption at this point, what are you going to do?"

Annabelle bit her lip. "Do you think I should tell him?"

Kate just gazed at her steadily. "Do you want to tell him?"

She thought about it for several seconds. "I don't want this secret hanging over our heads like a black rain cloud. I *want* to trust him with this."

Kate's smile had a wry twist to it. "But . . ."

She shrugged. "What if he's only after my dad's paintings? And I'm just the means to get them? Or what if it all blows up again? What if all the publicity is just too much? He shows up in the tabloids sometimes. I don't know that I want to live that life. Not with my past."

"Do you honestly think he's sleeping with you just so he can get to your dad's paintings?"

Damn, she really hoped not. But . . .

"The media was relentless after my parents were killed. They were vicious and cruel. I don't know that I could live through that again. I come with a lot of baggage, Kate. He's got family issues of his own, big ones. Maybe he just won't want to deal with my shit." Shaking her head, she sighed. "You know, I don't know why I'm even stressing over this. It's not like he's going to ask me to marry him. When we first met, he told me he was never getting married. Said he didn't believe in it and I think I understand why now. Maybe none of this will even matter. Maybe he'll just say 'See ya' and move on."

"But you don't want him to, do you?"

Kate's quiet question made her breath hitch in her chest. "I knew going into this that he didn't want a long-term relationship. And I wasn't looking for that either."

"But that's changed?"

Had it? Honestly . . . Yes, it had. Christ, why didn't she just ask to have her heart broken?

She stared at Kate, whose eyes seemed so sad.

"Hey . . . did something happen?"

Kate's gaze dropped for a second before she nodded. "I called off the engagement."

Annabelle's eyes popped wide and her mouth opened on a gasp. "Oh, God." She reached across the counter to take Kate's hand, lacing their fingers together. "When?"

"Last night. I knew I couldn't keep going like this. It wasn't fair to Arnie or me." She sniffed, blinking back tears. "He didn't even put up much of a fight."

"I'm so sorry."

"Me too, for letting it go on so long when I knew it wasn't right."

"Then it was right thing to do. And maybe that's what I need to do. Break it off now. Before it goes too far."

"Do you really want to?"

Kate's quiet question had Annabelle shaking her head, though not in denial.

"This day is totally fucked up," Annabelle finally said. "This calls for several bottles of Arbor Mist, Double Stuf Oreos, Cherry Garcia ice cream, and that first season of *True Blood* we've been meaning to watch. I think we deserve to forget about the world for a little."

* *

"Are you going to tell her? It was difficult to find but I *did* find it, Jed. If someone else decides to look . . ."

Jared spared Dane a glance as he read over the report Dane had prepared. How Dane had found a copy of the court order changing Graceanna Belle O'Malley's name to Annabelle Elder, Jared wasn't sure he wanted to know. He had no doubt the paper was legit, though Dane's means of retrieval were probably slightly less than legal.

It was the smoking gun. And it screwed Jared five ways to Sunday.

From outside, he heard the muted chaos of Philadelphia traffic. So different from the occasional buzz of traffic he could hear at Annabelle's place.

He'd called her last night to tell her he could come up today. She'd sounded . . . drunk.

Not sloppy, falling-down drunk. Just buzzed enough to slightly slur her words. And she'd sounded sad. Upset.

He'd asked what was wrong. She'd told him about Kate breaking off her engagement.

He knew how she felt about Kate's engagement. She wouldn't

have been so sad over just that. Did she suspect something? Or was that his own guilty mind talking?

Shit. He tossed the paper on the desk. "If I tell her I know, she'll be upset that I had her investigated. But if I don't, her identity's not safe and someone could use this to hurt her. And then I'll have to kill them. Christ, this is a fucking mess."

Dane laced his fingers over his stomach and stared at him. "So what are you going to do?"

Good question. After the horror she'd lived through, he understood why she'd wanted to be someone else, someone no one knew. It explained her reluctance to be seen in public with him. His family and his bank account made him a public figure. He'd never had a problem with it before. Now . . .

They may cost him the woman he . . . What? What did he want from Annabelle?

Jared raised a hand to rub at his temple. "Damn, my head hurts."

"You need to tell her what's going on," Dane said.

Hot anger that anyone might dare hurt her boiled in his stomach like acid. He'd do whatever it took to spare her that.

Including telling her he'd had her investigated. "And when she tells me to go to hell . . ."

Dane gave an amused snort. "The mighty Jared Golden thwarted by a beautiful redhead. I'm more impressed with her now than I was last weekend."

When Dane had been the second man in her bed. The remembrance of her passion that night made Jared hot as hell. He wanted to haul ass back to Adamstown, get her back into bed, naked and panting his name.

"See what you can do to hide the information. I need to clean off my desk so I can get the hell out of here."

* *

"Belle, we need to talk."

Because it was exactly what she'd meant to say to Jared when he walked through the door of the shop later that afternoon, it threw her for a second.

The smile that'd curved her lips when she'd first seen him froze before fading.

Some emotion passed through his eyes. Regret, remorse. She couldn't tell.

And her lungs seized into a tight ball of anxiety. He knew.

He took a deep breath. "Is anyone here?"

She shook her head, feeling a deadly cold chill encase her body. "The store's empty for now. What's wrong, Jared? Did something happen?"

He paused and took a deep breath. "I know who you are, Belle. I know who your parents were."

She actually felt like he'd kicked her in the gut. Even though she'd suspected it was coming, it still hurt like hell. "I don't know what you mean."

But she did. She knew exactly what he meant.

"You're Graceanna O'Malley, the daughter of Peter and Catrina O'Malley."

She hadn't heard anyone speak her real name to her face in years, and now it felt like tiny daggers in her heart to hear it coming out of his mouth. She wanted to feel a sense of relief that he knew her secret, wanted to be relieved that he knew. That she didn't have to tell him.

The relief never came. Only that ice-cold chill in her blood.

She didn't bother to deny it. Why should she, when she'd thought about telling him herself?

"How did you find out?"

His eyebrows lifted for a brief second, as if he hadn't expected her to admit it. As if he thought she'd at least put up a fight. Then he took another deep breath before saying, "Dane."

She understood what he wasn't saying. He'd had her investigated.

Okay, she'd known this was a very real possibility. She'd known Jared was smart enough to figure or at least wonder why she had so many O'Malleys in her collection. He'd seen the portrait of her mother.

So why did she feel so betrayed?

Her chin lifted. "How long have you known?"

"Since this morning. I left soon after he told me. Belle—"

"How long has he been investigating me?"

Jared paused now and she knew again what he was going to say.

"Since I saw the O'Malleys upstairs."

Her lips curved but it couldn't be considered a smile. "They're not for sale."

He straightened as if she'd offended him but he shook his head, his expression carefully neutral. "I'm not asking. I would never ask you to sell them. Listen, Belle, I know what you must think about me right now, and I probably deserve it but there's something else."

He moved closer and she took one step back. If he touched her, she might shatter. That ice was moving out of her blood and into the rest of her body.

Jared's mouth tightened then, the only outward sign that he'd noted her response. "Dane said he had trouble accessing the information but it wasn't impossible. Whoever hid you . . . You're no longer safe."

She wanted to laugh but could barely breathe. "I'll pass on that information. Thank you for letting me know. Is there anything else you need to tell me?"

He moved close enough to touch and she couldn't move fast enough to get away. He froze for a brief second before his expression hardened with determination. "Don't. Don't pull away. I know you're pissed at me and you have every right to be. But it doesn't change how I feel about you. God damn it, Belle, I care about you."

Her breath caught in her throat as she waited for him to say those three little words. The three little words that might make this all better.

But he didn't.

"We work well together. And I'm not ready to give this up yet. Let me make sure the information about your parents gets buried right this time. I'll make it all go away. No one will ever know who you are."

And his reputation would safe. No one would ever known he'd dated the daughter of one of America's most scandalous affairs.

Goose bumps covered her skin, the chill turning to a gut-churning, teeth-aching cold that encased her from head to toe. "I want you to leave."

"No way. We're going to figure this out, Belle. We're going to get past this."

Get past this to where? For what purpose? Did he want more than a sexual relationship with her? Or was his reputation more important? So far he hadn't said anything that led her to believe otherwise.

"There's nothing to figure out. Thank you for the information. I'll be sure to tell my lawyer. Please close the door behind you."

"Annabelle, we can—"

"There's no *we*, Jared. You made that perfectly clear at the beginning of this affair. No ties, no . . ." No love. "I look forward to continuing our business relationship but I'm sure you can understand if I'd like to work with Tyler from here on out. That might be better for both of us."

At least it would be for her. She'd already done the absolute worst thing she could have done by falling for Jared. To have to work with him now, after this . . .

She snapped her mouth shut to stop any other words that might escape. Or at least to hide the hurt she heard in her voice.

"Belle—"

She walked toward the door, her steps careful, but he caught her upper arm before she could get there. The heat of his hand began to seep through the cold but not enough. Her first reaction was to rip her arm out of his grasp but she refused to give him the satisfaction.

And he leaned closer to speak into her ear. "Go ahead. Get pissed off at me. I deserve it. Hell, I understand what you're feeling. The betrayal. It burns like hell. But I'm not going to burn you. Never, Annabelle. I would rather cut off my right arm than see you hurt again. I know this is my fault. Just give me the opportunity to fix it."

He couldn't. She could think of nothing he could do to erase the betrayal she felt over his investigation. Not unless he took that final step and told her he loved her.

He didn't.

She forced herself to look him in the eyes. "I want you to leave, Jared. I don't think we should see each other again. If I find out my personal information has been revealed, I'll call my law—"

He covered her mouth with his and kissed her. Hard.

She tasted his regret. And the heat of his passion.

She wanted to respond. But she felt only cold.

She pushed at his chest until he released her, withdrew her arm from his hand, and forced herself to walk, not run, to the door. Opening it, she turned to stare back at him.

For a second, she thought he wouldn't go, that he'd force her to break that icy shell surrounding her and scream at him to leave.

His stony expression made the beautiful lines of his face stand out in stark relief. Such a beautiful face. But she saw no love.

Only determination to keep her by his side.

And she wanted more.

"This isn't finished, Belle. This breach in your security needs to be taken care of. Let me have Dane fix it."

"I think Dane's fixed enough, thank you. And so have you."

"You're not safe."

She wanted to laugh in his face. "I know that. Now."

A tiny muscle in his jaw began to tic. "Belle—"

"You need to leave. Just go, Jared. I can't—You have to go."

He paused again but he must have seen something in her eyes that convinced him to give up the fight.

"I'll go. For now. I'll check back in a few days."

She didn't tell him not to bother. She didn't know what to think, how to feel. Everything was such a mess right.

"Don't hide, Belle. You'll solve nothing by hiding."

Her fingers itched to reach for him but she couldn't seem to get beyond the fact that he'd had her investigated behind her back. Her hands curled into fists at her sides. "I'm not hiding. I just need you to go."

He didn't move and the tension in her body drew her muscles into tight, painful bunches.

His hand lifted from his side and she flinched away from him. She couldn't help herself. She didn't know what she'd do if he touched her.

Probably break apart. And she'd done that once in her life. She didn't know if she could live through another.

He must have seen something in her eyes because he didn't touch her.

"Make sure the security system's set at night, Belle."

Her heart twisted at the concern in his voice but she didn't have anything to say.

When he finally shook his head and stalked out the door, she wasn't sure her legs would hold her weight. Flipping the open sign to closed, she forced herself up the stairs to her bedroom, closed the door, and let herself fall apart.

* *

"I'm not giving her up."

"Yeah, well, I don't think that's your choice, Jed. You screwed this one up good."

Jared considered flipping his brother the finger but knew it was an exercise in futility. And he didn't know if he'd get the right finger anyway.

His companion of the last several hours, Jack Daniels, had finally called it quits.

The empty bottle lay on its side, like a fallen soldier, on the floor of the Salon. Jared slumped on a chaise, figuring he'd be joining the bottle soon enough. The chaise seemed to have developed a definite angle that threatened to land him on the floor.

Of course, that could just be the Jack. Everything was off kilter. Or maybe that was just him.

Tyler sat at the piano, playing something slow and quiet that didn't grate on Jared's nerves. Tyler had found him holed up here about an hour ago. He'd poured himself a drink and hadn't said more than a few words.

"She won't let me take care of this for her. Why won't she let me take care of her?"

"Maybe because you went behind her back and had Dane investigate her?"

Jared grimaced. *Yeah, maybe that had been a bad idea.* But . . . "Why didn't she tell me?"

Tyler sighed. "For the fifth time, my answer to that is, 'Why should she?'"

Because she's mine.

Tyler's fingers came down hard on the keys, sending a bolt of pain through Jared's head at the discordant sound. "She's not one of your paintings, Jed. You don't own her."

Shit, had he said that out loud?

"I don't want to own her. I want her to . . ."

"Want her to what?"

To love me.

He wanted her to love him. He wanted her to be his.

"Shit, Tyler. I love her."

His brother snorted. "Ya think? Christ, I could've told you that two weeks ago."

His heart contracted in his chest, and he could barely breathe. "And she hates me. What the fuck am I supposed to do about that?"

With a sigh, Tyler closed the lid on the piano keys. "Well, first, you sleep off the Jack. Tomorrow, you fix it. You'll grovel, you'll beg, you'll throw yourself at her feet and tell her what an ass you've been and that you will do anything to make it up to her."

He'd groveled before. At least, he'd tried to. Maybe he wouldn't have to this time.

Maybe he'd just show her he could take care of her. He'd fix her information leak. He was good at fixing things.

And he never lost. When he wanted something, he got it.

He wanted Annabelle.

He'd do whatever it took to get her back.

* *

"Men are so totally not worth the aggravation," Kate declared as they made the rounds of the dealer tables at Renninger's Market way too early Sunday morning.

Annabelle ran her fingers over a rare piece of blue willow china and then spotted a box of costume jewelry on the jumbled table.

"Men are dogs," she agreed as she picked through the collection of '50s and '60s paste.

Jewelry had never been her area of expertise but she'd promised Beatrice she'd search for the missing pieces of her collection.

Just because Beatrice's grandson was an overbearing, no-good playboy didn't mean she would renege on a promise.

She'd shed enough tears over the guy for the past four nights. Cheap wine, sugar, and hot fictional guys. Perfectly . . . mindless.

Sighing, she moved on to the next table.

She hoped she found the damn ring soon. She wanted to put all of the Goldens behind her and out of her mind.

Especially one blue-eyed, blond, backstabbing—

"They're worse than dogs," Kate added as she paused to pick up a battered china doll from the table in front of her. "But . . . I still can't believe Jared left without a fight."

Annabelle rolled her eyes as she sifted through the jewelry, careful not to prick her finger on an unclasped pin back. "Oh, please, Kate, let's not go there. Obviously, the man was only interested in what he could get out of our relationship. When he realized he'd been caught and screwed his chance to get his hands on my paintings, he split."

Kate cocked one eyebrow at her. "And you're sure he only wanted the paintings?"

No but . . . "Positive."

"Did you even give him the chance to apologize?"

Grimacing, Annabelle returned to the jewelry box. "I won't be made a fool of again, Kate. He slept with me to get the pin. That should've warned me to stay far away from him. But I was stupid and let him get close to me again. And he played me."

"Don't you think he might really care for you?"

"No."

Annabelle moved on to another vendor's stall, not wanting to continue the conversation. It made her eyes burn with tears she refused to cry. She made a show of staring at the jewelry in the glass case but in reality, couldn't see a thing.

Kate moved up beside her and sighed. "I'm sorry. I just . . . I think Jared felt something more than just lust for you. I think he really . . . Hey, isn't this pretty?"

Kate reached for something in one of the cases and slipped a ring on her right ring finger. "What color did you say the stone was that you're looking for?"

She turned to see what Kate was holding out. "Oh, my God."

She almost grabbed Kate's hand to bring the piece into better light but stopped before she made a scene.

"Annabelle?" Kate frowned at her. "What's wrong? Are you okay?"

Annabelle leaned in and lowered her voice to a whisper, so she didn't attract too much attention from the seller. "I think you found Beatrice's ring."

Kate looked up, eyes wide. "No way. You're freaking kidding me."

"No, I'm not. Let me see it."

Kate slid the ring off her finger and dropped it into Annabelle's open palm.

The blue sapphire had the right shape and appeared to be the proper carat weight. Tarnish covered the plain silver band, and the teardrop stone looked dull from a coating of what she thought might be soot. Otherwise, it looked exactly like the picture Beatrice had sent her.

Could it really be that easy? It didn't seem possible.

"I haven't gotten a chance to clean that one yet." The dealer walked over with a smile on her face. "I found it in a box of jewelry I bought at an estate sale last week. The stone's real. A sapphire."

Trying not to act like an over-eager rube, Annabelle held it up to the light.

At the moment, it didn't look like it was worth five dollars, much less five hundred, which was actually closer to the truth.

To Beatrice, it was priceless. *If* it was her ring.

Turning her attention to the inside of the band, she swore she felt lightheaded when she saw the faint letters that looked like Greek. She wasn't positive they spelled the word *passion* but, really, what else could it be?

"How much do want for this?" she asked the vendor.

When she named a ridiculously high price, Annabelle settled into bargaining. She wasn't about to cheat the woman but she wasn't going to pay more than it was really worth. When they settled on $450, Annabelle walked away with a smile and the ring.

Which she handed back to Kate.

She took it with a confused smile.

"I think you should hold on to that for me," Annabelle said. "Just for a while."

She recalled Beatrice telling her about the legend associated with the jewels. Kate had picked it up first and put it on her finger. She should be the one to give it to Beatrice. Unless she saw Tyler first.

At least one of the Golden brothers was a gentleman and she had no doubt it was Tyler.

* *

The painting arrived Monday morning at nine by private courier.

From Haven Hotel.

Annabelle propped the crate against the checkout desk and left it there for an hour before she decided to open it.

When the shock of the address wore off, she realized she was pretty sure she knew what was in the crate. She couldn't decide if she was pissed off or touched. She didn't want to be touched.

"That bastard."

She'd barely managed to function on Sunday. Only the constant stream of customers had kept her mind off the mess her life had become.

And it'd taken an entire bottle of Arbor Mist to ensure she slept through the night.

Which she'd paid for today with a hangover she'd only managed to shake with three acetaminophen.

The sight of that crate made her temples throb again.

"Damn him."

She knew she wouldn't get any work done until she opened it, so she got her crowbar and pried it open.

Kate found Annabelle sitting on the floor of the shop in front of the painting an hour later.

"Annabelle? Hey, is everything okay?" A pause. "What're you doing on the floor, hon?"

"Hey, Kate. I got a present from Jared."

Behind her, she heard Kate walk over to her, then stop. "Is that one of your dad's?"

She nodded, letting her gaze trace the lines of her mother's naked back. "It's *Number Seven* in the Passion series. The one I needed to complete my collection. Jared sent it."

Kate paused. "Okay, back up. I'm thoroughly confused. I thought you said he wanted to buy your paintings."

"That's what I thought too."

"Then why did he send you this one?"

Good question. "You know, Jared accused me of hiding and he was right. I have been. And I'm so sick and tired of looking over my shoulder, waiting for my past to bite me on the ass."

Slowly, Kate nodded. "I get that, Annabelle. I do. But . . ." She sighed. "What are you going to do? I mean, do you just take out an ad in the newspaper and say, 'Hey, I'm Peter O'Malley's daughter.'"

"No, of course not. But I have to do something. And . . . I had this idea. It might be really stupid and if you think so, just tell me, okay?" She then let her idea tumble out in a rush before she lost her nerve. "I'm thinking about doing a showing here, a grand reopening. The renovations will be completed next week. I have that beautiful new gallery space. I'd decide who to invite and let the information just . . . slide out that way."

Kate's expression was solemn. "Sounds like you've given it a lot of thought, and I can see how having control over the event would be helpful." Kate turned back to the painting. "This one's beautiful. I wish I'd known your parents."

Annabelle wished for the same. "They were wonderful. All of them. And so much in love. I knew their relationship was different. Lots of kids had two dads and a mom but they didn't all live together and share the same bed. I knew other people thought they were freaks. And worse. But those people didn't understand. They just condemned. Then the way they died just made it all that much more titillating.

"But my paintings, the ones I've kept in storage all these years, they show the love, the affection. I think I didn't want to share that with anyone else after what happened. I wanted to keep it for myself."

"Understandable, considering. But you're not going to sell them, are you? Because you know people will be all over you to buy them."

"Of course not. But maybe I'll show some of the younger artists I've been collecting. Give others a boost."

"And dilute a little of the focus on your announcement. Sounds like a plan."

"I'm not ashamed of who I am. Or my parents. It's time to take back my life."

"Does that include forgiving a certain guy? You know he sent this as damn big 'I'm sorry,' right?"

Annabelle paused as she brushed a finger over her father's signature. "Yeah. I know."

She'd had a lot of time to think over the past week. A lot of time to calm down, think about what had happened. And to admit she missed him. And that maybe, just maybe, he'd had a valid reason for his actions.

"I guess that will depend on the guy."

* *

"So, have you heard from her yet?"

Jared shook his head as he stared out the window of his office, not bothering to turn around to acknowledge Tyler.

"The painting was only delivered Monday."

"Yeah, well, it's Friday. You're just going to give her a painting and hope she realizes how you feel about her?"

That was the plan, yes. She needed time. He understood that. Time to realize he wasn't playing her.

If it didn't work . . . Well, he had three more O'Malleys.

"You know you're an idiot, right?"

He opened his mouth to tell his brother to fuck off, then shut it again. Why bother? His plan would work. It had to.

Tyler shook his head. "It's not gonna work, Jed. So you sent her one of her dad's paintings. So what? She's supposed to read your mind? Did you even tell her you loved her?"

Of course he hadn't told her he loved her. She wouldn't have believed him. She'd have thrown it back in his face.

He lifted a hand to rub at the ache in his chest. "Do you have any advice that's actually useful?"

His voice sounded like a low, angry growl, and he clamped his mouth shut before he could say anything more.

"Yeah, I do. If I were you, I'd haul ass up to her place, throw yourself on her mercy, and beg her forgiveness for being a total douchebag."

"Tyler, dear, don't call your brother bad names."

Beatrice walked through the door of Jared's office and he gave a low whistle of appreciation. "Whoa, Nana. You look fantastic. Got a hot date?"

Dressed in a pale pink fitted suit, her hair a sleek bob of snow white, and her makeup impeccable, she walked into Jared's office with a grin. "Why, thank you, sweetheart. And no, I'm going to a gallery opening. I just thought I'd stop by and see if you received this same invitation. It looks like an interesting event."

Jared realized he recognized the envelope his grandmother held. He'd seen a similar one on the pile of mail on his desk this afternoon but he hadn't bothered to open it. He hadn't bothered to open a lot of his mail in the past week.

Another party didn't interest him. He'd only been able to think about Belle.

And how much he missed her.

Was this love? The ache in his gut? The pain in his chest?

Well, it sucked.

"Not interested."

Tyler snorted softly. "Since when are *you* not interested in a party, Jed? Sounds like someone's wallowing in self-pity, if you ask me."

The inflection in his brother's tone made him narrow his gaze on Tyler. "No one asked you for your opinion."

His brother pulled a piece of white paper out of his shirt pocket. "I got an invitation to the same party."

Tyler's gaze never wavered.

He walked to his desk, dug around the accumulated piles of papers, and pulled out the envelope.

The return address was Adamstown.

His jaw tightened as he ripped open the envelope and pulled out the card.

You're invited to the grand reopening of Elder Antiques
And the debut of the O'Malley Art Gallery
Featuring the work of
Peter O'Malley and selected artists

His gaze shot back to his brother. "This is for tonight. When did you get this?"

"Yesterday. And so did you."

Jared eyed his brother up and down. Tyler wore a suit and a tie. He didn't have a date. Tyler never had a date.

"We'll wait while you change, dear," his grandmother said. "Just make it quick."

* *

"What if no one shows up? I should have included an RSVP but it was such short notice. This was a stupid idea. I should have given myself more time to plan, for people to actually RSVP. No one's going to show up."

With a long-suffering sigh, Kate gave Annabelle's dress one last brush, then stepped up next to her so they were both framed in the mirror.

"Of course people are going to show up. You invited the entire town, in addition to all those artists and gallery owners."

"Maybe I shouldn't have invited anyone from town. I mean, what if they think I'm a freak? What if no one ever talks to me again? I'll have to leave. I'll have to—"

"Annabelle, knock it off right now."

Kate's sharp tone made her take a deep breath.

Whoa, okay. Panic much?

She had to get a grip or she'd never be able to go through with this.

And she refused to be a coward. Not now.

She could do this.

"Hello-oo! Annabelle? We're here!"

Teddy Walters's voice drifted up from the first floor, bringing a genuine smile to her face.

When she'd decided to do this, she'd made the decision to include her friends and neighbors. She wanted them to be here when she made her announcement. Might as well tear the bandage away all at once.

She'd hired Tracy and her staff from the café down the street to do the catering. She'd enlisted Teddy and his mother, Dolores, to check invitations and greet guests as they arrived. Dolores had been a meeting planner before she'd retired and opened her antiques shop. Annabelle couldn't have put this party together in time without her help. Or Teddy's. He had an incredible eye for arrangement and had helped her place all the artwork.

He'd done a better job than she could have imagined possible or ever accomplished by herself.

And considering the subject material, he'd never once blushed, cracked an inappropriate joke, or questioned her about the collection. He'd been a complete professional.

She hadn't been able to thank him enough, but he'd just smiled and said neighbors helped out neighbors.

Yes, it was high time she stopped shutting everyone out.

She looked down at her dress.

"You outdid yourself again," Annabelle said. "The dresses are amazing."

Kate's champagne-colored silk sheath hugged her slight curves like a glove yet covered her from neck to knee. Her hair fell in a sleek, dark wave over her shoulder, and her dark eyes held a faint trace of anxiety.

"Are you sure it's not over the top? I could change into the blue—"

"Don't you dare. You look beautiful."

Kate's lips slowly lifted into a smile. "So do you."

Her dress was a deep forest-green satin. The contrast made her

skin appear practically translucent. The style was deceptively sedate, with short cap leaves and complete coverage in the front. But
the back plunged in a vee, leaving her bare to the waist.

She looked . . . amazingly like her mother.

Kate slipped her hand through her elbow and squeezed her
arm.

"We should get downstairs."

"Thanks, Kate. You know I love you, right?"

Kate rolled her eyes but her smile was bright. "Of course you
do. Who else would put up with all of this?"

They headed to the first floor, where Kate veered off to check
on the food and Annabelle headed for the gallery. The rest of the
shop looked spectacular since she'd spent most of the week pulling
it all together.

But the gallery looked amazing.

"There you are, Annabelle." Dolores took her hand and held
her at arm's length. "Don't you look beautiful?"

"Dolores, I can't thank you enough for all your help this week.
It really means a lot to me."

"Oh, sweetheart, no need for thanks. That's what friends do.
We're just glad we're able to be here for you." Dolores motioned to
the walls. "I always did love this series. It was one of your father's
best, I think."

Annabelle nearly choked on her next breath as Dolores patted
her on the back. "Oh, now, none of that. Buck up, Annabelle.
Your grandfather would be very proud of what you're doing here
tonight. Your father's work deserves to be seen and you have nothing to hide. Don't worry. We'll all be here to hold your hand."

When she could breathe again, Annabelle asked, "How long
have you known?"

"Oh." Dolores waved a hand in front of her like the question was inconsequential. "Since shortly after your grandfather and you moved here. It was a painful time still for both of you and people in this town know everyone deserves their privacy to mourn."

"But . . . who else knows?"

"A few have put it together over the years. Most still don't. And it won't matter to them. At least, it shouldn't. You know there're going to be some idiots who'll try to use it against you but you're stronger than that. Now, I'm going to make sure Teddy knows what he's supposed to do."

Before she left, Dolores raised one soft hand to her cheek and patted her gently. "Everything will be fine. And if anyone tries to start something, we'll sic Teddy on them. That boy could talk a politician to death."

Dolores turned and walked away, a two-hundred pound, bleached-blonde mother tiger in a bright blue pantsuit.

Annabelle had no doubt Dolores would tackle anyone who tried to embarrass or humiliate her tonight.

Her eyes dampened and she blinked fast, biting her tongue so she didn't ruin her makeup. They'd kept her secret. All this time and no one had said a word.

Okay. No tears. This was no time for them. And no need for them.

Unless Jared never showed up.

Then she'd shed those tears in private.

＊ ＊

Nearly two hundred people mingled in the shop.

The turnout surprised Annabelle. Nearly all of the art crowd she'd invited had shown up. Dealers, gallery owners, agents, and artists mingled with her friends and neighbors.

Turns out she'd chosen a slow night in the art world for her grand reopening. It was a little . . . overwhelming.

Many of the guests had known her parents. And several recognized Annabelle immediately. Their amazement had turned to remembrance, and Annabelle had listened to wonderful stories about her parents.

Enough to keep her mind off the fact that Jared hadn't shown wup.

Maybe he hadn't received the invitation. Maybe he just hadn't cared.

If that was the case . . . Well, she'd live through that too.

An hour into the night, she walked into the gallery and, with a deep breath and a smile, she prepared to tear away any remaining bandages.

"I'd like to thank you all for coming, especially on such short notice. My name is Annabelle and my parents were Peter and Catrina O'Malley and Danton Romero. Peter O'Malley was an incredible talent and for many years, I've let fear dictate how I deal with my father's legacy. That stops here."

* *

"Jared, chill, dear. We're only an hour late. The flat tire didn't set us back that much."

Jared stifled a restless sigh as he reached into the backseat of Tyler's Mercedes to help Beatrice from the car.

"I know, Nana. I just don't want her to think we're not coming."

Beatrice patted his arm as Jared shortened the length of his stride to accommodate his grandmother's shorter legs. "I think she'll be more than pleased to see you."

Jared wasn't so sure. Yes, she'd sent the invitation, but it could have been more out of gratitude than a desire to see him again.

Judging by the amount of cars parked along the street and in the store's lot, she had a full house tonight, which was great.

He'd just wanted to be there from the beginning to make sure no one hassled her.

Which probably would've earned him a glare from those gorgeous green eyes.

He had no doubt she could handle herself and anything else thrown her way. The woman had a backbone of steel.

And he wanted her. All of her.

Christ, he'd been an idiot.

Opening the door to usher his grandmother into the shop, he checked out the remodel. She'd taken much of his advice but added her own stamp to everything. It certainly set the shop apart from anything else on the strip.

He didn't have time to take a close look though because he heard Belle's voice coming from the new gallery space.

Leaving Beatrice to his brother, he headed toward her.

"No, I won't be selling any of my father's work but I do plan to promote and sell the work of other artists, particularly new artists."

Stopping in the entryway into the gallery, he immediately saw Belle addressing the crowd, extending thanks to her friends and neighbors who'd helped her get ready for the night.

The sight of her hit him like a punch to the gut. A stunning vision in green satin, her gorgeous hair loose and curling on her shoulders.

When she flashed a smile at the audience, his cock responded by hardening almost painfully fast.

She looked confident, poised, and he wanted to throw her on her bed and ruffle all that calm.

He forced back the lust. He refused to embarrass her or make her uncomfortable.

When she locked her gaze with his, her smile remained,

though he thought he saw some darker emotion cross her expression. Would she forgive him? Maybe he'd be learning how to grovel after all. Should've asked his dad for a few lessons.

"I have one more person I'd like to thank. Without him, I don't think I'd be in this position. Ladies and gentlemen, Jared Golden was the catalyst for tonight's event. He provided me with the final piece to my father's Passion series. Thank you, Jared, and thank you all for coming tonight."

Annabelle turned and Jared realized Kate had been standing behind her the whole time. The women exchanged a few words, both of their gazes darting toward Jared before Kate's veered off to Tyler, standing behind him.

He swore he felt his brother tense.

"See, we're not that late at all." Beatrice slipped her hand through Jared's arm. "Why don't we go over and say hello, boys?"

Jared couldn't agree more.

Belle was speaking to another woman when they reached her but as soon as she ended the conversation, she turned to greet them with a warm smile.

"Mrs. Golden, I'm so glad you could come."

"I wouldn't have missed it for the world, Annabelle. Your shop is beautiful and the gallery is amazing."

"I have your grandson to thank for some of that. The design was mostly his." When she turned to him, her smile was a little warmer, though he still couldn't read her expression. "Jared, I don't honestly know how to thank you for the painting. I'd like to keep it for few months for display but I have to insist on returning it."

She didn't give him time to answer as she turned back to his grandmother and slipped something from the pocket of her dress. "And I must insist you accept this."

"I already told you, dear. The pin is yours."

Kate stepped up beside Belle and held out her hand, palm up. "But the set shouldn't be parted."

Beatrice gasped and her expression broke into a wreath of smile. "Oh, Annabelle, you found the ring!"

"Actually, Kate did. Amazingly, she picked it up at one of the stands at Renninger's Market. If you hadn't shown up tonight, I would have contacted you tomorrow."

Beatrice's smile couldn't be contained. "Well, now, I'm absolutely stunned." She turned to Kate with a smile Jared had learned to be wary of. "Kate, dear, why don't you give that to Tyler? He'll hold on to it for me, won't you?"

"Of course, Nana."

The hot look that flashed between Kate and Tyler as he reached for the ring didn't escape Jared's notice. But then Belle held out the pin to him.

He covered her hand with his, the pin trapped between them. "I want more than just the pin, Belle. You know that, don't you?"

She didn't say anything right away but she didn't pull her hand from his either. "I'm not really sure what to think, Jared."

Not an outright rejection. He could work with that. "Then let me convince you."

Her chin tilted up. "How?"

Good question. How did he convince this woman that he wanted more than a casual relationship?

"What do you want me to say? What do you need me to do? Whatever it is, I'll do it."

Disappointment flashed across her expression before she blinked and it disappeared. "I'm afraid I need more than you're willing to give."

A cold ache gripped his chest. He was going to lose her. He felt her drawing away emotionally, her gaze becoming more distant. The weight of strangers' stares, something that'd never bothered him before, now made him feel self-conscious. Exposed.

"I'll give you anything you want, Belle. Just tell me. The paintings—"

"No." She shook her head. "No, that's not what I meant. That's not . . ."

She grimaced, as if unable to put into words what she wanted.

Damn it, this wasn't how this was supposed to go. What did she want? What could he say?

He felt her tug on her hand, wanting to draw away from him. *No way.* "I love you."

She blinked and her expression began to thaw. But she didn't melt. "I'm looking for more than just a passing relationship. I want a partner for life, not just in bed."

"Then I'm your man, because that's exactly what I want. I promise no more secrets. I don't want to lose you. No matter what, you'll always be the most important person in my life. I love you, Belle. I can't imagine living without you."

Her smile made his heart pound and his mouth dry. "I love you, too, Jared."

He bent to kiss her, trying not to let his libido overcome propriety. His grandmother *was* standing only a few feet away from him.

But later . . .

He reluctantly drew back before he took things too far.

And was rewarded with one of Belle's amazing smiles.

"Later," she said.

"That's a promise."

* *

"How mad will Kate be if I just rip this dress off you?"

With Jared's lips on her nape and his hands working to divest her of the dress, Annabelle let herself drown in sensation.

She'd locked the door to the shop barely five minutes ago. As soon as she'd set the alarm, Jared had swung her into his arms and took the stairs two at a time.

He hadn't bothered with lights and moonlight bathed her bedroom in cool gray shadows.

Finally, the top of her dress loosened. They both groaned as it fell to her waist and his hands cupped her breasts.

Still dressed, she felt the smooth surface of his suit against her bare back, sending a shiver through her.

His fingers tweaked her already hard nipples, his erection nestled against her ass, and she hoped her knees continued to hold her.

But she knew if they didn't, Jared would catch her before she fell.

Then she hoped he'd throw her on the bed and fuck her until she passed out.

Burning lust bubbled low in her gut, spreading like lava into her pussy.

"Jared, hurry."

His hands tightened on her breasts, squeezing and molding. "We've got all night."

"Then we can do it more than once. I need you in me now. Please, Jared."

His answer was string of words she rarely heard come out his mouth and made her that much more insane for him.

With a cry, she twisted in his arms, her mouth lifting for his kiss as her fingers dealt with the buttons of his shirt and the zipper of his pants.

Taking a short, sharp bite of his lower lip, she pulled out of his arms, their gazes locking.

"Strip," she commanded. "And then fuck me."

His expression sharpened to one of pure male excitement, and he had his torso bared in seconds while she fumbled with the rest of her dress.

How could she be expected to make her fingers work when he was naked and beautiful only inches away?

Finally, she released the button that held the skirt at her waist and the green satin fell to her feet.

She reached for the garters holding up her stockings but Jared's growled "Leave them" made her fingers falter.

Before she could respond, Jared grabbed her hips and then tossed her onto the bed behind her.

She had time to bounce once before he was on her, his mouth plastered to hers and his knees spreading her thighs.

He nudged her with the head of his cock, testing her readiness, then plunged home.

Annabelle wrapped her arms and legs around him as he started to thrust with little of his usual finesse.

It was wild and passionate and she knew it couldn't last.

But it did.

Jared rode her hard, hips pistoning as he drove her closer to her peak.

Their joining wasn't only physical. The emotions between them elevated the act to a work of art.

And as she came apart in his arms, she knew her life had become complete.